the
perfect
husband

BOOK ONE OF THE
SYDNEY HARBOUR
HOSPITAL SERIES

CHRIS TAYLOR

LCT Productions Pty Ltd
18364 Kamilaroi Highway, Narrabri NSW 2390

ISBN. 978-1-925119-24-4 (Paperback)

The Perfect Husband is a work of fiction. Names, characters, places, brands, media and incidents either are the product of the author's imagination or are used fictitiously. Any resemblance to actual persons, living or dead, events, or locales, is entirely coincidental.

Published in the United States of America.

THE SYDNEY HARBOUR HOSPITAL SERIES

(in order)

THE PERFECT HUSBAND
(Book One)

THE BODY THIEF
(Book Two)

THE BABY SNATCHERS
(Book Three)

Find out more about all of Chris Taylor's books, including the hugely popular Munro Family series by visiting her website at: www.christaylorauthor.com.au/about/books

DEDICATION

*This book is dedicated to Pat Thomas and Grace Anselmo,
two extraordinary, courageous women who have
risen like phoenixes from the ashes.
You are stronger than you could ever imagine.*

And as always, to my beautiful husband, Linden.

ACKNOWLEDGMENTS

As usual, no book comes into being without a lot of help and support by my friends and family. A world of thanks must go to my friend and critique partner extraordinaire, Grace Anselmo and to my editor, Pat Thomas. Thank you for your courage and faith to entrust me with your story. My admiration for both of you is without measure. This book is for you.

To Detective Superintendent Michael Kilfoyle, thank you for lending my story credibility. Any mistakes are wholly my own.

To Grady, Alisha and all of the staff at damonza.com, thank you for yet another fantastic cover. To my sister, Nicole Guihot and to my friend, Ally Thomson, thank you for your excellent editorial comments, proof reading skills and suggestions. I hope you like the final result.

To Amy Atwell and her dedicated staff at Author EMS who are so much more than book formatters. Amy, once again, thank you for your magic.

To the fantastic writer organizations such as Romance Writers of Australia, Romance Writers of America and Romance Writers of New Zealand for all the help, support and encouragement they offer new and aspiring writers, including me.

To my readers, thank you for your support and love for my stories. Your encouragement and enjoyment make this journey all worthwhile.

And lastly, to my friends and family, especially my husband and children. Thank you for putting up with late dinners and even later conversations as I've emerged day after day from the sometimes scary but always enthralling world I've created on my computer.

PROLOGUE

Dear Diary,

It was everything I expected and more... The fairy tale wedding, right down to the last, perfect detail. My best friend, Jason, told me if my smile was any brighter, he'd be blinded by it and that was after he joked about having to wear his sunglasses to ward off the dazzling sparkle of my one-and-a-half-carat diamond ring.

I am married to the most beautiful man in the world. I'm the center of his universe and he is my everything. He professed to love, honor and cherish me in vows so sweet and tender they took my breath away and the depth of emotion in his eyes left me trembling. He loves me so!

I can still hear the string quartet playing on the terrace overlooking the beautiful, majestic lake and I remember every detail of the old restored mansion-turned-hotel restaurant where our guests laughed and danced under a glistening canopy of stars.

I'm blissfully in love and oh-so optimistic. I'm the luckiest girl in the world! This is what I dreamed of, what I yearned for. Every second, every minute by his side is wonderful beyond words...

CHAPTER 1

His fist came from nowhere and smashed into the side of her head. Pain exploded behind her eye, which had taken the brunt of the force. She should have seen it coming, but the truth was, she hadn't. While their argument had been growing in velocity and spite, she'd been distracted by three-year-old Sophie who'd been trying to fork up peas. She hadn't realized her husband had been so close to losing control.

"Mommy's head is bleeding."

Isobel Donnelly snatched a fine linen napkin from the table and dabbed it to her eye. "I'm fine, Ben. It's just a little cut," she hurried to reassure her five-and a-half-year-old son. "See, I'm fine." She held the napkin away from her face and forced a smile, secretly alarmed at the amount of blood that stained it.

"You should have kept your goddamned mouth shut like I told you," her husband growled from his place at the head of the table. "It's your fault, Isobel. How many goddamned times do I have to tell you? Don't get smart with me. It won't work."

Isobel clamped her mouth shut, now too scared to correct him. His fist had done the trick. They'd been discussing the pros and cons of traditional versus natural medicine. He hadn't taken kindly to her suggestion that natural remedies had their place in a doctor's arsenal. She'd forgotten during the heat of the discussion that Nigel always had to be right. The throbbing in her eye was a harsh reminder of her mistake.

He turned to look at her, his lip curled up in a sneer. "You're going to have a shiner in the morning. I wonder how you're going to explain it." He chuckled and shook his head and returned his attention to his meal.

Isobel gritted her teeth and blinked away sudden tears. She wouldn't cry in front of the children, no matter how much she wanted to. She couldn't believe her life had turned into the nightmare that it was. A never-ending rollercoaster of marital highs and lows that left her feeling bewildered, tense and exhausted.

She didn't even know how it had happened. One moment they were like any other young, happily married couple, living out their dreams. The next, she was existing in a state of constant fear, wondering when the next eruption of anger and violence would come.

The worst thing was, she didn't have a clue what to do about it. She had no frame of reference for this kind of treatment. And there was no one she could turn to, nowhere she could run.

4

Who would believe her if she did? For nine years now, she'd kept the dark and humiliating truth a secret, too ashamed to admit her perfect life was anything but. The cracks in her marriage had become huge chasms and the longer the façade continued, the harder it was to cover up what her life had become. She was more and more convinced she'd eventually be swallowed up by the pain, the hurt and the horror, and plummet into a deep, dark sinkhole, never to be seen again.

For the sake of her children, she kept up the pretense her marriage was made in heaven. Even her nursing colleagues at the Sydney Harbour Hospital where she worked three shifts a week were oblivious to the truth. Nigel had seen to that. He hadn't done it directly, of course. He was way too smart for that.

It was the endless criticism, the snide remarks, the downright offensive names he'd call her friends behind their backs. She'd started off defending them. After all, they were her friends. They didn't deserve that kind of treatment. She owed it to them to remain loyal.

But over the years, he'd worn her down until it eventually became easier to accept his biased opinion and let her friends drift quietly away. Even her best friend, Jason.

Openly gay, Jason was one of the sweetest, gentlest men she'd ever met. Right from the outset Nigel had set his mind against him. She'd lost count of the number of times she'd argued with her husband on Jason's behalf, but the spiteful words continued to pour out of Nigel's mouth. It got to the point where it was easier to refuse Jason's invitations and fail to return to his calls, rather than listen to the increasingly vitriolic diatribe that Nigel would give voice to at the mere mention of her friend's name.

It came as no surprise to Isobel that Jason was hurt and confused by her actions, but no matter how many times he pleaded with her to tell him what was wrong, she never found the courage to tell him the truth. The shame of admitting both her perfect husband and fairy tale marriage were so fatally flawed was simply beyond her.

She touched the napkin gingerly to her eye and winced at the pain. It was a good thing she mostly did the late shifts. At that time of night, all but a few of the lights in the hospital ward were turned down low. Along with the aid of some makeup, the dim lighting would help her conceal this latest assault.

"Are you okay, Mommy? You look sad," Sophie whispered from where she sat in her highchair, residual tension still shadowing her tiny face.

Isobel's chest went tight. Fresh tears burned behind her eyes, but once again, she refused to let them fall. "Of course, honey. Daddy and I were just having a little argument. It's fine. I'm fine."

"Why do you fight so much?" Ben asked, his voice scratchy with fear.

"It's your mother's fault. She doesn't know when to keep her mouth shut. She can't help herself. Why does she always want to disagree? I'm the man of this house and what I say goes. I won't have it any other way." Her husband turned his harsh glare on their young son. "You got that, Ben?"

Ben's lip wobbled, but he managed a nod before dropping his gaze to his plate. Isobel's heart broke in two. She wanted to go to her young son and tell him not to grow up and become like his father, and to offer him comfort— and she would, just not while Nigel was still in such a volatile mood. It was getting harder and harder to pretend to her children that their mommy and daddy were normal, let alone happy. It angered her to think she was teaching them that this was the way it should to be. This wasn't the way and it wasn't right, but she was helpless to change things. At least, that's the way it felt. She longed for the way things used to be.

They were high school sweethearts and had married a fortnight after their graduation. Isobel's parents had expressed their concern that the two of them were rushing into it, but she'd been head over heels in love with the hero of the football team. With his legendary charm and good humor, Nigel brushed away her parents' fears saying he and Isobel knew best, not them.

For the first three or four years of their marriage, life was all sunshine and smiles. It had been everything she'd imagined it could be. They were both busy with their college studies and had been blissfully in love. He was her moon and her stars. He brought her flowers every other day.

If they occasionally got into a disagreement, it was quickly over and the make-up sex was sublime. It wasn't until much later that she realized their arguments only ended when she conceded she was wrong. By then, it was too late to reflect more deeply on their relationship or remove herself: Their first baby had arrived.

Nigel hadn't wanted kids. Looking back, she realized it had been stupid not to discuss the question before they were married. She'd just assumed it was a natural progression; that at some time down the track, they'd start a family.

It had taken three years of begging and pleading to finally wear him down. He'd given in and Ben had been born, but her husband had made it clear he wanted nothing to do with the day-to-day job of raising their son. By then, Nigel had graduated from med school and was busier than ever meeting the demands of his new job.

It had been left to Isobel to feed and bathe and clean and do the laundry and sit with her son through the night when he had a fever. On top of all that, working long shifts at the hospital and then fighting with her husband was beyond her level of endurance most of the time. It was all she could do to keep her eyes open at the dinner table and listen and smile and nod when he regaled her with tales of all his successes, accomplishments and the stream of glowing accolades from others.

For all the praise and attention he received from his colleagues at the hospital, it didn't stop him from lashing out at her and accusing her of spending too much time with their son. She was shocked when she realized he was jealous of their baby.

"What's for dessert?" Nigel asked and pushed away his empty plate.

Isobel stared at it. She wasn't surprised he'd retained his appetite. If anything, their confrontations seemed to fuel his hunger, including his need for her. Later, there would be no escaping his attentions, no matter how disinterested she was.

Pushing that depressing thought aside, she stood up from the table and gathered up the dirty plates. "I made a pie."

Nigel merely grunted. Isobel turned to her son and forced a smile. "Ben, would you bring Sophie's plate to the sink, please?"

Her son obediently did as she asked and followed her silently into the kitchen. She set the dirty crockery down on the counter and then relieved him of his.

"Thank you, honey. Now, would you like to have some apple pie and ice cream?"

He nodded somberly, looking so much older than his five-and-a-half years. "Are you sure you're all right, Mom? Your eye looks kind of weird."

Reflexively, Isobel reached up and touched the tender spot. She could feel the swelling beneath her fingers. *Great, just what she needed.* She was rostered back on at work the next evening.

"I'm fine, honey. I already told you. Now, go and get everyone a bowl." She gave him a gentle push in the direction of the cupboard. He turned back to face her.

"Why does Dad hurt you like that?"

Her breath caught in her throat and she closed

her eyes briefly against the pain. When she opened them again, Ben was still regarding her with a solemn expression. Not knowing how to answer him, she bent down on one knee and drew him close. She held his gaze, silently imploring him to understand.

"Daddy and I love you and Sophie so much. You know that, don't you?"

His eyes glittered with tears. His tiny shrug sent shards of pain stabbing through her heart. "I guess," he whispered in a voice so soft she had to strain to hear him.

"Sometimes Daddy gets upset, that's all. He doesn't mean to hurt me. He works very hard as a doctor. He has a very difficult job. Sometimes he comes home after a long day at work and he needs to let off steam."

Ben frowned. "What does that mean?"

Isobel fished around for an answer. "It means, instead of getting angry at his work colleagues, he yells and shouts at me. We all treat our family worse than our friends. It's just the way it is."

"Well, I don't like it. I don't like it one bit."

She breathed through the tightness in her chest and hugged him. "I don't like it either, honey, but right now, we just have to let Daddy have his space. Now, where's the ice cream?"

She stood and moved away from him, wishing she could wipe the bleakness from his eyes. A moment later, he turned and opened the cupboard and retrieved the ice cream bowls. With a deep breath, she strode to the freezer and tugged out the tub of double-chocolate ripple.

"Let's have two scoops tonight, shall we?" She winked and was rewarded with the tiniest of smiles.

"Can we have some chocolate topping and cream and cherries on the top?" he asked quietly.

"Of course! Let's do it! I'll even let you go first."

His smile widened and chased the shadows from his eyes. Isobel breathed a sigh of relief and wondered how long his happiness would last.

CHAPTER 2

Dear Diary,

My name is Isobel Donnelly and I am married to a monster. I keep this diary as a record of the nightmare that is my life.

If I disappear without a word of good-bye or explanation, never to be heard of again, let these words be my witness and my salvation.

My name is Isobel Donnelly and I am married to a monster...

Doctor Mason Alexander rounded the corner at the end of the corridor and swallowed a lump of nerves. It wasn't that he was fearful about entering the pediatric ward of the Sydney Harbour Hospital, but the first day of a new job was always a little daunting. There were staff members to meet, politics to absorb and egos to stroke. The patients were the least of his worries. In fact, he found the patients were the easy part.

From the time he finished medical school and stepped onto a ward wearing a white coat that identified him as a doctor, he'd wanted to work in pediatrics. There was something about the hopefulness in sick kids when they had no right to feel that way that pulled at his heartstrings. It made him so much more determined to heal them.

"Good-morning, you must be Doctor Alexander. We've been expecting you." The woman who greeted him stuck out her hand and he shook it firmly. Her navy-blue uniform and the badge pinned to her lapel identified her as Georgina Whitely, the Nursing Unit Manger.

"Please, call me Mason. It's great to be here."

The nurse smiled and touched her hair. A faint blush stole up her cheeks. She looked close to his age and a glance at her left hand showed that she didn't wear a ring. She was far from unattractive, but he wasn't in the right headspace for a flirtation, even an innocent one.

The woman offered him another smile. "Welcome to the Sydney Harbour Hospital, Mason. I'm Georgie."

"Thanks, Georgie, it's nice to be here. I've moved from up north, in the country. The last hospital I worked in was tiny compared to this one," he told her.

She waved away his comment. "Seen inside one hospital, you've seen inside them all. They're all the same. Don't worry, I have everything covered. I've worked on this very ward for half a decade. If there's anything you need, just let me know."

She winked and Mason blushed. It wasn't exactly a come on, but there was an obvious interest in her warm brown eyes. He hurried to move the conversation to a less personal footing.

"I have eight children on my patient list. Do you mind joining me on ward rounds? The sooner I get acquainted with them and their parents, the better. I try to get kids in and out of hospital as soon as possible. Everyone's happier that way."

"You won't get any argument from me. I'm all for a quick turnover. They generally do better at home, surrounded by their family and their own things."

"Good. Shall we?" He indicated with his head toward the corridor that stretched out before them with rooms coming off on either side. Georgie glanced at her watch.

"I'll introduce you to the staff along the way. It won't be long before there's a change of shift. If you're lucky, you might be able to meet the evening staff, too."

Mason nodded. Familiarizing himself with the nursing staff so quickly was ideal. As far as he was concerned, nurses were the front line of healers. The doctors depended upon them and their ability to relate accurate observations of a patient's condition over the phone. If the nurse's observations could be relied upon, it made the doctor's job a lot easier, particularly if the doctor couldn't be in attendance on the ward at the time.

His outstretched hand indicated Georgie could precede him. "Lead the way."

Forty-five minutes later, Mason made the last notation on his patient list and smiled farewell to the young boy in the bed in front of him who'd been admitted to the hospital two days earlier suffering with pneumonia. The IV antibiotics were doing the trick and the boy's chest sounded almost clear. His fever had subsided and his cough had improved. In another day or so, he'd be right to go home.

"That's all for now, Mason," Georgie said as they walked back toward the nurses' station. She smiled. "We'll see what the evening brings."

"You run a tight ship, Georgie. I'm impressed. And I can see how the staff look up to you. You're a good nurse."

She blushed at his words and looked away, but he'd meant every word. It wasn't always the case that staff held their boss in such high esteem. Of the five nurses he'd already met, they each appeared devoted to their patients and to their job. It was refreshing to see and all of a sudden, he knew he was going to enjoy working at the Sydney Harbour Hospital.

"The staff rostered on the evening shift have just arrived. If you have time, and you're not all peopled out, I'd like to introduce you to a few more of our nurses."

He nodded at Georgie. "Of course. It might take me a few days to get all the names straight, but I'd like to meet as many of them as I can. I want to make sure they know how important they are to my team."

Georgie looked at him sideways. "You're a rare breed of doctor, Mason. It's not often one of your kind recognizes the contribution the nursing staff make. I like it."

He smiled. "I can't speak for my colleagues, but the way I see it, without competent nursing staff, there's chaos. There's no way we'd be able to provide the quality day-to-day care you guys do. I admire and respect you for your ability to do what needs to done. It isn't always pretty."

She chuckled. "You certainly have that right." She led him around the corner and came to a stop outside a door that had a handwritten sign reading: Staff Only. With a gentle push, she opened the door and he followed her inside.

The room was on the small side and was painted a nondescript gray. A large table filled most of the available space. Nurses in uniform sat around it, talking and drinking coffee. Upon Georgie's entry, the chatter subsided.

"People, I'd like you to meet Doctor Mason Alexander. He's started with us today and will no doubt get to know all of you over the coming weeks. I'd like you to make him feel welcome."

A chorus of friendly greetings followed Georgie's announcement and Mason nodded in response. His gaze wandered over the women gathered around the table. One of them remained still, with her back to him. When his gaze fell upon her, his heart skipped a beat. Even from the back, she looked so much like... *No, it couldn't be. It was some other woman with the same shade of red hair. It was just wishful thinking...*

The nurse turned to face him and he swallowed a gasp. Looking as stunned as he felt, she stared at him, her eyes wide with shock.

"Isobel West? Is that you? I don't believe it!" Forgetting for a moment where he was, he stepped forward and reached out to her. She shrunk back against her seat and his movements came to an abrupt halt. Confused and embarrassed, he turned away.

"I'm sorry, I must be mistaken. I... I thought you were someone else."

"There's no mistake," came a soft reply from a voice he hadn't heard for a decade. "But I'm Isobel Donnelly, now. It's good to see you, Mason."

Georgie looked bemused. "Do you two know each other?"

"Yes," he replied. "That is, we knew each other in high school. We haven't seen each other since the night of our graduation."

"Wow, what a small world," one of the other nurses said and pushed away from the table.

"Yes," Isobel murmured and offered him a tentative smile.

"We'll leave you to catch up," Georgie offered and the rest of the nurses followed her out the door.

Too soon, the room had emptied. Mason's heart thumped and all of a sudden, he was right back in high school again, yearning for the love of the girl he could never have. "So, you and Nigel got married."

Isobel nodded and her smile looked a little forced. "Yes, we married straight out of high school and then headed to college. I studied nursing at the University of Western Sydney. Nigel studied medicine."

Mason was filled with surprise. "Nigel's a doctor? I'd never have believed he had it in him. He didn't seem to have time to remain focused on anything other than sports."

"Yes, being a doctor's a long way from a football jock, but that's what he wanted to do. He's now an orthopedic surgeon."

"Good on him," Mason forced himself to say. "Where does he work?"

"Here, at the Sydney Harbour Hospital."

"That must make things easier?"

"You'd think it would, having us both working at the same place, but it hasn't worked out that way." She sighed and dropped her gaze.

"Oh?" he asked, stepping closer, but once again, she moved to put distance between them. He was caught between wanting to know more, yet not wanting to listen to another word about her life with another man.

"We have two young children," she explained in a lighter tone, staring at the bright plastic sheet that passed for a tablecloth.

Kids. She and Nigel had kids. Mason's heart squeezed with pain and an old, familiar longing tightened his chest. He struggled to breathe. All these years he'd thought he was over her. Had convinced himself of that and moved on. *He'd even married Sue Ann, hadn't he?* And he'd cared for his wife. Just not enough.

Suppressing a weary sigh, Mason forced himself to respond. "Two kids. That's great. How old are they?"

"Ben's nearly six and Sophie's just turned three."

"Wow, they must keep you busy."

She nodded and turned her head toward him for a brief moment. This time, her smile seemed genuine. "Yes, they do. It's why I only work part time. I didn't want them spending every day in care. Nigel looks after them on the evenings I work."

"So this is one of your regular shifts?"

"No, actually, I'm rostered to work the night shift, but I received a call from staffing a little earlier. They're down on numbers. There's a flu going around. We're not the only ward short-staffed. I agreed to come in and work a double."

Mason whistled, impressed. "That's very accommodating of you, given you're a busy mom. You're lucky Nigel was available to pick up the slack."

She grimaced and this time when she turned her head his way, he noticed the slight swelling around her eye. Was that bruising beneath the layer of makeup, or was it something else? *Had someone hit her?* He frowned, but she spoke quietly again, giving him no time to contemplate the disquieting thought.

"Actually, I was out of luck. Nigel's apparently

stuck in the operating room until six. I had to phone the daycare center. Fortunately, they were able to squeeze them in for the few hours until Nigel gets off work."

Mason shot another look in Isobel's direction, but she'd turned her head away. His chest constricted on a sudden surge of anger. If that asshole had touched her...

He gritted his teeth and shook his head. *What the hell was he thinking, drawing such a wild conclusion?* He couldn't even be sure what he'd seen was a bruise. It was churlish to blame Nigel for something that was probably no more than a figment of Mason's imagination—because he realized, despite what he'd told himself for years, he was still in love with the football star's girl.

No, she hadn't been hit; he had to have been mistaken. There was no way Nigel Donnelly would beat up his wife. He might have been an asshole in high school, but that was a long time ago and a long way from becoming a violent husband.

Mason wasn't prepared to admit his willingness to think the worst of his former teammate had nothing to do with any real belief Nigel was an abuser and everything to do with the fact Nigel had married the only girl Mason had ever loved.

Dragging his gaze away from the woman in question, he made a conscious effort to relax his clenched jaw. Isobel's marital status was none of his concern. She'd married Nigel. They had two kids. Mason's marriage might have ended badly,

21

but he'd never purposefully set out to break up someone else's marriage—no matter how badly he wished he could.

He'd spent the best part of a decade trying to forget about her and now, without knowing it, he'd relocated from his hometown a half day's drive away to the very hospital where she worked. The irony wasn't missed on him and it was something he'd have to get his head around.

He wished he'd known beforehand that she was a nurse at the Sydney Harbour Hospital. He would have headed in the opposite direction. Hell, he could have applied for a job in far North Queensland and visited with his parents every now and then. It would have put him more than a thousand miles away from the woman who still haunted his dreams.

If he tendered his resignation now, he'd appear ludicrous. Today was his first day on the ward. Questions would be asked and even more considered in private. It would set his career back further than he cared to think. The Sydney Harbour Hospital was the most prestigious hospital in the country. People vied for jobs there like children fought over favored toys. No one accepted a position and then passed it over the very first day they started.

No—resigning his position wasn't an option. All he could do was steel his heart against the woman he loved and push aside any hope he had of making her his. He had to steer clear of Isobel Donnelly, no matter how strong his feelings still were. In fact, that was even more reason to stay the hell away from her altogether. Nothing good could come of yearning for another man's wife, and especially not the wife of Nigel Donnelly.

CHAPTER 3

Dear Diary,

I am losing myself. I am terrified one day I'll look into the mirror and see a complete stranger...a woman I no longer recognize. I am being pulled under, into the dark, silent depths and each time I manage to resurface and snatch a breath, I am pushed down again.

I am slowly dying from the inside out and don't know what to do, or even if anyone cares. It's surreal how much I loved my husband in the early years of our marriage and yet now, I am frightened by his touch.

He has become a stranger to me and one of whom I am scared. There was a time when I felt safe and secure in his arms. Now I can't imagine ever feeling safe near him again...

Isobel pulled her car into the driveway of her impressive North Shore home. Although it wasn't on the water, she could glimpse the harbor between the leafy trees that lined the lower shore. The rendered brick façade, painted in a modern shade of gray, sat comfortably beside its similarly grand neighbors', but right then Isobel was way too tired to appreciate it.

After completing a double shift, she could barely drag herself from the car, but knowing Nigel would be waiting for her to get home before he could leave for work, she collected her handbag from the seat beside her and slowly got out. She climbed the stairs to the porch and the usual sense of dread began to grow. She'd hardly stepped through the front doorway before he started in on her.

"What the hell took you so long? I'm going to be late because of you!"

Even though she'd anticipated such a welcome, his narrowed eyes and the angry red flush that stained his cheeks took her aback. It was only a little past seven. He still had at least twenty minutes before his normal departure time. She couldn't understand what he was so worked up about, but she held her tongue as she'd learned to do so well. She turned away and placed her handbag on the table that stood against the wall in the hallway.

"Don't ignore me, Isobel." He grabbed her arm and spun her around to face him. She gasped in alarm at the menace in his eyes.

"Where have you been?"

"I told you, I've been at work."

"Who were you working with?"

She sighed, way too tired to deal with this right now. "Jacquie and Ronald."

"Ronald? Who's Ronald? Do you like him?"

She shook her head. "He's gay."

"What doctors were on?"

"Mark Wild and David Hamilton."

Nigel's eyes narrowed. "I know David Hamilton. He thinks he's pretty special. Works out all the time. Pretty proud of his muscles." His fingers tightened around her jaw. "Do you like him? Do you like the way he looks?" He loomed over her, his eyes mere inches from hers. His breath was hot on her face. "Do you want to fuck him?"

Her stomach clenched in fear and revulsion. "No! Of course I don't! Where's all this coming from, Nigel? I don't understand."

His breath hissed in and out between his teeth. "If I ever catch you with another man, I'll kill you. And then I'll kill the kids. Slowly. Painfully. They'll feel every second of the torture."

Isobel gasped. His tone was as deadly as the expression on his face. Fear paralyzed her. The only sounds she heard were the rushing of her blood through her ears and the pounding of her heart. Each of his words inflicted fear so icy she was frozen to the spot. Useless tears burned behind her eyes and she wanted so much to let them fall; to wash away the shame and guilt; to bring even a moment of relief.

And then her husband laughed. It should have eased her tension, but his laughter sounded crazed and there was a dangerous glint in his eye. She remained as taut as ever. He released her jaw and turned away. She rubbed at the soreness he'd left behind.

He suddenly turned back to face her and sneered down at her. "Not that I have anything to worry about on that score. You're way too ugly for anyone to want to fuck. Look at you, scrawnier than a prairie dog. No tits or ass to speak of. Fucking you is like fucking a bloke. In fact, I'd probably get more pleasure screwing a man."

She gasped again in shock and horror. Her hand came up to her mouth in an effort to contain her disgust, even as hot shame flooded through her. She lowered her head and stared at the carpet, knowing that at least part of what he said was true. She was thin. Too thin.

She'd lost a lot of weight over the past few years from the continuous stress and strain of her marriage. Nigel craved endless reaffirmation that he was the best husband, father, doctor, friend— the list went on and on. She equated her current state of affairs to living with a drug addict.

When Nigel was in a buoyant mood, the high was nothing less than blissful, but after the highs came the inevitable lows and once that happened, her life became hell on earth. The constant tension was exhausting.

Her stomach was always in too many knots for her to eat more than the tiniest of morsels. She tried to force herself to eat more, but her stomach didn't agree with her head. It was little wonder she was always so tired.

Then of course, there were the countless nights when she was too scared and upset to sleep. Even with Nigel snoring beside her, she rarely did more than doze. She didn't want to roll over and touch him by accident. She didn't want to risk waking him and having him at her for hours and hours on end. She was terrified of their grueling sex sessions where she'd end up crying and just lying there, feeling demeaned, exhausted and abused. She'd stopped saying no, years ago.

And last week he'd come home from work, talking about the marathon sex his colleague was having with his new girlfriend. One session had lasted three hours. To her horror, Nigel had seemed driven to want that for them. She'd lain there, praying to God to have him ejaculate early. Her prayers went unanswered and the longer it lasted, the more angry he'd gotten. Angry at her, for not exciting him enough to come.

For one hopeful moment, she thought about how wonderful it would be if he were never interested in her again. If he could take a lover; she didn't care whether it was a woman or a man, just so long as he never touched her, never forced her again. Nothing about their life, their relationship was healthy. It was all so horribly, awfully wrong. There was no way she could sustain this way of living, but she had no power to change it.

Instead she'd become numb and maybe that was a good thing. It was better to feel nothing than to feel the truth of their situation. In the meantime, she was as jumpy as a mouse in a hole with a cat prowling around and around. She'd begun to think it was only a matter of time before the cat pounced and consumed her whole...

With a snort of impatience, Nigel pushed past her and headed for the front door. Collecting his keys and briefcase from the hall table, he grabbed his suit jacket from the coat rack and left without another word. Isobel looked around for the kids, but apparently they were both still in bed. Hot tears pricked her eyes.

Familiar feelings of helplessness and despair overwhelmed her. With dogged steps, she shuffled toward the couch and collapsed onto its soft leather seat. With her head in her hands, she gave in to the urgent need to cry.

Desperate tears ran down her cheeks and dripped onto the knees of her stockings. Her injured eye burned from the makeup she'd applied with a heavy hand. She recalled how Mason had stared at her in the tea room and how for a moment, she'd thought her cover was blown.

Mason.

Of all the men to run into. It had been years since she'd seen him. The night of their high school graduation, to be exact. The night he'd begged her to come away with him. The night he told her he loved her. She remembered it like it was yesterday, just like she remembered how, without a qualm, she'd politely turned him down, choosing to end the night wrapped in Nigel's arms.

CHAPTER 4

Dear Diary,

I took a good long look at myself in the mirror today. The sight momentarily startled me, enough that I felt compelled to inch forward and take a better look. I scrutinized the reflection, analyzing each feature and detail, looking for some anomaly, some mark that would prove this wasn't me. But I didn't find what I was looking for.

The woman staring back at me looked older, pale... And those eyes, they were expressionless, blank. Dear God, I hate who I've become! I will the tears to pour out because I want to feel sad and hurt and angry. I want to mourn the loss of me! I want to feel something...anything... But I feel nothing. I'm numb from the inside out. My whole world is consumed by infinite shades of black....

Mason stared at the large, legal-sized envelope in his hands and tried to find the courage to open it. The logo from his lawyer's firm graced the top left hand corner. *Harton & Sharpe: We get results.*

There were no guesses as to what the envelope contained. His lawyer had called a week ago to tell him it was on the way. He remembered the exact moment: He'd been in the middle of packing the last of his belongings in his car before leaving his hometown of Maitland for the glamor of the city lights. Maybe forever.

His three brothers had left Maitland long before him and his parents had retired to the coast. They were currently up in far North Queensland, embracing their retirement, sailing in a yacht from Port Douglas to Cairns. He was happy for them and wished them all the best.

Drawing in another deep breath, he eased it out between lips that were suddenly dry and turned the envelope over again. Knowing he couldn't put it off forever, he tore it open. Inside was a single sheet of paper.

The official-looking document had been issued by the Family Court of Australia. He scanned the typed words, each one bold and black and succinct. The court had issued a *decree nisi*. His divorce had been officially approved.

He tossed the paper aside. He didn't need a court order to tell him his marriage was over. It had been over before it began. He thought Sue Ann could help him put his past behind him and make him forget the girl he could never have, but it hadn't worked out that way. He'd felt badly about it almost from the beginning, when it became clear he'd made a mistake. He'd been unfair to Sue Ann and his conscience didn't let him forget it. She'd never done him wrong. All she did was have the bad sense to fall in love with a man who didn't love her in return. The rest was history.

Isobel did her best not to look at the reflection she knew she'd see in the bathroom mirror. Even a glimpse reminded her of the shell she'd become. The young, optimistic, vibrant, *happy* woman she used to be had disappeared and she was terrified she was never coming back.

Taking a soft cotton pad from the vanity drawer, she carefully removed her makeup in preparation for bed. Her eye was still tender to the touch. A glance in the mirror showed her the bruise had morphed into a darker shade of purple, making it very difficult to conceal. It was lucky she was on her usual rostered days off.

She hadn't seen Mason since she'd run into him at the hospital a few days earlier and was relieved about that. She'd seen the way his gaze had snagged on her face and the frown that had marked his brow. She couldn't help but wonder if any of her nursing colleagues had noticed. The last thing she needed was people wondering about whether her eye had taken a hit.

Not that anyone who knew Nigel would ever suspect he was handy with his fists. He was the pin-up boy of the Sydney Harbour Hospital; the talented surgeon who had a ready smile and a charming word for everyone else. It was only his wife who saw the aggressive, darker side. Now she couldn't help but wonder what life would have been like if she hadn't turned down Mason's offer all those years ago...

She shook her head sadly at the memory. Mason hadn't stood a chance. She'd been under Nigel's spell from the very beginning; his pull stronger than anything she'd ever felt before. If she'd only known back then how his grip would tighten to the point where she was choking and that how every now and then—too often—she actually wished she were dead.

As if sensing her thoughts were on another man, Nigel came up behind her and threaded his arms around her waist. When he pulled her backwards against him, she realized he was naked. His erection pressed against her buttocks, with only her thin cotton nightgown separating them. She tensed involuntarily and did her best not to shudder. His hands reached up to cup her breasts.

"Come to bed."

His fingers found her nipples and pinched them hard. She gasped from the pain. "Nigel, please, don't be so rough."

He laughed and nuzzled her neck, biting her soft skin. "You like it rough. You pretend you don't, but I know you do. It's just another one of the games you like to play. Lucky for you, I like to play this one, too."

Bending her over the sink, he caught her nightdress in his hand and dragged it upwards. Moments later, he spread her legs wide and forced himself inside her. Pain and humiliation brought tears to her eyes, but she knew better than to resist. Any sign of defiance only served to arouse him further. She'd learned that the hard way.

"You could appear a little more excited," he growled in her ear as he continued to thrust inside her. "How about a moan or two?"

He took hold of her hips in both hands and increased his frenzied attack. This time, she didn't have to force the sounds from her throat. She groaned in discomfort and bit her lip until she tasted blood. She gripped the sides of the vanity and prayed for the assault to end.

"Does David Hamilton fuck you like this? I bet you groan for him." Releasing her hips, he brought his hands back around to knead her breasts. A moment later, his hands were around her neck.

"Nigel!" she gasped. "Let go of me! I can't breathe!"

His laughter sent chills down her spine. "Some people get off on this kind of thing, Isobel. It's called autoerotic asphyxiation. The trick is to let go before you suffocate. I thought we might try it."

Her vision narrowed and stars burst behind her eyes. She reached up and tried to loosen his grip, but his fingers were like iron.

"Nigel! I mean it! I can't breathe!

Please…please…" Her heart thumped as hard and as fast as the pounding of his hips. A moment later, he found his release and let out a shout of triumph. His hands fell away and he collapsed against her, bending her further over the vanity.

With her head mashed against the cold sink, Isobel sucked in desperate mouthfuls of air, her lungs screaming for oxygen. She wheezed and coughed and swiped at her tears, too distraught to even speak. Nigel moved away from her and blew out his breath on a satisfied sigh.

"Phew! That was something special, don't you think? We ought to try that one again."

As if only just noticing her distress, his gaze narrowed on her face. "Why the fuck are you crying? Plenty of women would be glad their husbands still want to fuck them after nine years of marriage. You ought to be grateful. There is an ample number of other willing takers, let me assure you." He smirked.

"That young blond theater nurse with the perky tits can't wait to suck my cock. I can see it in her eyes. Today she was all over me, laughing at everything I said, brushing her tits against my arm. I should have just taken her into the changing rooms and fucked her."

Isobel wanted to press her hands against her ears and block out his filthy words, but instead, she stood in silence with her hands fisted by her sides and waited for it to end. Nigel just looked at her. A moment later, he shook his head and stalked out of the room. She collapsed onto the toilet seat and held back a fresh rush of tears.

Where had she gone wrong? Why was she being punished? How had her life gone so far off the track?

It was a long while later when she finally found the strength to stand and finish her preparations for bed. She longed for another shower to scrub away the feel of Nigel, but didn't want to risk waking him. Already, his snores filled the silence.

Instead, she stumbled to the sink and splashed some cool water on her cheeks. She opened up the cabinet above the sink and checked for a bottle of Tylenol. She usually kept one in there. Her hand closed around an unfamiliar bottle and she pulled it out into the light. She looked down at the label and frowned.

Diazepam. Otherwise known as Valium. Why would there be sleeping tablets in her bathroom cabinet? She certainly hadn't requested them and Nigel had no trouble sleeping. She turned the bottle over in her hands, but there was no name attached to the prescription. The bottle hadn't been issued by a pharmacist. Which meant Nigel had brought them home. He'd stolen them from the hospital. There wasn't any other explanation. The question she asked herself was, why?

All of a sudden, she recalled the pile of books she'd found on the desk inside his office. *How to Get Away with Murder, Secrets of a Serial Killer,* and others similarly themed. Her mind returned to their violent sex—when she'd thought she was going to die. A coldness settled deep in her belly. Her legs went weak, no longer able to support her.

As the terrifying realization hit her, she gasped and slid slowly to the floor.

The truth was there for all to see, but she was the only one who could. The tablets were meant for her, she was sure of it. Nigel was planning to kill her...

CHAPTER 5

Dear Diary,

Work has been my salvation and I thank God for this escape. When I'm at the hospital, I can forget about the horror of living at home. Apart from my children, taking care of sick kids makes me feel human and gives me a purpose. It's the only time a little of my constant fear and paranoia leave me.

Sometimes I catch a glimpse of my former self in my patients' laughter or see it in their eyes. I used to laugh and smile like that and I used to hope I could make the world a better place. Seeing Mason has been like having a life line thrown at me. I can look at him and remember the girl I used to be, so long ago. I miss her so much and I've lost hope that she'll ever come back.

I feel something today, something more than the usual numbness. I feel sadness and heartache and...yearning. Maybe that's a good thing? Because finally, I'm starting to feel again.

Mason glanced through one of the windows in the children's ward and sighed inwardly. Mid-afternoon sunlight streamed through the opening and landed on the linoleum floor in a maze of colorful geometric patterns. He'd spent another busy day tending to sick children and to their parents, who were almost as needy. He understood their concern, of course, and how the worry and uncertainty about the health of their children could eat away at their souls. He didn't have to be a father to empathize.

He looked out the window again and realized that since his arrival in Sydney a week earlier, he hadn't had an opportunity to explore. Today, the beautiful city, with all its early December splendor, beckoned to him from outside the window, but his chances of finding time to enjoy the warm summer afternoon were next to none. His patient list was full.

Rounding the corner at the far end of the ward, he walked into the room that contained his latest patient. Charlie Alsop had been admitted via the Emergency Department, or ED as it was known among staff. The boy's mother had brought him in complaining of acute stomach pain. Appendicitis was the preliminary diagnosis, but a CT scan had ruled that out. Charlie had been admitted and brought up to the ward for further investigation.

Mason looked up from the clinical notes in his hand and smiled at his patient. He opened his mouth to greet the child and his mother, but the greeting got caught in his throat. A pretty nurse was bent over the boy, a blood pressure cuff in her hand. It took his brain less than a second to recognize Isobel and her trademark red hair.

As if alerted to his presence, she turned to look at him and then quickly averted her gaze. He was relieved to find no lingering sign of the trauma to her eye, even though her face was drawn with fatigue. He couldn't help but wonder about her reluctance to meet his gaze.

"Mrs Alsop, I'm Doctor Mason Alexander. I'm going to look after Charlie while he's in hospital." The boy's mother nodded in acknowledgement and Mason perched himself on the side of Charlie's bed, a mere two or three feet from Isobel. She tensed and then visibly relaxed, as if she'd willed it. Another wave of curiosity surged through him at her odd behavior, but now wasn't the time to give voice to his concerns.

"Now, Charlie, your mom told the doctors downstairs that you had a terrible pain in your tummy. Is that right?"

The seven-year-old nodded solemnly.

"How does it feel now?" Mason asked, his tone gentle.

Charlie shrugged. "It's still sore, but not quite as bad as it was before."

"That's good to hear," Mason replied. "Do you mind if I have a feel of your tummy?"

Charlie shook his head and wiggled further down in his bed. Isobel packed up her equipment and moved out of the way. When she inadvertently brushed against Mason's sleeve, his heart skipped a beat. Her perfume teased his nose—familiar, warm, sweet, feminine. She continued past him without pause, perhaps oblivious to her effect on him. She'd never given him any indication in high school that she regarded him as anything more than her boyfriend's teammate, even after Mason had risked all and declared his undying love.

The decade-old memory burned him with as much humiliation now as it had then and his fists tightened in response. Forcing a deep breath into his lungs, he made a deliberate effort to wipe the memory from his mind. After all, he was at work, in the middle of an examination though the object of his pain stood less than ten feet away. He had to get a grip.

"I'm just going to lift your T-shirt so I can have a look at your tummy. Is that okay?" He included Charlie's mom in his gaze. Both of them nodded. Mason pressed gently on the boy's abdomen and palpated it beneath his fingers.

"Does that hurt, Charlie?" he asked.

"No."

"How about here?"

"No, not really."

"What about here?"

"Ouch," Charlie complained and a wave of concern washed over his mother's face.

Mason continued his examination. When he was finished, he pulled down the boy's shirt.

"How long has it been since you went to the toilet, Charlie?"

The boy shrugged. "I don't know. I did a pee while I was still downstairs."

"No, I mean a poo. Do you remember when you last went to the toilet for a poo?"

Charlie frowned in thought. His mother sat forward in her chair.

"Have you been today, Charlie?" she asked.

"No."

"What about yesterday?" Mason asked.

"No. I remember because I had to go, but it was in the middle of class and I didn't want to ask the teacher if I could leave, so I just held on. Later, in the break, I didn't feel like going."

"Do you normally do a poo most days?" Mason asked.

Charlie's mom nodded. "As far as I know. He seems to spend an awful lot of time in there."

The young boy's cheeks turned red and he stared down at the sheet. "It's only because I take a book in there, Mom. I like to read. It helps pass the time." His blush deepened and Mason couldn't help but feel sorry for him.

"I like to read in the toilet, too, Charlie," he said and the boy shot him a grateful look. "Sometimes it's the only quiet time I get."

"Yeah," Charlie replied with feeling, shooting Mason a grin. "It's the only place I can get away from my pesky little sisters."

"Charlie, that's not very nice," his mom admonished.

"It's true, Mom," Charlie insisted, unabashed.

Mason cleared his throat and brought the conversation back to point. He stood and folded his arms across his chest.

"I'm pretty sure I know what the problem is," he

said and both Charlie and his mom turned to him, expectant looks upon their faces.

"I think your tummy ache is being caused by constipation."

Now it was the mother's turn to blush. Charlie just looked confused. "What's constipation?"

"It's when your bowel gets hard and full and tight because you're not going to the toilet often enough," Mason explained.

"What's my bowel?"

Isobel moved nearer and Mason steeled himself against her closeness. She smiled down at his young patient.

"Your bowel is a storage compartment in your tummy," she explained with a soft smile. "It holds all the food waste that you've eaten. It's really important to go to the toilet when you feel the urge. That's your brain telling your body it's time to go and empty out. If you ignore it too often, your poo ends up hard and impacted and your tummy gets really sore. Doctor Alexander thinks that's the reason for your tummy pain."

Mason shot Isobel a look of gratitude and then offered Charlie a wink. "I couldn't have put it any better myself."

"How do you fix it?" Charlie asked.

"Well, the easiest way to fix it is to go to the toilet," Mason replied.

Charlie frowned. "Will it hurt?"

Isobel squeezed his hand. "A little bit, but we can give you a special medicine that will soften things up and help it on its way."

Mrs Alsop shook her head, her cheeks still

slightly pink. "I can't believe we rushed here in such a panic when it was only constipation."

Mason was quick to reassure her. "It's always better to be safe than sorry, especially with children. They can go downhill very quickly. You were right to bring him in."

She offered him a smile filled with relief and gratitude. "Thank you, Doctor Alexander. I appreciate your understanding. Now we know what the problem is, we can go home and get it seen to."

"There's no rush," Mason replied and glanced over at Isobel who nodded in agreement. "It's nearly four o'clock. He might as well stay the night. I'll chart the medicine he needs to help him do what needs to be done. The nurse will administer it shortly and with a bit of luck, he'll be as good as new in the morning."

Charlie's mother issued a soft sigh of relief and reached out to shake Mason's hand. "Thank you, Doctor, for everything. You don't know how comforting that is."

"My pleasure," Mason replied and looked away, uncomfortable with the praise. As far as he was concerned, he was merely doing his job.

"I'll leave you to it," he said and offered a brief wave of farewell. At the same time, he turned and addressed Isobel, pitching his voice low: "Nurse, can we speak for a moment?"

Isobel's eyes widened in alarm, but she quickly regained her composure. "Of course, Doctor."

He moved far enough away that they wouldn't be heard by the other patients in the room. Isobel followed slowly behind him.

"What is it, Doctor?"

"Please, call me Mason."

"All right. Mason. Is something the matter?" she asked fearfully.

He stared down at this timid woman and wanted to shake her and demand to know where the fun-loving, spirited Isobel of old had gone. She was quiet and withdrawn and solemn—nothing like the brash girl he used to know. Instead, he asked gently, "What's happened to you, Belle? What's happened to change you so much?"

Her jaw tightened and crimson inched across her face. She gnawed on her lower lip. He heard her soft intake of breath a second before a single silver tear slid slowly down her cheek. His gut clenched in an agony of pain and regret. She was crying and it was his fault... Or maybe it wasn't? When he was this close to her his mind was in such a whirlwind, he no longer knew what to think.

"Belle?" he croaked. "Please, Belle. Please, don't cry. I never meant to make you cry."

She sniffed and swiped at the offending moisture and then drew in another breath. "It's not you, Mason. You haven't done anything wrong."

He shook his head, flooded with confusion. "Then what? Please, tell me what's wrong and what's happened to make you so sad. I want to know. I need to know."

Something in the earnestness of his tone must have finally registered because a moment later, she lifted her head and her eyes met his desperate gaze. The deep well of sadness in her beautiful green eyes snatched his breath away. Once again, he was flooded with the desire to help.

He wanted to obliterate her sadness and bring sunshine back to her face. He wanted to pull her into his arms and promise she'd never feel this unhappy again.

But she was married to Nigel and was a mother to their children. She wasn't Mason's to love and protect and cherish. She'd turned down his love and now belonged to someone else.

The reality of that came crashing down on him and he took a step back. The action seemed to snap the fragile bond between them. When she looked up at him the next time, her eyes were blank again and the pain he'd spied in them only moments earlier had disappeared.

"Belle?"

"I'm fine, Mason. It's nothing. I-I'm just a little tired. I've been working extra shifts to cover the staff shortages. What I need is to go home and get a decent sleep. Lucky for me, I'll be out of here in about ten minutes."

She offered him a brief smile, but he could tell it was an effort. Whatever was troubling her hadn't gone away; rather, she'd decided not to share it with him. He bit down hard on the surge of hurt and disappointment.

"Where did you go to college?" she asked, her tone now light and curious as they headed out of the room.

He stared down at her for a moment, willing her to find the courage to confide in him, but then reluctantly let it go. It wasn't his place to force her. They hadn't seen each other for a decade; though he'd thought about her every day. He was like a stranger to her and had no right to expect her confidence or trust.

"The University of Queensland in Brisbane," he finally answered and couldn't help but notice her relief that he'd dropped the other topic.

She pursed her lips. "A fair way from home and a move interstate. What made you choose UQ?"

Mason shrugged. "I have family who live in Brisbane. An aunt and an uncle on my father's side. They have a bunch of kids—cousins I spent a fair bit of time with when we were young. One of my cousins, Jake, went to med school with me."

She nodded and her smile seemed to come a little easier. "That's nice. Family's good. I'm glad you had someone to help you through it. When Nigel was at college, he had no one—no one but me. I was his study buddy, his take-out girl and everything else he needed. It was lucky I was studying nursing. At least I had some idea what he was trying to learn. Some of that biology..." She shook her head and this time, her grin seemed real. "It nearly did my head in."

He smiled back at her, relieved that her sad mood had lifted. "Oh, yeah! You and me, both."

"How are the rest of your family? Your parents and brothers?"

"They're all good. My brothers are spread around the state, doing what they do. Mom and Dad retired awhile ago. They moved to far North

Queensland. They spend a fair amount of their time on a yacht."

"Sounds like a nice way to pass the time."

"Yes, it does, doesn't it? Maybe some day, I'll earn enough to buy one of my own. Do you like to sail? Maybe we could go out on the harbor some time? With Nigel and the kids, of course," he added hurriedly, his face aflame.

Her withdrawal was immediate. The soft smile disappeared; the easy air between them suddenly became tense and her gaze remained fixed on the floor. He didn't know what had done it, but the mood was well and truly gone.

"I'm sorry, Belle, I didn't mean to upset you."

She brushed him off. "It's fine, Mason. I'm fine. I... I have to get back to work. I'll see you later." She turned and walked away.

Isobel gripped the sides of the kitchen counter and forced herself to breathe. Nigel had been in a mood all evening. First he'd complained that the children were spending too much time in daycare because she'd accepted extra shifts.

"Why the hell can't they call someone else?" he'd yelled. "Why is it always you?"

"There's a flu bug going around, Nigel. There *is* no one else. I'm surprised the surgical staff haven't been affected. It seems like every other department in the hospital has."

Then it was the dinner she served. She'd worked

until four that afternoon, and by the time she collected Ben and Sophie there hadn't been enough time to prepare the usual fancy meal. She'd ducked into the shops and bought a pre-prepared stir-fry and had microwaved a dish of rice. She should have known it wouldn't be good enough for Nigel.

"What do you call this crap?" he'd snarled when she set it down in front of him. Ben looked up from his spot at the table, his body tense. Sophie fell quiet.

"It's beef and garlic stir-fry."

"It's premade crap from the supermarket. How the hell do you expect me to eat this?" He shoved it to one side and turned his back on her.

"I-I'll see what else I can find," she said and pushed away from the table.

Now, she drew in another deep breath and slowly counted to ten. With a huge effort, she pushed her exhaustion aside, relaxed her fingers and stepped away from the counter. Pulling open the door to the freezer, she searched for something else to cook. It wasn't easy. The extra shifts had meant that she hadn't had time to go to the supermarket. The freezer was almost bare. She spied a steak toward the back and reached for it.

"Don't bother. I'm not hungry."

She gasped and slowly closed the freezer door. Nigel stood a few feet away, a churlish expression on his face. She swallowed a sigh and braced herself for another round of complaints.

"I'm happy to grill a steak, Nigel. It won't take long to defrost. I could peel some baby potatoes and steam some of those sugar peas you like so—"

"I said forget it." His tone had gone from annoyed to deadly in the few seconds since he'd complained.

Her heart leaped with fear, but she bravely held her ground. The children were in the next room, able to hear every word. Then she remembered that the presence of his son and daughter no longer had the usual restraining effect. A little over a week ago he'd hit her at the table, right in front of them. *How had she forgotten?*

Feeling like she'd come to a sudden halt right at the very edge of an eroding cliff, she stood stock still and snatched only the tiniest of breaths. One move in the wrong direction and she'd be plummeting over the other side.

She waited for Nigel's next move. She didn't have to wait long. He stalked across the room and wrenched a long-bladed knife from the knife block. Seconds later, he was back at her side.

Fear like she'd never known turned her limbs leaden. She stared at the knife like it was a cobra, poised and ready to strike. Her breath came fast and her chest felt tight. Nigel stared back at her, a knowing grin twisting his lips.

"That got your attention, didn't it?" he snarled. A moment later, his tone softened and became almost conversational. He turned the knife over in his hands, examining it with interest.

"Do you know how many ways there are to kill someone?" Without giving her a chance to answer, he continued in the same, calm voice. "Let me tell you; more than you can imagine. I have to admit, my night-time reading has proven quite beneficial and...entirely enlightening."

His gaze, intense and ugly, traveled over her and she shivered from the menace in his eyes. He took a step toward her and she gasped and automatically moved back. She came up hard against the door of the freezer. Once again, she was paralyzed with fear. A triumphant expression lit up his eyes and he closed the distance between them, his gaze never leaving hers. He leaned in close and she whimpered, way beyond forming even the simplest of words.

With his mouth just inches from her ear, he whispered, "All it takes is a flick of the wrist and a sharp blade and we both know I have access to some *very* sharp blades. I know just where to cut. One slice across your carotid and you'd be dead before you hit the floor." He smirked. "Trust me. I'm a doctor."

He pulled back a little, but still crowded her space. Her heart thumped and her mouth went dry. She could hear nothing over the rush of blood in her ears, but still she heard everything that mattered, including her husband's humorless chuckle.

"Like I said, I've been doing some very interesting reading. I've already learned so many fascinating tricks. I think I could stage a believable break-in. Of course, when it happens, I'll be conveniently at work. The roster will show I'm there and it will be verified by my staff. No one will think it strange if I disappear for an hour or so. I'm entitled to lunch, after all and everyone knows I can't abide the crap they serve up in the cafeteria. Yes, I think an hour should do it."

He made a sudden movement and she cried out in fear. A second later, the cold, hard blade of the knife pressed against the fragile skin of her neck. She stared up at him, petrified.

His breath came fast. A wild look filled his eyes. His face morphed into something so ugly and distorted, she barely recognized him. Terror gushed through her veins and filled her heart with ice. She stared at him, too frightened to make another sound.

"Daddy! Stop! What are you doing?"

Ben stood in the doorway to the kitchen, his eyes filled with tears. Isobel cried out at the terrified expression on his face.

"Get out of here, Ben, or you'll be next," Nigel growled and Isobel's heart stood still.

"Please don't hurt Mommy. Please, Daddy, please. Please don't hurt Mommy." Ben's sobs came harder and his body shook with fear, but he bravely held his ground. Isobel bit down hard on her lip to hold back a torrent of tears.

"Ben, baby, please go back inside. Daddy and I... We...we..."

With a savage curse, Nigel stepped back and turned and moved away. He threw the knife across the room and it clattered loudly into the sink. Isobel collapsed back against the freezer door and dropped her head into her hands, sobbing out of control. She trembled so violently, her legs gave out and she crumpled to the floor.

In some distant part of her mind, she registered

the sound of Nigel's boots on the tiles and then she spied them inches from where she sat. One foot came out and connected hard with the side of her leg. She cried out in pain and buried her head harder against her knees. She didn't know where her son was, but she could no longer hold back the flood.

Tears poured down her cheeks. Nigel hunched down beside her and she whimpered in fear and squeezed herself into a tighter ball.

"One hour, Isobel. You and the kids. That's all the time I'll need."

CHAPTER 6

Dear Diary,

They say a person's eyes are the windows to their soul. A deep hidden place which contains every one of their secrets. Look long enough at someone and eventually you'll see their hidden truth; that little something everyone tries so hard to mask behind layers and layers of falseness.

I know this truth: If someone stared at me long enough, they'd see a woman caught up in the terror that her own life has become. They'd see the reflection of hell.

Damn you, Father O'Dell! Even after all these years, I still remember your dark, evil eyes, flashing with hell and brimstone. The perspiration dripped from your skin and became entangled in your thick beard. With your piercing gaze, you preached to us sixth graders all those untruths during catechism class. You scared me enough to envision hell as some hot, fiery hole, a place of banishment for sins committed...

I might have believed hell was like that then, but I know better, now. It's not hot and fiery at all. It's a dark, desolate, lonely place, barren and cold and empty. Shrouded by a silence so deep and impenetrable, one's mind skitters between sanity and madness and the seconds, minutes, tick away... A lonely place, even in a crowd.

How did I get here? What awful sin did I commit that God chose this as my punishment? I have no answers. All I know is that I woke up one morning and found myself here. The only sound I hear is the ticking of the clock: tic toc, tic toc, tic toc... And it suddenly comes to me: I'm stuck. No matter how much time passes, there's no escaping him...

I sobel glanced over her shoulder, but the staff car park was empty. She was late. No doubt the other staff rostered onto the evening shift had already made it to their wards. She was meant to start work at two-fifteen and it was now going on for half-past. She'd fallen asleep beside Sophie right after lunch and had woken tired and disoriented and in a panic.

After her nightmarish skirmish with Nigel, she hadn't been able to bring herself to go to bed. She'd spent the night curled up on the couch in a ball of tension and fear. She'd wracked her brain for a plan, for some hope that she could escape with her children, but as the hours rolled over, she'd been overwhelmed with hopelessness.

She had no one to turn to. The few friends she'd had from her past were now a distant memory.

Since arriving at the Sydney Harbour Hospital, she'd resisted any attempts her colleagues made toward friendships. They would only end in an agony of embarrassment and disappointment as Nigel worked his evil magic once again.

Behind the protection of their closed front door, he'd belittle and criticize and offend until Isobel couldn't bear to listen to it and would let even the nicest of them go. It had happened time and time again.

In the early days, she thought it was just another way Nigel had found to hurt her, but now she knew the truth. He'd isolated her from each and every outside influence. Even her family wasn't spared. It was part of his need to control, to own her and her every single thought—and he'd won. He'd *won*.

Even her sister didn't know what her life was really like. Kat thought Nigel was the perfect husband. She had no idea what went on when the door was closed. No, Isobel was on her own. There was no one she could call. No one who could help her. Except, perhaps the police.

The police. She'd go to them in her break and tell them what was happening, the threats, the beatings, the...everything. She'd beg the police to help them, to arrest Nigel and lock him up. And then, for the very first time, she'd be safe with her children. *Safe.* She could barely fathom how that would feel.

But for now, the police would have to wait. She was already late for work. With a bit of luck, Nigel would be too busy in the operating room to check on her during her breaks. More often than not, he called the ward. She'd try and get one of the other nurses to cover for her, in case her interview with the police went overtime. Provided her courage held, by the end of her shift, the nightmare might be over. She lived in hope...

"Isobel, wait up!"

Mason spied her up ahead of him and hurried to catch up. He'd been hoping she was working the evening shift. It had been nearly a week since he'd seen her, but she was never far from his thoughts. Over and over again, he replayed the scene when she'd looked so sad and hopeless—and the growing suspicion that there was something very wrong in her life just wouldn't go away.

He thought again of seeing what had looked like bruising around her eye and his jaw tensed. *If that bastard was hurting her...* His fists clenched. He couldn't even bear to complete the thought. She turned slowly to face him and he couldn't help but notice the sadness and resignation that yet again shadowed her face.

"How are you?" he asked gently, coming up close.

"I'm fine," she replied in a voice that was far from sounding fine.

He tilted her chin up with his finger so that she was forced to make eye contact. She flinched away. The desolation in her gaze broke his heart. "You're not fine, Belle. I don't know who you're trying to convince, but it's not working on me. I know you. I *know* you. Remember?

"Your colleagues might think that the quiet and subdued nurse with the flaming red hair is the woman known as Isobel Wes...Donnelly, but I know better. I know the real Isobel, the one who laughed and danced and hummed sweet tunes, the girl who was always surrounded by friends. Over all the years we spent together in high school, I never once saw you sad and alone." He shook his head.

"And yet, a decade later, I run into you and it's like you're someone else. On the outside, though you're a lot thinner, you still look much like the girl I knew, but on the inside, when I look into your eyes, all I see is an emptiness, like the spark, the spirit inside you has died."

He drew in a breath and a sense of urgency rushed through him, as if he had to solve the mystery, to discover the secrets behind her green eyes and if he didn't, all would be lost. He didn't know where the feeling came from, but it was too strong to deny.

"Talk to me, Belle. I want to help. I want to take away your pain. I want to bring back the Belle of old. I want to hear you laugh again." In an effort to convince her, he took her by the arms. His grip tightened unconsciously, a little more with every word he uttered. She stepped back and rubbed her arms.

"I'm sorry, Belle. I hope I didn't hurt you. I just—"

He broke off with a sigh of resignation. He had to let her go. She wasn't his to love and to hold. She wasn't then and she wasn't now and the odds were she never would be.

When he'd told her a decade ago that he loved her, she'd smiled kindly and brushed his declaration away. He was certain she didn't have a clue he was still in love with her and it wasn't right or fair for him to let her know now. She was married to Nigel, the man of her dreams. Together, they were the perfect couple. He only wished he saw even a little of the same joy in her gaze that he had ten years ago. Defeated, his shoulders slumped and he turned away.

She surprised him then when she reached out, and stopped him. He couldn't help the sudden traitorous leap of hope.

"I'm on a break in ten minutes," she whispered. "Will you meet me in the cafeteria?" She stared at him and he stared right back. Her eyes pleaded with him.

Hoping he wouldn't live to regret it, he nodded.

As if she'd been holding her breath, she exhaled in a rush. "I'll see you there."

Isobel made her way across the crowded cafeteria and tried to still her trembling limbs. Ever since she'd agreed to talk to Mason, she'd worried over her decision. He'd called her Belle— his childhood nickname for her. His words, and the sweet endearment, had reminded her of everything she'd lost, of a time she didn't live in fear of her husband, or anyone else. Those days seemed so dim and distant now.

Other than when she immersed herself in work, she couldn't remember the last time she hadn't felt afraid. And now she wasn't just afraid for herself. His latest threat to the children sapped any strength and peace of mind she'd had left.

She found an empty table in the far corner of the room. At least she wouldn't have to worry about running into her husband. Nigel never ate in the cafeteria. Instead, he preferred to dine at a nearby café. Besides, there were enough people around her that it would be unlikely he'd spy her sitting inside if he happened to walk past.

She glanced at her watch. Unless he'd been waylaid, Mason should arrive any minute. Once again, a wave of nerves tightened her belly. She'd invited him to meet with her for the express purpose of confiding her troubles, but the more she thought about it, the more she questioned the wisdom of getting him involved. She had no right to expect his help or his sympathy.

Okay, so they'd known each other in high school and he'd confessed to having a crush, but that was a decade ago. He owed her nothing. If they hadn't run into each other at work, she would never have thought to contact him.

It was just that he'd surprised her and he'd been so kind and gentle and sweet. He'd looked at her with such concern. It had been a long time since anyone had done that, so well had she hidden her pain. She was the needy one, the one who was living a lie. Was it fair to drag him into the sorry, sad mess that was her life?

And there was also the question of trust. She'd watched him on the ward, interacting with the staff and patients. He was a good and honorable man, full of kindness and compassion, but could she depend on him to keep her confidence? She wanted to believe she could, but she'd been so wrong about her instincts before.

The whole time she'd dated Nigel, she'd never once felt the slightest bit alarmed. Not a single warning bell had sounded. A few times, she'd been annoyed at his occasional pettiness or the way he'd criticized her friends, but nothing that gave her even an inkling of the man he would become.

She wanted to believe Mason was different. He exuded goodness and safety and strength. She'd never noticed it in high school, but back then, safety and security were a long way down on her list. She'd been all about having fun and enjoying life to the fullest, working hard and reaching for her dreams—and most of all, making a home with Nigel, the man she'd loved.

As she sat there, considering the dreams she'd had as a teen, the awful realization of how far her life had drifted off course hit her with a sickening jolt. The knowledge that her children were growing up in such an unhappy, dysfunctional household, filled her with sadness and more than a little panic. She hadn't seen it coming, so different was the reality of her life from how she'd grown up and what she'd imagined for her future.

She remembered how Nigel had tightened his hands around her neck until she was certain she would black out, and then most recently, when he'd held a knife against her throat. She recalled the way he'd bragged about what he'd learned in the books about serial killers and murder and other nameless horrors and shuddered.

And then there were the sleeping pills...

The idea that her husband had it in him to kill her filled her mind with so much horror she tried to block those thoughts, but try as she might, she couldn't. She was living a nightmare with no avenue of escape.

"Why the sad face? You look like your dog just chewed up your favorite Jimmy Choos."

She looked up and saw Mason grinning down at her, but even his lame attempt at a joke failed to penetrate her misery. As if sensing her fragile emotional state, his grin faded and when he took a seat opposite her, his expression was solemn.

"I'm sorry, Belle. I shouldn't have joked like that. It's obvious something's wrong. Why don't you tell me what's going on?"

She dropped her gaze and was once again flooded with indecision. Was she really ready to leave her husband, walk out on her marriage? And what about her kids? It appalled her to think that if she did leave Nigel, they'd just become children from another broken home.

But what choice did she have? If Nigel carried through on his unspoken plans, she'd more than likely be dead and her children along with her.

She couldn't take the risk that he'd follow through on his threats and there was no way she was going to leave her babies alone to live with Nigel without protection...

Was she being overly dramatic? Reading things into Nigel's actions that just weren't there? She was so confused and tired and uncertain, she no longer knew what to think. Her thoughts were a jumbled blur and she felt like she was caught in some complicated maze, retracing the same steps over and over again and getting nowhere.

Mason squeezed her fingers. The contact startled her. She pulled her hands away and averted her gaze.

"Talk to me, Belle. I can see you need a friend. Tell me what's wrong and I'll do everything I can to help."

She shook her head in bewilderment. "How can you say that? We haven't seen each other in years. How could you possibly know that there's a problem? I appreciate your concern, but we might as well be two strangers meeting for the first time for all that we know about each other right now."

"It doesn't matter. Something's upset you. I can see it in your eyes. There's a sadness there that you never had before and it tears me up inside. I want to help you, Belle. I want to bring back your smile."

She looked at him and thought again how good and kind he was. Did he see her as she saw herself in the mirror? Was it obvious to the world now? She didn't think she could bear to know.

"Why do you call me that?" she asked softly in an effort to delay the real purpose for their conversation.

He gave her a look that told her he knew exactly what she was doing, but answered her anyway. "The name Isobel always sounded so formal and proper. Belle seemed to suit you so much more. Besides, everyone called you Isobel. To me, Belle was unique and special."

His voice had grown husky over the course of his explanation and emotion now shadowed his face. It dawned on her that his feelings for her from all those years ago might not have been buried over the passage of time. The thought unsettled her and yet at the same time, warmed her through.

He glanced at his watch and the spell was broken. He wasn't being rude or signifying he wanted to be somewhere else. She understood time was at a premium. He was a senior doctor in a busy hospital and there was always plenty to be done. Knowing if she didn't find the courage to tell him now, she might never feel brave enough to approach it, she spoke again.

"Mason, it's hard for me to trust anyone right now, at times I don't even trust myself. What I'm about to tell you will shock you. In fact, if I wasn't the one living through this, I'd have a hard time believing it, too."

His gaze remained steady, but his expression turned guarded. "Okay."

She drew in a deep breath and eased it out between lips that were parchment dry. "Nigel and

I have been married for nine years. The last five of them have been a living hell."

He didn't move. Not even a blink. His tone remained conversational. "In what way?"

Hot shame boiled up inside her, but she forced herself to answer. "He's controlling, manipulative and selfish and... And more and more lately he uses his fists."

That got his attention. He visibly paled beneath his summer tan and swallowed uneasily.

"What are you saying, Belle? That Nigel *beats* you and the kids?"

She bravely held his gaze, though it was the hardest thing she'd ever done. "Not the kids. So far, he's only threatened them. It's me he beats."

Mason stared at her and did his best to control his fury, knowing instinctively that any loss of control would frighten her. Under the table, his fists were clenched and anger gushed through every vein. He wanted to rush away and find Nigel Donnelly and pummel him to a pulp. He was so angry, he could imagine killing the man with his bare hands. The bastard deserved that and more. So much more.

A man who beat up on his wife and threatened his kids. What kind of goddamned cowardly asshole did that? He couldn't believe it was a man he knew—although looking back, the early warning signs had been there.

He could still remember seeing Nigel after a game, angry because they'd lost. His mom had swung by to pick him up and Nigel had shoved past her so hard, he'd pushed her against the wall. She'd cried out, but his pace hadn't slowed.

It was Mason who'd walked over to her to check that she was all right. He could still remember the glint of her tears, but what was worse was the shame that had filled her eyes. It was the same look that flooded Belle's gaze now.

"It's not your fault, Belle. There's something missing in Nigel. He's sick. He needs help."

She nodded, but he could see she didn't believe him. Her lip trembled and she averted her eyes. He took her hands in his again and squeezed them, trying to reassure her, to make her see. She cringed at the contact and once again, pulled her hands out of his. He didn't press.

"It's a common reaction to blame yourself. It's what a lot of victims do," he continued gently. "You're a health professional. You know this stuff as well as I do. It's not your fault." He spoke slowly and succinctly, doing his best to convince her of the truth. The reality was, it would take a lot more time and skill than he had to make her believe it.

"I'm going to hunt that prick down and hit him so hard he'll never want to beat you again." He said it calmly, but with enough force that she'd know he was serious.

She shook her head as if to protest, but a tiny

smile tugged at the corner of her lips. "What good would that do?"

"Probably nothing, but I'd feel a hell of a lot better."

She fell silent and busied herself rearranging the napkins. He stared at her, willing her to meet his gaze.

"You have to leave him," he said. "There's nothing else you can do."

It took awhile, but eventually, with eyes downcast, she nodded. "Yes, I know that now. I've been searching for the courage to do it, but somehow every time I think I'm ready to leave, the doubts creep in. Then I remember the constant threats, the murder books and the bottle of Diazepam..."

He frowned in confusion. *Murder books? Diazepam?* She wasn't talking sense. He quietly told her as much. He heard her shaky, indrawn breath and just as shaky release. As if the action had fortified her, she raised her gaze to his and told him what she'd found. The bleakness in her eyes and voice lacerated his heart.

When at last she fell silent, it was all Mason could do not to howl out his anger at the man she'd married. Instead, he forced a few calming breaths through the tightness of his chest and breathed out slowly, silently counting to ten. She interrupted his mammoth attempts to hold on to his self-control by speaking again.

"Will you...help me?" she whispered brokenly. "I... I can't do it on my own."

He replied without hesitation. "Of course."

"It's not only me..."

"Your kids. No problem," he said and meant it. "Kids are good."

"Do you have any?"

"No, Sue Ann wasn't able to."

"Sue Ann? You're married?"

"Not anymore."

"What happened?"

He sighed. "It didn't work out."

She frowned and he could see she wanted to know more, but she surprised him by saying, "Thank you for helping me, Mason. You're a good man. Until I saw you again, I didn't have anywhere else to turn."

She looked at him with so much gratitude, he wanted to curse. It wasn't her gratitude he wanted, but he knew it would take her awhile to reach a point where she was open to anything along the line of a normal relationship. Regardless, he knew in that moment that he wanted to be part of her life—and that he'd have to be patient. What she needed right now more than anything was a friend.

"It's fine," he said and then winced inwardly at his dismissive tone. He was being churlish and it wasn't fair. In a much milder voice, he spoke again. "We should talk about how this is going to work. First, we're going to the police to file a report and get an apprehended violence order. What time do you finish work?"

She looked doubtful and more than a little scared. "Eleven, but Nigel will be expecting me home. He finishes around six tonight and then swings by the daycare center to collect the kids. He knows how long it should take me to get home. If I'm late, he'll wonder why. He'll ask questions. It could get...nasty."

Mason stared at her and his jaw clenched with the effort of holding in his anger. Once again, he wanted to bury his fists into Nigel Donnelly's face and pummel him into oblivion. He drew in a deep breath and eased it out. "Could you get away a little earlier?"

She nodded. "I'd planned to do it tonight during my dinner break. I'm off between seven and eight."

"No problem. I'll come with you."

The relief on her face was palpable. Once again, he had to tamp down on his anger. It wasn't right that any woman should feel so scared of her husband's reaction. He couldn't believe it was happening to someone he knew and cared for. With reluctance, he checked his watch again.

"I have to go, but I'll meet you in the hospital car park just after seven. We can go in my car to the police station."

Fresh tears welled up in her eyes, but she blinked them away. "Thank you, Mason," she whispered.

He nodded once and then stood and walked away.

CHAPTER 7

Dear Diary,

I don't know where I'd be without Mason's support. He has given me courage, he is the light in my darkness and for that I will be forever grateful. I do not know how I will repay him for his kindness. I should be thanking You, God, for him, but I have lost my faith in You. I can't help but question what it is that I have ever done wrong to have earned this living hell.

How many times have I prayed to You for help, for direction, for comfort? My prayers have gone unanswered. But maybe I've misjudged You, too? Maybe You were waiting to send me Mason all along or maybe You knew what I didn't—that I could bear this cross on my own, that it wouldn't destroy me and that in the end I would have my own triumphant resurrection and come out of this a better, stronger person. Only time will tell. Because aside from time, what do I have left?

I want so much to trust Mason, but how can I trust another when I no longer trust myself?

As Isobel entered the sterile surrounds of the Sydney City Police Station, she was encompassed in a rush of cool air from the air conditioner vents. Even though the sun had disappeared half an hour earlier, the night was still warm. She drew in a breath and tried to ease the tension that had doubled her stomach up in knots.

Mason offered her a smile of reassurance and she took courage from his quiet strength. Squaring her shoulders, she approached the reception desk and forced herself to make eye contact with the young female constable who stood behind the counter.

The woman greeted her with a friendly smile. "Hi, what can I do for you?"

"I-I need to report an assault."

"Okay, are you the victim?"

"Yes," she whispered. Mason moved up beside her and she was grateful for his comforting presence. The officer looked from one to the other and then nodded to Isobel.

"I'll have one of the senior officers come and speak with you. They won't be long. You can take a seat, if you like."

Isobel turned and looked at the row of hard plastic chairs behind her. They were stained from years of ground-in dirt. She shuddered and turned away. "I'm fine, thank you. I-I'm happy to stand."

Mason moved to put his arm around her shoulders, but she deftly slipped out of reach. She was sure he'd only meant to offer her comfort, but she was uneasy with unexpected physical contact. Just another part of her that her husband had damaged.

A moment later, a door opened at the far end of the room and a male officer appeared. His graying hair and quiet air of authority reassured her that he would listen to her fears. She only prayed he'd take them seriously.

"I'm Senior Constable Gavin Rogers." The officer put out his hand and Isobel shook it. Mason followed suit and introduced them.

"If you'd like to follow me, we can talk inside."

Isobel murmured her thanks. With Mason right on her heels, she followed the officer through the doorway and down a corridor that eventually led to a series of empty rooms. Each was furnished sparsely with nothing more than a plain wooden table and three chairs. They all took seats, in silence.

Thirty-five minutes later, she was done. Her throat felt dry and scratchy and her eyes were hot and pulsing from the pressure of unshed tears. Mason reached for her hand and this time, she let him take it.

He squeezed her fingers and she returned the gentle pressure. It had been reassuring to have him there by her side, though what she'd told the officer had been pretty graphic. Now that Mason was aware of what her life was really like, she believed he would stand by her and she gratefully accepted his comfort.

"I can apply for an apprehended violence order first thing in the morning," Senior Constable Rogers said. It will need to go before a judge, but it shouldn't be difficult to get the order. We'll then set about serving your husband with his copy." He cleared his throat. "I assume you have somewhere else to stay tonight?"

The question was enough to undo her. The reality of what she was about to do hit her all of a sudden with enough force to leave her gasping. Panic surged through her. Fast on its heels was a fear so debilitating, she was sure she wouldn't even have the strength to leave the station.

The more she thought about what would happen as soon as Nigel was served with the AVO, the more she knew she couldn't take the risk. She shook her head with increasing vehemence, willing the men who watched her with concern in their eyes to understand.

"No, I'm sorry. I-I can't go through with it. Forget I said anything. I'm so sorry for wasting your time."

"I understand your fear, Mrs Donnelly," Senior Constable Rogers responded quietly, "but from what you've told me, taking the children and leaving your husband to go somewhere safe is the best thing you could do."

Isobel drew in a shaky breath and willed away her panic. She tried again to make him grasp the gravity of her situation. "With all due respect, Senior Constable Rogers, you don't understand. I have to go home, at least for tonight. My children are there. Even now, Ben's brushing his teeth. Sophie will already be asleep. I can't just not show up. Nigel will go berserk. He's never hit the kids before, but after his recent threats, who knows what he might do? And once he finds out I've left him, he'll never let me near them. I can't leave without them." Her voice broke from the strain. Tears poured down her cheeks. "I just can't."

Mason's arm snaked around her shoulders. After a slight hesitation, she relaxed and leaned on him for support. Her sobs came harder until she wasn't sure if she could ever stop. Mason stroked her back in wordless comfort.

"*Shh*, Belle. It's all right. We'll think of something. He won't take your kids. I'll come home with you and we can face him together. I'll make sure he doesn't hurt you. He's not going to hurt you again."

"If you'd rather, I can have an officer escort you home and wait while you collect your kids. Would that help?"

Isobel lifted her head and gazed at the policeman. He meant well and she was grateful for his offer, but he still didn't understand. Nigel wouldn't care if Mason or even a police officer were present. If he knew what she planned, he'd go crazy. More than once, he'd threatened to kill her and the kids if she even thought about leaving. What if he tried something and the officer and Mason couldn't stop him? It would be too late for all of them.

No, she had to return home tonight and pretend that nothing had happened. She'd act like it was just another night and in the morning, after Nigel had left for work, she'd pack up their things and leave with her children. Haltingly, she outlined her plan to the men.

"I'm not letting you go back there alone, Belle!"

Mason protested, his expression reflecting his alarm.

"It doesn't sound like the best of plans," the officer agreed, his tone full of doubt.

"I agree, it's not what I'd prefer." She shivered. "I'd be happy not to spend another moment under the same roof with my husband, but he has my babies and I'm not leaving without them. He won't have any idea what's transpired tonight and I'm certainly not going to breathe a word." She eyed Senior Constable Rogers. "You said it will be some time tomorrow before the court approves the AVO?"

"Yes. Court doesn't sit before ten, so it will be some time after that."

"Then tonight I should be safe. Nigel has no reason to suspect what's happening and the earliest he'll know anything about it is after ten tomorrow when he's served. Returning home tonight is the best plan I can come up with. I'll leave with my children after Nigel leaves for work in the morning."

Mason still looked doubtful. His lips were pressed in a mutinous line, like he wanted to argue with her some more. She glanced at her watch and noted the time. She had less than ten minutes left of her break. Pushing away from the table, she held out her hand to the police officer.

"Thank you, Senior Constable Rogers. I appreciate your time and efforts and I'll be even more grateful tomorrow when you've obtained the AVO."

The officer nodded in response. "I'll go first thing

in the morning and I'll call you on your cell as soon as it's done."

"Thank you," she murmured for the second time and turned to leave. Mason stood and together they left the room.

———————

Isobel was quiet on the short return ride to the hospital. Mason could understand her silence. She'd been through so much at the station, having shared all of the horrible details of her life. The anger that had settled in the bottom of his gut like an icy block of cement, stirred and twisted and once again, the cold, burning fire of fury surged through his veins. He wanted to take Nigel Donnelly apart, limb by limb and torture him as he did it. Knowing what he'd done to Belle...

"I can feel your anger and frustration from here," Isobel murmured and Mason gritted his teeth. She turned to him and through the dimness, he saw a quiet strength and determination in her eyes.

"I'll be fine, Mason. It will be no different from any other night. A thousand other nights."

"But knowing what he's—"

"One more night. That's all it is. I can do it. If it means leaving peacefully with my children during Nigel's absence tomorrow, I can do it."

He stared at her, his lips compressed, not trusting himself to speak. Even one more night was more than he could bear to think about, but he understood her reasoning. Nigel had become so unpredictable where she was concerned, it was impossible to know how he'd react to having Mason and/or a police officer turn up on his doorstep as a protective detail for his wife. The last thing Mason wanted to do was tip off a man who was clearly on the edge.

The kind of things Belle had spoken about at the station... He shook his head, still in shock at the depravity she'd revealed. He drew in a deep breath and blew it out between taut lips and forced himself to relax. He glanced across at her.

"Let's talk about tomorrow. We need a plan. Do you have any idea where you're going to go?"

"My parents are still living back home in Maitland, but they're not in the best of health. Dad has dementia and Mom's just plain worn out. She's been his primary caretaker for years." She paused and then added, "My sister Katrina will take us in, but she's living in a shoebox in Bondi. Kat and I are close, but I... She thinks Nigel is the perfect husband and I haven't told her he's anything but. Besides, Nigel knows where Kat lives. He'll look for us there and once I've left for good, there's no way in the world I can let him find us..."

All of a sudden, the fear was back. She looked terrified at the prospect. Mason's hands tightened on the steering wheel.

"It's probably best if we go to a hotel," she continued quietly. "There are so many in the city. I could register under a different name..."

Mason listened to her suggestions and his heart

rebelled against every one. His head told him the best thing to do was to stay the hell away from her and the temptation she represented, but his heart was having none of that. Some might call him a fool, but there was no denying the pull Isobel West still had on him. He'd let her walk away ten years ago. He wasn't about to repeat the same mistake.

"You can stay with me," he blurted out. "I have plenty of room and Nigel won't come looking for you there. He doesn't even know I'm in Sydney, let alone that we've reconnected."

Isobel shook her head. "I can't ask you to do that for us. Besides, if he does find out, you'll be at risk, too. It's not fair for me to do that. It's bad enough that I asked you to come with me to the police station and help me leave."

Mason waved her concerns away. "Don't worry about me. I can take care of myself. I'm a big boy. Nigel won't find it so easy to intimidate me or leave marks for all to see. And in the unlikely event that he's stupid enough to try, it won't be me wearing the bruises." He stared at her and she gazed right back. A moment later, she lowered her head.

"I thought I'd done a good job with the makeup."

"You did. I'm sure no one else noticed. I had particular reason to pay attention."

She looked up and searched his face—for what he couldn't be sure. A tiny frown marred the perfect paleness of her skin. The silence stretched out and she continued to stare. She was so close he could count her freckles, even in the dimness of the car.

His heart took off at double time. The air around them was suddenly charged. She reached across the gearshift and briefly touched his hand. His heart stood still. Her expression remained serious.

"Thank you, Mason. For everything."

He acknowledged her thanks with a brief nod and returned his attention to the road. As much as he wanted to shout it from the tallest city office block, now wasn't the time to tell her he was still in love with her and that there was nothing in the world he wouldn't do for her. He cleared his throat.

"What time does Nigel leave for work in the morning?"

"He usually leaves around seven-thirty. On a normal day I give the kids breakfast. Sometimes we go to the park. I do laundry, clean the house, organize dinner. The usual stuff."

"What time does he come home?"

"It depends upon emergencies and how his theater list has gone, but it's usually around seven in the evening."

Mason nodded. "Good. That gives us just under twelve hours from the time he leaves until he returns home."

Isobel stared at him, her green eyes wide and solemn. Once again, fear chased itself across her face, but she nodded. He couldn't help but feel a surge of admiration for her courage.

Despite the horrors she'd relayed to him and the police officer, he knew the decision to walk out on her marriage hadn't come easily. It pained him to think that even now, after all she'd been through, she was still second guessing the choice she'd made. Remembering the errand he'd run earlier that afternoon, he reached into the pocket of his coat and pulled out a cell phone. He handed it to her.

"This is for you. It's prepaid, so there's no account or paper trail for Nigel to follow. Keep yours in case he calls you."

"Oh, he'll call all right."

"Once he knows for sure you're gone, you won't need to answer his calls. You can get rid of your cell and use this one. I'll be at work tomorrow. It's important that I act as if nothing is out of the ordinary. The fact that he doesn't know I'm in Sydney is a good thing, but still I want to be cautious. I don't want him to link us in any way. That will only endanger you and I sure as hell don't want that. Unfortunately, it means I won't get home before seven tomorrow night, so you'll be on your own until then."

She sat forward in her seat, a look of concern in her eyes. "But I don't know where you live or how to get there."

"I've programmed directions to my apartment into the new phone. Just go to Google maps and follow the prompts."

"But, what about your neighbors? Won't they wonder about a woman and two children moving into your house?"

He shook his head. "I haven't had time to do more than greet one or two people in the building with little more than a passing nod. They don't know anything about me. They won't question you."

"Is there a key?"

He reached into his pocket and pulled out the spare key he'd had cut while he'd been out purchasing the phone.

"Here." He pressed it into her palm and closed her fingers around it. He tried not to think how soft and warm her hand felt. She stared at him, her eyes dark with emotion.

"Thank you," she whispered.

CHAPTER 8

Isobel checked her side mirror and changed lanes. It was way past late. At eleven, her shift had finally ended. In a daze, she'd headed for home and in half an hour, she'd be there. Home. With Nigel. With her kids. Her lips trembled at what could lie ahead for her, but she refused to give in to her fear.

After the meeting with Senior Constable Rogers, when Mason had pulled up into the hospital car park with only minutes to spare, her stomach had been tight with nerves and a headache pierced her eyes. She'd swallowed some Tylenol, but it had barely taken the edge off. The last thing she wanted now was to drive home to Nigel, but she didn't have a choice.

Somehow, she had to carry on as normal, as if nothing momentous had occurred—or was about to. She'd never been good at lying and especially not to her husband. The few times she'd attempted to, it ended with him slapping her hard across the face. Somehow, he'd always been able to detect any hint of her deceit.

The thought of pretending all was well made her even more tense and anxious. Hot tears burned behind her eyes. She bit her lip and tried to stem the flow, but despite her best efforts, they made a slow, desperate path down her cheeks. She lifted her foot off the accelerator and eased the car over to the side. With her head in her hands, she sobbed.

She wasn't sure how much time passed, but the clock on the console told her it was almost midnight. Panic surged through her. Her husband was waiting for her. He hated it when she was late. She hadn't been lying when she'd told Mason how difficult Nigel got over things like that. She had to get home. Fast.

Searching through her handbag for a tissue, she swiped at the moisture on her cheeks. With a determined blow of her nose, she pulled her Toyota Magna back onto the road. Like she'd told Mason, it was only one more night. Then she could make good her escape. But she was so scared he'd somehow discover her plan. She was even more terrified the planning was too late.

At last, she pulled into the drive outside her house. The building was silent and dark—not even the porch light was on. She was upset that Nigel hadn't shown her even that smallest consideration, but couldn't help but also feel relieved that he'd gone to bed. Taking care to bury Mason's cell phone and house key deep inside her handbag, she climbed out.

The half moon provided enough light that she

could make out the front step. With her door key in hand, she cautiously made her way up the porch steps and inserted it into the lock. The knob turned and the door opened without a sound. She breathed a tiny sigh of relief and crept into the house.

"Where the fuck have you been?"

She yelped in fright. Her heart leaped into her throat. In growing panic, she felt around for the light switch. Nigel sat on the couch in the dark, nursing a glass of scotch. His cheeks were flushed and his breath came fast. It obviously wasn't his first drink. He stared at her, his hard eyes glittering with anger.

"N-Nigel! You scared me half to death!" she said, silently willing the trembling from her limbs.

His gaze narrowed. "I said, where the fuck have you been?"

"N-nowhere. At work."

"Bullshit. I called there. You left more than an hour ago. You should have been here well before now."

He stood and stalked toward her until he was little more than a breath away. He loomed over her. She held her ground, even while her heart thumped hard enough to cause pain. She tilted her head up and stared at him.

"Who have you been with?" he spat. "It's David Hamilton, isn't it? You've been fucking him, haven't you? That's the reason you're late."

She shook her head, anxious for him to see reason. "No! No! You're wrong, Nigel. It's like I told you, I've only been at work."

His hand flashed past her face and grabbed a fistful of her hair. Tears sprang to her eyes. She whimpered against the pain.

"Nigel, please. You're hurting me."

His grip only tightened. He forced her head back until her face was inches away from his. She shivered at the malice in his eyes.

"Don't lie to me, bitch! I asked one of your colleagues. David was working tonight. Do you think I'm an idiot?" he screamed, spittle flying out of his mouth. He yanked her hair again and she bit down hard on the pain.

"Do you think I'm *stupid*? You were fucking him, weren't you? Probably in the back seat of his car, like the filthy, little slut that you are. That's why you're late, isn't it?" He shook her again. "*Isn't* it?"

Fear turned her limbs leaden. Tears streamed down her cheeks. She tried to shake her head, but his grip on her hair made it impossible. "No! No! It was nothing like that," she sobbed.

He brought his face so close to hers she could feel his hot breath against her skin. The smell of alcohol turned her stomach. She swallowed hard to hold back the bile.

"Then what?" he growled, his voice now low and deadly. "There must be some reason you're more than half an hour late."

Her thoughts turned frantic. She had no idea what to tell him. Certainly not the truth. With as much courage as she could muster, she settled on a lie.

"There was a traffic accident on the freeway. I had to wait."

He stared at her with narrowed eyes and she could tell that he wasn't sure whether to believe her. After what seemed like a lifetime, he loosened his grip and released her.

"You'd better not be lying to me."

"I'm not, I promise." She moved across the room, well out of his reach. As much as she wanted to turn and walk right back out, she couldn't. Her children were asleep down the hall. There was no way in hell she'd leave without them. No, her only hope was to pacify him, ease his anger; calm him down.

"It's late, Nigel. We're both tired. How about we go to bed?" While everything inside her screamed out against what that meant, she held out her hand to him.

He stared at her, his eyes full of suspicion, but a moment later, he stepped closer and put a heavy arm across her shoulders. He held her close against his side as they walked together down the hall. Isobel counted her footsteps to keep herself from turning and running in the opposite direction.

"I just want to check on the children, Nigel. I'll be there in a minute."

He looked down at her for a moment, studying her, and then shrugged. His arm fell away and he continued on in the direction of their bedroom.

Isobel quickly opened the door to the bedroom shared by her kids. Slipping inside, she closed the door behind her and collapsed against it. Her breath came fast and her heart pumped wildly. She tried hard to get both under control. Knowing Nigel would get impatient if she took too long, she hurried over to the twin beds where Ben and Sophie lay.

The soft moonlight streamed in through the window and found its way through the half-opened blinds. She stared at her babies, both sound asleep and blissfully unaware. A fierce surge of maternal protection flooded through her. She'd do anything to keep them safe. Nigel had never turned his anger on them, or suggested he might until the other night, but what if she wasn't around to take the brunt of his rage when something else set him off?

What if he gave her sleeping pills? What if he made her disappear? What then? Would her babies become his next targets? She couldn't take the chance. They needed her. She had to get them all out of there as soon as Nigel left in the morning.

Her thoughts drifted to Mason almost against her will and she recalled the escape plan they'd discussed. She wanted to call him, to seek reassurance, but she couldn't. Not only was it very late, but she couldn't risk Nigel hearing her on the phone.

Mason. What a fool she was, having romantic thoughts about him as her knight in shining armor... She shouldn't even be thinking about him.

He looked much as he had in high school. Tall and athletic, with an easy smile that reached all the way to his eyes. She couldn't remember the last time she'd smiled freely at anyone like that for fear Nigel would misinterpret it.

Mason was the ultimate boy next door, the boy everyone trusted. But could *she*? Sadness flooded through her. Trust no longer came easy to her, even in herself. Something else Nigel had stolen.

With a quiet sigh, she leaned over and pressed a gentle kiss against the soft cheeks of Sophie and Ben and reluctantly left the room.

When she got there, their bedroom was empty. Her tension ratcheted up another notch. She wondered where Nigel was, but forced the thought aside. She went into the bathroom and removed her makeup and then picked up her toothbrush.

She opened the cabinet above the sink to look for the tube of toothpaste and froze. The sleeping pills were gone. She glanced through the open doorway toward the bed. A glass of water sitting on her nightstand caught her attention.

Icy fingers of fear clawed at her heart. Panic filled her veins. Her throat went tight and she could barely breathe. She had to get out of there. Had to escape. Before it was too late.

A moment later, Nigel's large form filled the door to the bathroom, his eyes flashing with anger. She bit back a cry of alarm and braced herself against another attack, wondering desperately what she'd done this time to set him off.

"You fucking liar!"

She shook her head in confusion, but forced herself to remain calm. "Quieten down, for goodness sake. You'll wake the children. What are you talking about?"

"You know what I'm talking about!" he

shouted, ignoring her plea. "There wasn't an accident on the freeway. I just checked on the Internet with traffic control."

A sinking feeling centered in her belly and icy dread flooded her veins. In panic, she thrust around in her mind for something to say. "I... I'm not sure what you want me to say. Your information's wrong. There *was* an accident. It's the reason I was late."

His fist came out from nowhere and connected with her face. Blood, hot and acrid, filled her mouth. A second later, it was followed by stinging pain. She gasped and brought her hand up to her lip. It came away wet and sticky with blood.

Tears filled her eyes and ran down her cheeks. She tried to keep the sobs in check, but it was no use. She heard Sophie crying and somehow, that made everything worse. Nigel stood over her, breathing hard.

"What's the matter, Mommy? I heard Daddy shouting. Sophie needs you. Why's your face bleeding?" Ben asked from the hallway.

Ben stood, small and uncertain, in the shadows by the bed. Fear pinched his features. Tears glinted in his eyes. She hastily wiped her mouth with the back of her hand and hurried to reassure him.

"It's all right, baby. Daddy just..." She stopped midsentence and struggled to find the words to explain.

"I know," Ben finished quietly. "You were having another fight."

"Oh, for fuck's sake! You're nearly six years old!

Don't be such a cry baby." Nigel threw their son a look of disgust and stormed out of the bedroom. A moment later, the front door slammed.

Isobel stared after him. Usually, she'd follow him outside and try to pacify him, beg him to come back inside. But tonight, she couldn't find the strength and his departure provided a level of relief she welcomed. Besides, her babies needed her. She swiped at the tears on her cheeks and used a tissue to dab at her lip. With a wobbly smile, she went to Ben.

He threw himself against her and she gathered him in her arms. Burying her nose in the softness of his hair, she tried hard to regain control.

"It's okay, baby. I promise. Mommy's okay."

"But you're bleeding!"

"Only a little bit. I... I just cut my lip. It's nothing for you to worry about."

"I hate it when Daddy yells at you. I don't want him to hurt you. He's mean."

He said it so quietly, she nearly missed it. When his words penetrated the turmoil in her head, hot tears burned behind her eyes. Yes, leaving couldn't happen soon enough.

She squeezed him tightly and pressed a kiss against his cheek. "I hate it, too, baby and I'm going to do something about it."

"I talked to Jack at daycare and he said his dad doesn't yell at his mom like my dad yells at you."

She sucked in a breath. "Jack's right, honey. Most dads don't yell like that and I'm going to make sure your daddy doesn't do it again, either."

Ben pulled a little away from her and looked up, his dark eyes solemn with uncertainty and hope. "Do you think he'll stop when you tell him?"

She stared down at him and prayed she'd convince him. "Yes. Don't worry, honey. Daddy's never going to yell at Mommy again."

After tucking him back up in bed, and taking a moment to comfort Sophie and get her back to sleep, Isobel pulled down two suitcases from the shelf in her closet. Knowing Nigel could return any minute, she had one ear tuned to listen for the sound of his key while, with her heart pumping hard, she threw clothes and shoes and toiletries into one suitcase and then took the other into the bedroom shared by Sophie and Ben.

Quickly and quietly, aided only by moonlight, she filled the second suitcase. With a sigh of relief, she dragged it into her bedroom and hid both cases under her bed. The glass of water on her nightstand caught her eye.

With one eye on the door, she picked up the glass and emptied it down the drain. Then she quickly refilled it and placed it back on the nightstand and climbed into bed.

It was almost two in the morning when she heard Nigel's key in the door. She forced herself to lie still and quiet under the covers and prayed his mood had improved. He walked into the bedroom with a heavy tread.

From the dim glow coming from the street light outside the window, she saw that his shoulders were bowed, along with his head. She swallowed a sigh of relief. He switched on the light on her nightstand and then perched himself on her side of the bed. It was all she could do not to scream.

He stared at her swollen lip and his expression flooded with remorse. His head dropped into his hands.

"I'm sorry, Isobel," he sobbed. "I'm so sorry. I don't know why you drive me to hit you like that. Why do you make me so mad? You know I don't handle it well!"

He shook his head back and forth. His hands fell away and he turned back to look at her. "I love you so much. I don't want to hurt you. Sometimes...I just go crazy. I know you're not seeing David Hamilton, but the thought of you with another man... It sends me over the edge."

Anger over the injustice of his treatment of her ignited way down deep inside, but she couldn't give it voice. The best thing to do was to agree with him and keep things calm. That way, he'd get over his suspicions—at least for the time being—and hopefully go to sleep.

"I'm sorry, Nigel. I wish I'd gotten home earlier. There was nothing I could do."

He stared at her, as if trying to gage her sincerity and then reached for the glass on her nightstand.

"Here, take a sip of water. You'll feel better." He held the glass to her lips and she took a small drink.

"Have some more."

She shook her head. "I'm fine, thanks. Come to bed."

It took everything she had inside her, but she

reached out for him and drew him into her arms. He collapsed against her and sobbed against her chest. She held him through the long minutes while he cried himself to sleep. Every second of it, she prayed for the morning to arrive.

CHAPTER 9

I sobel flipped the bacon over in the pan and checked the toast. It popped up just as she reached for the button and she jumped. Telling herself not to be so jittery, she pulled it out and quickly spread it with butter, just the way Nigel liked it.

A headache had begun behind her eyes. It had been there since she'd woken. Having spent an uncomfortable night with Nigel snoring on top of her, she'd barely managed to doze between bouts of consciousness where she'd gone through her plans to leave—over and over. Now the sun was up and the birds were singing. Soon it would be time to put her plan into action. The thought made her tense. Nausea swirled in her stomach.

"Why the hell didn't you wake me? I'm going to be late for my rounds," Nigel grumbled by way of greeting.

She smiled and prayed he couldn't tell it was forced. "Good morning. You got in so late last night, I thought you might appreciate the extra sleep."

He stared at her with narrowed eyes, as if deciding whether to trust the concern in her voice. His gaze skimmed over her injured lip and then skittered away. She picked up the plate of bacon and eggs and a separate plate with the toast and set them at his usual place at the table.

"I don't have time for breakfast." He looked back toward her and a sneer curled up his lip. "Besides, it looks like shit." With that, he turned his back to her, picked up his briefcase and jacket and left.

Isobel stared after him, a little taken aback. He'd been rude to her on many occasions and had often made derogatory comments about her cooking, but it was usually when he was spoiling for a fight. She touched her finger to her bruised lip from the night before.

He'd returned home full of remorse, but any guilt he'd felt in those dark hours had dissolved in the light of day. It had never been like that before. Normally he was full of sorrow and repentance for his bad behavior—at least for a few days after an assault. The fact that he'd gotten over this one so quickly was a strange new development and one that was more than a little alarming.

"Yum, have you cooked bacon?"

Isobel turned to see Ben wandering into the kitchen, his hair all askew. She smiled and bent down to hug him.

"Good morning, honey. Yes, I made bacon and eggs for Daddy."

Ben cast a wary gaze around the kitchen. "Where is he?"

"He had to leave for work, baby. He didn't have time to eat."

His expression cleared. "Can I have it?"

"You certainly may." She removed the plate from the table and took it over to the counter to cut into more manageable pieces. She transferred some of the food to a smaller plate and took it back to Ben. "Here you go."

"Thanks, Mom." He looked up at her and once again, his expression grew taut and troubled. "What happened to your lip? It's all red and puffy. Is that from last night?"

She averted her face and tried to think of an answer. "I... I..."

"Did Dad hit you again? It was scary last night to wake up to hear you fighting."

He said it so matter-of-factly Isobel felt an immediate rush of tears. She did her best to blink them away and quickly changed the subject. "Is Soph up yet?"

"Yeah. I think she's in the bathroom."

Isobel glanced at the clock that hung on the kitchen wall above the sink. It was going on for eight. She thought of what Mason said about having twelve hours before Nigel realized they were gone and felt a fresh wave of nerves. Every minute they wasted took them closer to the time Nigel would return and discover her betrayal.

And that's how he'd see it. And why wouldn't he? She was walking out on her marriage. She'd sworn to love him in sickness and in health, for better or worse, 'til death did they part. At the time, she couldn't imagine how bad it would get, but the thought that she was about to irrevocably break her vows filled her with sadness and guilt. She was about to split up her family and after taking the first step there would be no turning back. All of a sudden, she was paralyzed with indecision again.

Perhaps she should try harder to make him happy? Maybe she could try again to convince him to seek professional help? They had two children to consider. Was it fair to deprive them of their dad?

The questions tumbled around inside her head until she wanted to scream out loud. It was only Ben's presence at the table that stopped her.

"Did Dad promise he wouldn't hurt you anymore?" The words came out of nowhere and she gasped.

"He was in a hurry to get to work, honey. It's up to me to change things," she said, buying time.

"You said last night you'd make sure he didn't yell at you anymore. I wondered if you'd asked him not to hurt you, too."

Past scenes of violence that seemed like an endless horror movie scrolled through her head. She closed her eyes against the pain of it. Her heart thumped like it did when she and Nigel were in the middle of another fight and all of a sudden her determination from the night before solidified.

If she didn't go now she'd have no hope for a future. She'd forever be a victim and the victimization would continue until she could no longer recognize it for what it was. Either that, or she'd be dead. If she lost her nerve now, she'd lose her chance for any kind of normal life with her children. There was no question that she had to leave.

"Listen, honey, can you finish up here and go and get dressed? We're going out today."

"Where to?"

"Um... We're going to a friend's house."

"Will there be other kids?"

"No, Ben, but I'm sure you'll have a good time."

"Who—?"

"Honey, I really need you to hurry. Just finish what you're eating and go and get changed. I want to leave in fifteen minutes."

He looked like he wanted to ask more questions, but eventually gave a shrug. A moment later, he slid off his chair and padded back the way he'd come.

Hurrying now, she cleared away the plates and pans and quickly stacked the dishwasher. Out of habit, she switched it on. Not that she'd be here to unpack it. Nigel would have to learn how to do it.

She imagined Mason would be a little handier around his place. She didn't know how long he'd been divorced, but he now lived on his own. She presumed he'd picked up at least a few tips on the basic domestic activities of daily living.

The thought of staying in his apartment suddenly brought her movements to a stop. What would happen when he got tired of playing host to her and her children? They weren't his family, after all. They couldn't hide out there forever. And what about work? Would Nigel come marching up to the pediatric ward and cause a scene?

He'd always gone out of his way to keep up appearances at their place of employment, but would he continue to have that much self-control? A lot of her colleagues had jokingly expressed their envy over what a perfect husband he was. Attentive, considerate, he called the ward two or three times a day to ask after her and still regularly sent her flowers. Only Isobel knew all of that was a form of control, just another way he kept tabs on her.

Perhaps she should take some time off? Wait until the worst of Nigel's anger had been spent? She had a few weeks of holidays owing and she could take that leave with pay. But what about afterwards? How would she pay the bills without Nigel? She couldn't expect Mason to support them.

She didn't have any money. Nigel had always controlled all of their finances. Even her wages were deposited into an account in his name. In the early days of their marriage, he'd told her it was because he didn't want her to worry about trivial things such as money. He was the brains. It was his job to keep her comfortable and he assured her he'd see to that.

Over the years, he'd forgotten his promise. She'd been forced to beg for every dollar and quite often, her requests were refused. There was never anything to spend on frivolous things—at least what Nigel deemed frivolous. She couldn't help but notice the same rules didn't apply to him. Only a month earlier, he'd come home with an eight-hundred-dollar briefcase that apparently he just couldn't do without.

She'd have to go to a bank and open an account and then have her wages redirected, but she didn't have time to do those things right now. She glanced at the clock again and noticed another six minutes had slipped by. Wiping her hands on a cloth, she hurried into her bedroom and finished packing the last-minute things. Her hairbrush and toothbrush; toothpaste, vitamins and her contraceptive pills. She went into the kids' bedroom and collected a few of their toys.

"What are you doing, Mommy?" Sophie asked, sitting up in her bed.

Isobel forced a smile. "We're going on a little trip."

"Yay! Is Daddy coming?"

"Not this time, baby. Now, I need you to get out of bed. I'll help you get dressed. We're in a bit of a hurry."

"Why?"

"We just are. Here, how about you put on this dress? It's going to be warm outside today."

"I want to wear my jeans! The ones with the flowers on the pocket."

"Soph, it's far too hot for jeans. Now, come over here so I can get those pajamas off you."

Her daughter shot her a frown so familiar, it nearly broke Isobel's heart. The little girl was a mirror image of her father. Not that Isobel would ever hold that against her. Still, she used her no-nonsense voice, aware time was ticking away.

"You're wearing this pretty dress, Sophie. Now, come over here."

With a melodramatic sigh and an eye roll that

would put the best actress in the world to shame, her little girl climbed out of bed and moved over to where she stood.

"Lift up your arms." Her baby did as she asked without any further fuss and Isobel swallowed a sigh of relief.

"What's for breakfast?"

"Bacon and eggs. Or cereal. Whatever you like, but we have to be quick. We're leaving very soon."

Ben appeared in the doorway.

"Hey, buddy, can you go and brush your teeth? We're leaving as soon as your sister's finished breakfast."

He nodded and turned to leave.

"Oh, Ben?" she called out after him.

He stopped and turned back to look at her. "Yes?"

"Bring your toothbrush to me when you're finished. I need to pack it."

He frowned. "Are we staying overnight?"

"Yes, honey. We are."

"For how long?"

"I'm... I'm not sure. Right now, I need you to brush your teeth, find your shoes and get ready to get into the car, okay?"

He stared at her a moment longer before slowly turning back toward the door. He left without another word.

"Okay, Soph. You're all set. Now, where are your shoes?"

She shrugged. "I don't know. I think I left them near the front door."

"All right, I'll go and look for them. You head into the kitchen. Did you decide whether you're having cereal or bacon?"

"I want blueberry pancakes and maple syrup."

"We don't have time for pancakes, honey. It's bacon and eggs or cereal."

"But I want pancakes."

"Not today, Soph. I guess bacon and eggs it is."

Not giving the child any time to argue, she left the room. She hurried toward the front door and found her daughter's shoes. After putting them on Sophie's feet, Isobel set out a small plate of food. Murmuring her thanks, her baby began to eat.

"I'm ready," Ben announced and flopped down on the chair opposite his sister.

Isobel threw him a smile. "Great. We won't be too much longer. Did you brush your teeth?"

"Yes, I left my toothbrush on your bed, near the bag you've packed."

His stare was pointed. She did her best to ignore it. "We're staying with my friend for a few days. I'm not sure how long, exactly, but I thought we should take a few things."

"Does Dad know where we're going?"

Her smile faltered. "Of course." She averted her gaze. "Soph, hand me your plate. It's time to get going."

After quickly rinsing her daughter's things, she hurriedly brushed the little girl's teeth and tossed her toothbrush into the bag. On her hands and knees, she tugged the suitcases out from beneath the bed.

"There are more? I thought you said we were

only going for a few days?" Ben asked in an accusing tone.

Isobel jumped guiltily. "I did. But I also said I wasn't sure exactly how long we're going to be away. I like to be prepared."

"How far away does your friend live? Is it outside the city?"

"No, honey. Not very far. It shouldn't take us too long to get there."

"Then if we run out of clothes, why can't we just come back?"

Impatience surged through Isobel, but she forced herself to keep her temper in check. The clock on her nightstand told her it was way past eight. Nigel would be almost finished his ward rounds and would then be headed to the operating rooms. As if on cue, the house phone rang. She hurried back into the kitchen to answer it.

"Hello?"

"It's me. Just thought I'd call and see how you are."

The tension inside her ramped up its efforts to tighten her belly into knots. She forced a breath between her clenched teeth. "I'm fine, Nigel. Thanks for asking."

"What are you up to today?"

"I... I thought I might take the kids to the park. It looks like it's going to be a nice day."

"I wouldn't know. I've been inside since I left."

"Well, I'll make sure I tell you all about it when you come home. What time do you think you might get away?" She asked the question as casually as she could and hoped he wouldn't wonder about it.

"Not before seven. I have a full list today."

"Right. Well, have a good day." She ended the call, her heart thumping, and strode back into the bedroom. With a suitcase in each hand, she made her way to the car.

It took another ten minutes to pack all the bags and the kids into the Toyota. She made sure all the lights in the house were off and then locked the door behind her. With hands shaking, she fitted the key into the ignition and then heard the *ding* of her phone. *No, not her phone.* The phone Mason had given her.

She dug into her handbag and pulled it out. There was a new text message on the screen.

Thinking of u. UR the bravest woman I know. I'm here 4 u. Don't forget, the address of my apartment's in the phone. Make sure u have the key. C u tonight.

Isobel read through the message twice and her breathing gradually slowed. Checking in her handbag, her fingers closed around the house key he'd given her. With renewed determination, she opened Google Maps and found the address. She absorbed the details and turned on her GPS. Her hands tightened around the steering wheel. She reversed out of the driveway and didn't look back.

CHAPTER 10

Dear Diary,

I have forgotten the pleasure of my husband's touch. There was a time when I was the center of his universe, his moon and stars. He put me on a pedestal so high it was only a matter of time before I toppled off. When I couldn't give him what he needed, without a second thought he knocked me to the ground and trampled me into the dust.

This isn't how love is supposed to be.... Love is patient and kind, not hurtful or controlling. He's taken everything I have—my sense of identity, my self-esteem, my ability to trust and to love. I am nothing more than an empty shell, like a conch that has washed up on the beach.

I hope and pray one day someone will see that shell and look close enough to find the beauty that used to be me. I yearn for someone to hold me close so that they can hear my whispered plea...

Mason glanced at his watch and swallowed a sigh of irritation. The day was going way too slowly. No matter how he tried to concentrate on his duties, his mind remained focused on Isobel and her planned escape. She'd come to him for help.

The weight of responsibility to protect her and ensure her safety was enormous and it didn't matter how many times he told himself she wasn't his wife or his sister or even someone to whom he owed a debt. There was no reason for him to feel so much pressure to keep her safe, but he did. She wasn't his and she probably never would be, but the simple fact was, that despite all her trials, she was the same person he knew as a teenager, and he loved her still and he'd do anything he could to help her and her children escape.

Knowing the extent of the abuse she'd suffered ignited a fury inside him such as he'd never known and his anger scared the hell out of him. He was normally a peaceful, fun-loving kind of guy who'd rather join people in a laugh than an argument, but hearing first-hand the treatment Nigel Donnelly regularly inflicted upon his wife simply enraged him.

He wanted to make Nigel suffer like Isobel had suffered. First and foremost, he wanted an all-out brawl where he intended to punch the prick as hard and as often as he could. Smash the asshole's perfectly aligned teeth—the best that money could buy.

They hadn't been friends in high school, but they'd both played on the same football team.

Nigel had been the star and had always gotten the girl—even Isobel West, the only girl Mason ever really cared about.

It had started in junior high when the contents of Mason's locker had spilled out all over the floor. It had been a joke played on him by some of the boys in the football team, but he'd still been as embarrassed as hell. Especially when some of the stuff that had fallen out included a handful of dirty magazines. He didn't know where they'd come from; they sure as hell hadn't been his, but he nearly died from humiliation when Isobel West happened by.

He knew who she was, of course. She was the prettiest girl in his year. But not only that: She was smart and sweet and seemed to have a nice word for everyone. She was the head of the junior high debating team and volunteered at an animal shelter on the weekends. He could still remember Nigel complaining that she barely had enough time to come to his games.

While he'd been scrambling to pick up everything, she'd come to a halt outside his locker. Mason had wished the floor would open up and swallow him whole. Crouching on the floor, surrounded by books and pencils and the scattered magazines, he'd stared at her feet, too embarrassed to do anything more. Silently begging her to walk on by, he'd flushed from head to toe when she knelt down beside him and helped him gather his things.

She chatted the whole time she did it about the upcoming game and the players. She even made a comment about the weather. If she noticed the magazines in her hands, she didn't once make mention of them and it was at that point, he knew he would love her forever.

It still hurt when he remembered how she'd smiled in surprise and thanked him politely after he'd declared his undying love the night of their graduation. Later, when he saw her leave with Nigel, the asshole's arm draped possessively over her shoulders, the pain had been too much to bear. He'd spent the night sad and alone, convinced he'd never feel happiness again.

Of course, as the years went by, he threw himself into his studies and did his best to get on with his life. He finished med school and secured a good job. He met and married Sue Ann. But the truth was, he hadn't moved forward at all. His heart was still firmly caught up in everything that was and always would be Isobel West and there wasn't a damned thing he could do about it.

The child on the bed in front of him whimpered in pain and he forced himself to refocus. The four-year-old had stepped on a pile of hot coals that had been used as a campfire the night before and had badly burned the soles of his feet. The accident had happened that morning when the fire had barely smoldered. Covered in white ashes, the dangers had been invisible to the young child. Mason was only glad he could help him and that the boy's feet would heal with time.

As he finished replacing the final dressing, he checked his watch. It was nearly eight-thirty. If Nigel had left for work at his usual time, Isobel should be on the road by now. She might even be at Mason's apartment, settling in. The thought sent a warm rush of happiness surging through him, but he quickly put an end to his optimistic thoughts that one day they could be one big happy family.

She'd turned to him as a friend and he was more than willing to help her out. There was nothing else between them other than his desire to protect her—it wouldn't be fair to expect anything more.

The day stretched out before him. It would be hours before he could clock off and welcome her properly to his home. His only hope was that his shift was busy. It always helped to make the time speed by. He'd sent her a text a few minutes earlier, but hadn't received a response. He only hoped it was because she was driving and unable to answer her phone.

After giving the nurse a few final instructions about the patient's care, he gave the boy a cheery wave and left the ward. Stopping by the cafeteria, he bought a cup of coffee and then headed down the corridor toward the elevators, his mind still on Isobel and her kids. He wondered if either of them looked like her. It would be interesting to see her in miniature form.

"Mason Alexander? Is that you?"

The booming voice snagged his attention. He turned, taking care not to spill his coffee. A tall man with dark hair, broad shoulders and a wide smile strode toward him. Mason's gut somersaulted with shock. Nigel Donnelly stretched out his hand in greeting.

"Nigel, what a surprise," he managed and returned the man's handshake.

"I wasn't sure if it was you. I haven't seen you since high school," Nigel replied, shaking his head in bemusement and looking him up and down. "And you're a doctor. Who'd have guessed? Don't tell me you're working here?"

Mason nodded. "Yep. I started here a little over a week ago."

Nigel grinned. "Well, I'll be damned! What's your speciality?"

"Pediatrics." Mason watched Nigel closely for a reaction, but apart from a slight frown, Nigel didn't comment.

"How about you?" Mason asked, knowing it was expected.

"I went into orthopedic surgery. You know how much I used to like playing with those chisels and saws. Apart from playing football, for me getting into the woodworking room was one of the highlights of school. Now I get paid to do it."

Mason grinned, along with Nigel and prayed the man wouldn't sense the strain.

"So, are you married? Got a family?" Nigel asked.

"No, mate. I was married, but we went our separate ways. No kids. How about you?" he forced himself to ask.

A wide smile creased Nigel's face. "I'm still with Isobel West. You remember her from high school, don't you? She was the hottest piece of ass in our year. I still remember the first time I fucked her. It was behind the school bleachers, after the grand final. She was worried the whole time that we'd be caught," he scoffed. "She's still a worrier. That hasn't changed, but she's still a good fuck, too, so I guess that makes up for it."

Mason found it hard to contain his anger. To hear the casual and disrespectful way Nigel referred to his wife sent fury surging through Mason's veins. He clenched his fists to prevent himself from plowing them into the asshole's smug face.

His breath came fast and he did all he could to slow it down. He couldn't allow the prick to see his anger. It would blow everything and might even put Isobel and her kids in jeopardy. He forced a smile and extended his hand once again to Nigel.

"I'd love to stay and chat, mate, but I'm needed on the ward."

"Yeah, I have to get going, too. Listen, when do you have your next day off? We must get together for a beer."

Mason thought frantically for a suitable response. He couldn't imagine a single circumstance that would force him to drink with the man. "Um...I'm not sure. I'll check my roster. I'll let you know when I'm free."

Nigel threw him a jaunty wave good-bye and turned away. Mason unclenched his fists and forced deep breaths all the way down to the bottom of his lungs. He pulled out his phone and sent another text to Isobel.

Isobel heard the beep of her new phone, but she was in the middle of a busy intersection and the phone was buried in her handbag. A moment later, her old phone rang. It was lying on the passenger seat. She glanced across at the screen and her nerves went into overdrive.

Nigel. Shit, she was going to have to answer it.

With panic increasing her pulse rate, she accelerated away from the traffic and pulled over a short distance away. She scrambled for the phone and forced a lightness to her tone that she was a long way from feeling. "Nigel, how are you doing? How's your day been so far?"

"Where are you? Why aren't you at home? I tried to call you. There was no answer."

Fear tightened her vocal chords, but she forced herself to reply. "I told you. I'm at the park."

"*Hm.*"

He sounded far from convinced. Isobel hurried to alleviate his suspicions. "It's such a lovely day outside. I'm sorry that you're missing it."

"How long will you be there?"

"I'm not sure, maybe an hour or two. The kids are having a great time on the swings."

"Well, don't stay out too long. I might even get home early today. A couple of patients have been scratched from the list because they're suffering from the flu." His voice dropped lower and was full of innuendo. "We could put the kids to bed early and get up close and personal. Make sure you shave your legs and get ready for me. You could wear that new outfit I bought you. The one with all that leather. Fuck, I'm getting a hard-on just thinking about it."

Bile climbed up Isobel's throat and she gulped hard to keep it down. Panicked, she looked around for something to throw up in, but there was nothing. Terror iced her veins. She didn't even want to imagine the scene when he arrived home and discovered she was gone.

"Did you hear me?" he asked, his tone now petulant.

"Y-yes, I heard you."

"I've got a fat cock and it's all your fault. I'm about to head back to the theater. What the hell am I going to do with this hard-on? Too bad you're not working today. I'd come up to your ward and fuck you in the bathroom."

Isobel's breath came fast. She did her best to slow it down. Nigel chuckled in her ear.

"That got you panting, didn't it? You like the idea of me fucking you at work, don't you? You like the idea of being fucked, where any moment, someone might walk in. You're a dirty little slut, just like I always said."

She hurried to set him straight. "No, Nigel. That's not it at all."

"You can't lie to me, Isobel Donnelly. I know you inside out and right now I've got a big hard cock. What do you want me to do about it? Do you want me to ask that young nurse I was talking about to get down on her knees? I'm sure she'd be more than happy to put her lips around me and do what needs to be done. I might even tape it for you. I could play it back for you when I get home. You could watch her suck me 'til I come. We could have a threesome via video link." He sniggered.

Isobel held her hand tightly against her mouth, horrified by his disgusting words. All she wanted was for him to find someone else, to leave her alone. But she couldn't tell him that. She fished around for something to say, but right then and there, saying anything was beyond her.

"Are you still there, slut?"

She gasped. "Nigel, please, the children are nearby. Can't we finish this at home?"

"Oh, we'll finish it at home, all right. The end of the day can't come fast enough. You make sure you have the kids in bed early." His voice held a less than subtle warning.

"O-okay. Sounds good. I'll...talk to you soon." She nearly choked on the words, but managed to get them out. But before she could end the call, Nigel spoke again.

"You wouldn't believe who I ran into a little while ago."

She had a sudden terrible premonition. Icy tendrils of fear clawed at her insides. She swallowed and forced herself to reply.

"Who?"

"Mason Alexander. Do you remember him from high school? We were in the same year and played football together. Of course, he was just a—"

The rest of Nigel's words were drowned out by the roar of panic in her head. She sucked in a breath in a desperate bid to regain control. *Nigel knew about Mason.* He'd found out about *them.* It was all over before it had started. She was sure of it.

"Isobel? Are you still there?"

She gulped and did her best to answer him. "Y-yes, I'm still here. Sorry, Ben just fell off the slippery dip. I was helping him to get up. What were you saying?"

"I was telling you Mason Alexander's working at the hospital. He's a pediatrician. I thought you might have run into him."

"N-no, I can't say that I have, but that doesn't mean anything. I only work three shifts a week."

"Yeah, well, anyway, I invited him out for a drink. We might have him over for dinner soon."

Her heart thumped so loudly, she was sure Nigel could hear it, even over the phone. Once again, she forced out a suitable reply.

"That sounds nice, Nigel. I'm sorry to cut things short, but Sophie needs help to get off the swing. I'll speak to you later."

Before he could respond, she ended the call. She tossed the phone away like it was suddenly red hot and gulped in mouthfuls of air. Sweat popped out on her forehead and her hands started to shake. She knew enough about medical issues to recognize that she was about to go into shock.

He knew about Mason. It was only a matter of time before Nigel connected the dots. She couldn't go through with this. She couldn't leave him and she couldn't put Mason in danger. The thought of what awaited her upon Nigel's arrival home that night disgusted her, but knowing how he'd react if he found her gone, filled her with abject terror. He was sick in the head. He was unstable. There was no telling what he might do.

If she turned the Magna around now, she could still make it back home in plenty of time to unpack and put things back where they belonged. She'd call Senior Constable Rogers and tell him not to apply for the AVO. Nigel wouldn't be any the wiser. She'd be safe from his wrath, at least for a little while.

The new phone in her handbag beeped again and she remembered it had gone off before. She tugged it out of her handbag. There were two new messages from Mason.

Hope u like the flowers. I remembered how much u like lilies. I bought them early this morning.

Tears flooded Isobel's eyes. She shook her head, overwhelmed with emotion. It had been a long time since someone had shown her that much kindness. She couldn't remember the last time Nigel had. Mason hadn't seen her for the best part of a decade and he treated her better than the man she'd given the last nine years of her life. With trembling fingers, she scrolled to the next message.

Hey there, call me. Text me. Let me know ur OK. Please, Belle. I need 2 know ur safe.

Safe. That's how she felt when she was with Mason. The feeling was so foreign, she had barely recognized it and though it was lovely she had no idea if she could trust it. Trust *him*. After all, she barely knew him.

"Mom, why are we stopped?"

Isobel glanced at Ben and then at Sophie, who'd fallen asleep in her car seat. Her children trusted her to keep them safe. If she stayed with Nigel, neither their safety nor hers could be guaranteed. Each day would be fraught with more danger and uncertainty and fear.

It wasn't right for them to live like this. They were too young to understand it now, but there would come a time when they did and they'd wonder why she'd put them through it. And they'd be right to wonder. With a surge of determination, she composed a reply to Mason.

Got away a little later than I thought, but all now on track. Will text u when I arrive at ur place. Thx again 4 letting us stay. PS. Thx 4 the flowers. UR right. Lilies r my favorite.

Before she could change her mind, she pressed 'send.' Feeling lighter than she had for a long time, she switched on her indicator and pulled back out into the traffic.

CHAPTER 11

Dear Diary,

There isn't one piece of me that isn't broken. My mind, body and soul have been obliterated into the ether, lost in a vast darkness, unrecognizable and forever gone. Yes, I am lost.

There are days when I cling to anything around me to ensure my survival: my work, my children...Mason. What a burden I must be to them...

It's my husband's fault. He did this to me! He gave me dreams and then he snatched them away with so much gleeful maliciousness, the memory leaves me fighting for breath. I have no doubt that if he ever finds me, he will kill me. I am intimately acquainted with his wrath, and its fury is beyond anything I can ever hope to survive...

———————

Nigel sped through the final intersection and swung his car into their street. Despite his best efforts, he hadn't made it home early. Not that it mattered too much. Isobel would be sure to have the kids in bed by now. She might even be in the bedroom waiting for him like he'd asked, dressed from head to toe in black leather.

He hadn't been lying to Mason when he'd bragged how good she was to fuck. Her tits and ass were as perky as they'd been in high school, although she was a little skinnier than he liked. He wished women didn't get so hung up on the pictures they saw in those glossy magazines. He'd always preferred his women with a little more meat on their bones.

He swung into the driveway and frowned. The house was in darkness. Okay, so it wasn't exactly dark outside, but dusk was approaching fast. He'd have thought the dimness warranted at least a light or two. Shrugging off his disquiet, he climbed out of his shiny red Porsche Boxster Cabriolet and headed into the house.

Deepening darkness greeted him. He peered through the dimness, more and more bemused. Perhaps she'd surprised him, after all, and was even now spreadeagled across their bed, waiting for him. The thought propelled him forward and he strode down the darkened hallway and into their bedroom. Flicking on the light, he stared at the bed. It was empty.

Anger stirred in his gut. *Where the fuck was she?* And where were the kids?

His long legs ate up the short distance to the

bedroom shared by his children. Once again, he found another empty room. He returned to the kitchen and opened the internal door that connected it with the garage. Her car was gone.

Perplexed, he shook his head and tried to think where she might be. She obviously had the kids with her. Perhaps she'd gone to the shops to pick up something she'd forgotten? She knew how cross he got with her when she called him on his way home and expected him to do it. If she couldn't get organized in all the time she had over the course of the day, it was her problem.

He went over to the stove and put his hand over the burners. They were all cold. Next, he opened the door of the fridge. The usual assortment of items crowded the shelves. There was nothing that looked like it had been prepared for dinner.

He went back into his bedroom and flung open the doors to the closet. Isobel's clothes still hung neatly from their hangers, but upon closer inspection, he noticed some of the hangers were empty. His anger rose. He tore into their bathroom and ripped open the door on the cabinet. The empty shelves stared back at him.

Toothbrush, hairbrush, perfume—all missing. Even her contraceptive pills were gone. He dashed into the second bathroom, the one that the children used. Once again, the place where they kept their toothbrushes was empty.

She was gone. And she'd taken his kids.

Rage like he'd never known tore through him. He screamed like a man possessed. He burned so hot it felt like he was going to combust from the inside out. He only had one thought: There was no way in hell she was going to get away with this. She was his wife and he'd never let her go. The bitch would learn the meaning of *'til death do us part.*

He snatched the phone out of his pocket and hit her number. The call dialed out and eventually went through to voicemail. He screamed down the phone.

"You filthy slut! You ungrateful bitch! You fucking whore! Get yourself and my kids back here *now!* I'm going to kill you, Isobel. I'm going to fucking *kill* you!"

He vented some more, gasping with rage and disbelief. A sob tore from his throat. He hurled the phone across the room and it landed with a thud against the wall. He spun on his heel and upended lamps; he smashed pictures across the door. Glass flew every which way, some of it getting caught up in his hair. With his head in his hands, he slowly sank to the floor. He rocked back and forth, his sobs coming faster and harder. His breath was harsh in his ears. *It was happening all over again...*

The woman he loved had abandoned him. Just like his mother.

Isobel stood outside on Mason's balcony, soaking in the red and orange and purple hues of the sunset. From inside the apartment, she heard her phone ring. Her old phone. It was a little after seven. It had to be Nigel. Terror surged through her. *He was home.* She was sure of it. And he'd worked out she was gone. Frozen with fear, she let the call go through to voicemail.

The sun's dying rays sparkled like diamonds. It was so beautiful and so surreal after the torturous morning hours. She breathed in and out slowly and made a concentrated effort to relax. The scent of the heavily perfumed oriental lilies which stood in a vase on the table wafted in the air. She was still touched over Mason's thoughtfulness.

Ben and Sophie were settled into one of the spare rooms, watching cartoons. She'd found a tin of soup and some crackers in Mason's pantry and had prepared them a simple dinner. Earlier, they'd had ham and tomato sandwiches for lunch. She was sure Mason wouldn't mind that she'd helped herself to his food. She'd replace anything they used.

Senior Constable Rogers had called a few hours earlier with an update on the AVO. He was pleased to report the court had made an order in her favor. It was anticipated a copy of it would be served on her husband sometime the next day. She didn't have to imagine his response. She'd been on the receiving end of his fury too many times to guess at the way he'd react. She was only relieved she'd managed to escape when she had.

Her thoughts returned to the recent phone call. Knowing she had to get it over with, she stepped back inside the living room and picked up her cell. With shaking hands, she dialed into her mailbox. Holding the phone up to her ear like it was a poisonous snake, she listened to Nigel raging at her and flinched.

The succinct threats that followed weakened her knees. With a cry, she slid down the wall to the tiled floor. Sobbing now, she held one hand up to her mouth while she listened right to the end, unable to help herself. Even now, he controlled her.

Though it was irrational, and she knew Nigel was at home, she cringed and cried harder when a key turned in the lock. From the corner of her eye, she saw Mason appear, but still couldn't stop the tears. He frowned in concern. She saw the questions in his eyes, but she was beyond making a coherent response. Without hesitation, he stepped forward and took the phone from her hand.

He held it up to his ear and his frown turned ferocious. With a curse, he tossed the phone away and squatted down beside her. Gently, he pulled her to her feet. A moment later, she was held close against his chest. Instinctively, she tensed, but his breath was warm and comforting against her skin. Gradually, she relaxed.

"*Shh, shh*, Belle; don't cry, honey. It's going to be all right."

She lifted her head and stared at him, her face awash with tears. "It-it's not going to be all right." She hiccupped. "Nothing's ever going to be all right again. I'm sorry. I should never have come here. I should never have dragged you into this."

"Don't do this to yourself, sweetheart. And for your information, you didn't drag me into anything. I offered, which means I'm more than happy to help. Now, I'm taking your phone. You won't ever have to listen to that kind of rubbish again. I'll give it to the officer we spoke to last night. He can keep it as evidence in case Nigel wants to defend himself against the AVO."

Fear and uncertainty flooded through her. "You mean he can ask the court to reverse their decision?"

"Yes. I did a little research online last night, but don't worry, if he does choose to take issue with the order, the police prosecutor will present any evidence you have against Nigel and I'm certain they'll continue to see things your way. Especially after they listen to *this*."

She looked at the phone where it now lay on the sofa and gave a shaky nod. "Take it and give it to the police. Let's hope we never need to use it." She listened to her words and wished they brought comfort, but she was still a bundle of fear. In spite of Mason's reassurances, she'd never forget the fury in Nigel's voice—or that he'd threatened to find her and kill her.

———————

Mason led Isobel over to the couch and drew her back gently into his arms. In an effort to ease the tension that still held her body in a tight grip, he stroked his hand up and down her back, hoping to comfort her, wanting to ease her pain.

Her breaths came in short, sharp gasps and tears slid down her cheeks. He could hear the television and children's voices coming from the direction of one of the spare bedrooms and hoped for now that they'd stay where they were. Their mother didn't need the added strain of having to put on a brave face for her kids. He wasn't sure what explanation she'd given them for being in his house, but now wasn't the time for them to see their mother like this or ask their questions.

Her gasps turned into full blown sobs and a moment later, she buried her head against his chest. She cried like her heart was broken. The sound of it moved him way down deep inside. How anyone could be expected to endure the kind of pain she had was beyond him. Fresh anger surged through him at the thought of her husband and all that he'd done. Mason had seen the doubt in her eyes and prayed that Belle had the strength to overcome her fear and come through this intact.

He couldn't say how long she cried, but it was fully dark when she finally lifted her head. Her eyes were swollen and red and deep shadows haunted her gaze. A cut on her lip had reopened and was oozing fresh blood. She stared at him as if only now becoming aware of her surroundings. Almost instantaneously, she pulled away from him.

"I-I'm sorry," she stammered. "I shouldn't have done that. I-I don't know what came over me. I'm so sorry."

Irritation surged through him and he did his best to tamp it down. "Would you stop apologizing? You've been through a horrendous time—too terrible for anyone to imagine. Cut yourself some slack."

She inched further away from him and stared up at him with eyes filled with doubt and confusion. She appeared unsure about trusting his support and that somehow she'd thought, instead of offering advice, he'd given her an order.

He moved closer, choosing to ignore her sudden tension, and cupped her cheek in his hand, wanting so hard for her to understand. "I only want to help you. Protect you. You're safe, Belle. It's okay. He'll never hurt you again."

The shadows in her eyes didn't lessen and once again, she moved out of his reach. Fresh tears filled her eyes and slid silently down her cheeks. Mason's heart clenched. He couldn't bear to see her so...broken. In this moment, she seemed nothing like the beautiful, vibrant girl from high school, the girl who even now continued to haunt his dreams. And he would do everything he could to bring her back, even if it wasn't going to be to him.

"Let me take care of you, Belle," he whispered. Unable to help himself, he reached for her again. This time, she stood and crossed her arms defensively over her chest. She walked across the room in the direction of the bedrooms. "I need to check on Sophie and Ben."

He nodded and ignored the stab of hurt her withdrawal caused. He understood her reticence to let another man get close. She'd just escaped a violent relationship. What more did he expect?

"I'd like to meet them," he said quietly.

Her eyes widened. She stared at him for a long moment, but eventually nodded and then turned away.

Mason stared after her, nervous, excited and uncertain. What had he gotten himself into? He'd loved her for as long as he could remember. He'd yearned to be a part of her life, but he couldn't help but wonder if it were too late, perhaps even impossible. She was so badly broken. *What if she never healed?*

He pushed the unwanted thought aside. He was determined to help her any way he could. Failure wasn't an option.

CHAPTER 12

Nigel threw back two fingers of scotch and once again pored over the phone bills that were strewn out all over his desk. The sun had barely poked its head above the horizon when he'd started looking for something out of place. An unfamiliar number, a lengthy conversation—anything that might indicate where Isobel had gone and who knew about it. He was sure she had an accomplice. She wasn't capable of walking out on him on her own.

He'd managed to pull himself together long enough to pay a visit to her sister in Bondi. Katrina thought the sun shone out of his ass. He made sure to plaster on the charm when he knocked on her door and asked to see his wife.

She'd shaken her head in total bewilderment and had told him Isobel wasn't there. He made up some story about Isobel calling him the day before to say she was catching up with her sister and was going to spend the night. He'd been in the neighborhood and thought he'd surprise them.

Katrina had once again shaken her head and he was sure her confusion was real. She told him she hadn't spoken to Isobel for a couple of weeks. Katrina assumed she'd been busy at work and with the kids and all the other things that sucked up her time every day.

Perhaps he'd misunderstood, she'd wondered aloud. Perhaps it was another friend her sister had been referring to?

Nigel had forced a smile that showed all of his teeth and agreed that he must have gotten the conversation confused. After sharing a few more moments of casual repartee, he'd taken his leave. All the way home, he'd cursed the woman he called his wife.

Now, the memory of his humiliating visit to her sister came back to him and he flushed anew with anger. If she and the kids weren't with Katrina, then where the hell were they? Surely she wouldn't have gone home to Maitland? Her parents were frail and poor in health.

No, she must have had contact with someone else in the days or even weeks leading up to the day she abandoned him. There was no other explanation. The bitch was too stupid to have planned the whole thing by herself. Besides, why now? They'd been living this way for years and she'd never once looked like she considered packing her bags.

He'd made it clear on many occasions what he'd do to her and their kids if she ever left him. He reminded her of it every chance he got, and yet, she'd run away. With his kids. The bitch would pay for that.

With a vicious curse, he thrust the pile of phone bills aside. He'd found nothing out of the ordinary and neither had there been any unusual texts on her cell. She didn't know it, but he went through her phone every night. It was important for him to know who his wife was spending time with, even if it was only via texts.

He glanced at his watch and cursed again. He was going to be late for work. Pushing away from his desk, he found his briefcase and keys and headed out the door.

The traffic was heavy as at least a million people made their way to work. He slammed his fist against the steering wheel. One of the things he hated about Sydney was the peak-hour traffic. It started before seven in the morning and didn't let up until ten. The trip home was just as bad. There were few things he missed about his hometown, but the slower pace of country life was one of them.

Thoughts of his hometown triggered memories of running into Mason Alexander. He hadn't seen him since graduation. It had to be ten years or more. Mason hadn't changed a bit—maybe filled out a little. His football body was still taut with muscle. There hadn't been a sign of fat. He obviously kept himself fit, like Nigel did. He wondered if he worked out at the hospital gym.

Nigel frowned. Mason worked at the Sydney Harbour Hospital, on the same ward as Isobel. She'd told him yesterday she hadn't run into him.

Yet Mason told him he'd been there over a week. It seemed odd they hadn't met. Perhaps as strange as the fact his wife disappeared the day Nigel ran into their mutual friend.

Coincidence?

Nigel didn't believe in coincidences.

———————

Mason made a notation on the chart in his hand and maintained his focus on the three-year-old patient in the bed beside him. The little girl's renal infection had finally settled. The antibiotics had done the trick.

"Guess what, Ellie? I think you're well enough to go home."

She squealed with excitement and clapped her hands. The child's mother threw him a grateful smile.

"Thank you, Doctor Alexander. I'm so relieved she's okay."

"She'll be fine. No doubt back to her usual self in a day or two. I'll give you a script for another course of antibiotics that she can continue when she gets home, just to be on the safe side. I checked her history. It appears she's a little prone to these kinds of infections."

The woman nodded. "Yes, she's suffered from them on and off since she was a baby. It seems like every time she catches one, we end up in here."

"It can't be easy. I understand you have other young children at home."

"Yes, a two-year-old boy and a seven-year-old girl. I'm lucky my husband's self-employed. He runs his own software business from home. He's amazing with the kids, especially at times like this. There's no way I'd leave her in here alone."

"No, of course not. Well, your husband will be pleased to hear you're both heading home."

"Yes, thanks to you and the wonderful nursing staff. They always treat Ellie so well. It makes it so much easier for both of us."

"We're just doing our jobs. I'm glad I could help." Giving both her and her daughter a wave of farewell, he left the room and walked into the one beside it. A nurse stood near one of the patients, checking the child's observations. Mason's thoughts turned to Isobel and he was helpless to stop them.

He recalled how she'd introduced him to her children, quiet pride shining briefly in her eyes. Sophie had lifted her head momentarily off her mother's shoulder and given him a sleepy look. Ben's face was lively with curiosity.

"Mom says you're her friend," he'd stated matter-of-factly. "We've never met any of Mom's friends. Have you known her long?"

Mason was happy to answer him, although he was surprised to discover Isobel hadn't introduced her children to any of her friends. Was it because of Nigel? Was she scared her friends would notice something amiss? He had no idea, but he filed the information away for further contemplation.

"I've known your mom *forever*." He'd

responded with an exaggerated eye roll and a big grin. Ben had smiled back at him.

"Forever? Really?" the young boy asked.

"Well, maybe not forever, but it feels that way," Mason replied with another grin. "Your mom and I went to high school together and believe me, high school was a long time ago. Are you at school yet, Ben?"

"Not yet. I'm five-and-a-half. I go to school next year."

Isobel had reached for her son, drawing him in close against her side. She smiled down at him tenderly.

"You're growing up way too fast, Ben Donnelly. I'm flat out keeping up. Now, how about you say goodnight to Mason and I'll tuck you into bed."

"But I haven't had a shower, Mom!" he protested.

"You can have one in the morning," Isobel had replied. "It's too late to have one now."

"But Mom, I want to stay up and talk to Mason. I—"

"You can talk to him again in the morning. Come on, honey, it's time for bed."

She'd adjusted a sleeping Sophie in her arms and had headed in the direction of the bedrooms, with Ben trailing behind her.

"'Night, Ben," Mason called after them.

Ben turned and waved. "Goodnight, Mason. See you in the morning."

The smile the little boy sent him had warmed Mason all the way through. He waited for Isobel to reappear, but she didn't. He'd been disappointed they wouldn't get to share a meal or otherwise celebrate her first night of freedom, but he understood her need for privacy in order to settle her kids and come to terms with the reality of her new life.

The truth was, he needed to be careful. All the years of hard-won effort spent trying to forget her had disappeared the moment he'd seen her again. It was like they were back in high school and she was the most beautiful girl in the world. He wanted to protect her, cherish her and keep her safe from harm, every day for the rest of their lives and yet he also needed to keep his distance and protect his heart from being trampled on all over again.

She hadn't given him any indication that she saw him as anything other than a friend. True, she'd called on him in her hour of need. But that's what friends did. They were there for each other when they were needed. It didn't mean she wanted anything more. Hell, he didn't even know if she found him attractive.

No, right now, Isobel West needed to find herself, regain her confidence and take care of her children. Everything else would have to wait.

"Where the fuck is he? Get the hell out of my way! Mason! Mason Alexander! Come out and show yourself like a man!"

Mason heard the commotion in the corridor. He set down the chart he'd been reading and left the room, trying to locate the origin of the angry voice. He rounded a corner and nearly collided with Nigel. The man was almost foaming at the mouth.

"You fucking asshole! You stole my fucking wife! You always wanted her. Did you think I didn't notice the way you used to look at her? You've had a hard-on for her since high school!"

Before Mason realized what was happening, Nigel threw a clumsy punch in his direction. He neatly sidestepped it and almost gagged at the smell of liquor on Nigel's breath. It was nine in the morning. *What the hell was the man thinking?*

Two nurses came to a sudden halt, shock flooding their features. A burly security guard materialized and Mason breathed a sigh of relief. Not that he feared getting beaten. In fact, there was nothing he'd enjoy more than to knock Isobel's husband off his feet, but the man was obviously drunk and needed to be removed before any patients got wind of it or some bystander was hurt.

Mason should have known Nigel wouldn't go quietly. The furious man broke away from the loose hold the guard had on his arm.

"You're not even going to deny it!" Nigel spat. "You fucking bastard! You're the reason she left! It took me awhile, but I finally twigged to what happened. She was fine until you arrived in town, sniffing around her." He sucked in an angry breath and once again, Mason caught a whiff of alcohol.

"I want you transferred to another ward, effective immediately," Nigel shouted, getting up in Mason's face. "I want you to stay the fuck away from my wife!"

Mason worked hard to control his temper. He replied as calmly as he could. "I'm a pediatrician,

Nigel. I work on the pediatric ward. As far as I know, it's the only one in the hospital."

Nigel stabbed a finger in Mason's direction. It barely missed his face. "You *knew* she was a nurse here. Don't fucking try and deny it. You're here because this is where Isobel works. My wife! *My* fucking wife! I got home last night and the house was empty. She's run off and taken the kids and now I know where she is!"

Mason stared at him, his eyes narrowed. Anger swirled low in his gut. "If you hadn't hurt her, and had treated her as a loving husband should, she wouldn't have had reason to leave. Did you ever think of that?"

Nigel spluttered and waved his hands. Mason's lip curled up in disgust. "You're a disgrace, Nigel Donnelly. You don't have the right to call yourself a man, let alone lay claim to someone as fine as Isobel West."

Nigel's eyes blazed, but Mason stood his ground. "It's Isobel *Donnelly* to you. *Mrs* Isobel Donnelly," Nigel shouted and then his expression turned into a sneer. "I see you haven't denied knowing where she is."

Mason shrugged. "Why would I bother? You've already made up your mind about what happened. I can see you don't make the mistake of letting the truth get in the way of what you want to believe. It must be tough beating up on a defenseless woman."

His calm statement seemed to infuriate Nigel further. The man growled deep in his throat and lunged at him, but this time, the security guard's hold remained firm. Mason stared at Nigel and silently dared him to hit him. He'd love to have an excuse to drive his fist into the bastard's handsome face.

From the corner of his eye, he saw Georgie Whitely striding toward them, a look of concern on her face.

"Doctor Alexander, would you mind checking in on Sam Perkins?" she asked when she reached them, ignoring Nigel. "He's not responding as well as we hoped to his medication. His fever's still high and—"

"Go on, do it. You know you want to," Nigel goaded him.

Fury burned through Mason and his hands clenched into fists. The roar in his head urged him to punch the bastard and wipe the smug look off his face. The only thing that stopped him was the knowledge that hitting him was exactly what Nigel wanted. Mason's career at the hospital would be over just as soon as it had begun. He'd be lucky to secure a job elsewhere in the state if he threw a punch.

"Doctor Alexander—" Georgie tried again.

To Mason's relief, the security guard jerked Nigel around and frog-marched him out of the ward. Mason dragged in a deep breath and waited for the emotional haze to clear. He still shook from the force of his anger, but was relieved he'd kept his cool. The only other thing that gave him comfort was the knowledge that Isobel would never have to put up with abuse from the prick again.

Isobel's breath caught at the sound of the door banging and turned to scold Ben as he ran toward her down the hall. She'd been jittery all morning, ever since Mason had left. She guessed it was normal to feel so jumpy, under the circumstances. In her mind she'd fantasized once she was away from Nigel she'd feel safe. But the reality was much different than that. It was only twenty-four hours since she'd walked out on her violent husband and though he couldn't contact her by phone anymore, she still worried he might show up.

The fact that her fears had no grounding was beside the point. No matter how many times she told herself Nigel had no idea where Mason lived, she still couldn't shake the feeling that somehow, her estranged husband *would* find out and come after her.

When he'd mentioned oh-so-casually about running into Mason the day before, she'd nearly died from fright. Of all the days for Nigel to discover his high school football buddy now worked in the same hospital... She couldn't believe it was on the same day she'd chosen to make her escape. She could only hope he'd bought her line about not knowing Mason was there. The alternative sent shivers running down her spine.

The shrill ringing of her new cell phone jarred

her thoughts, but then she smiled. Mason was the only one who knew the number. Hurrying across the living room, she picked it up from the kitchen counter and quickly answered the call. "Mason, how are you?"

"I'm fine. I...I just wanted to call you and let you know Nigel's on the warpath."

Dread congealed in her belly and her mouth went dry. "Wh-what do you mean?" she forced herself to ask.

"A little while ago, he came charging into the kids' ward like a bull with a bee up its butt. He reeked of alcohol and was so consumed with rage, I thought he was going to blow a gasket. He threw a punch at me and was escorted away by security."

Shock surged through her. She put her hand up to her mouth to hold back a gasp. "Oh, Mason! I'm so sorry! This is all my fault! I should never have involved you in my problems. You... You could have been hurt! And what will the staff think? I bet there was an awful scene."

"Trust you to think of everyone but yourself," Mason replied. "And for the record yet again, I got involved in this of my own free will. Nobody held a gun to my head. It's you and the kids I'm worried about," he added in a somber tone.

Isobel drew in a deep breath with his reassuring words and did her best to quell the fear and panic that had immediately taken hold. "We'll be fine," she said and wasn't sure which one of them she was trying to convince. "He doesn't know we're here."

"I hate to say it, but I think he probably suspects I'm hiding you. But don't worry. He doesn't know where I live and I'm not listed in any of the directories. I've only just moved to the city. I haven't had a chance to make the type of friends I'd trust with my address. I'll keep an eye on the vehicles around me in case he gets it in his head to follow me, but I'm certain it won't come to that. What kind of car does he drive?"

"A bright red Porsche Boxster Cabriolet. It's quite distinctive."

"Even better. I'll spot him from a mile. Hopefully he'll waste a lot of time driving around the city streets and will come up without a result. The odds of finding my building amongst the thousands in Sydney are almost non-existent."

She listened to his reassurances and her breath eased a little. She wanted so much to believe Mason was right.

"Thank you for calling and letting me know," she said softly. "I appreciate it."

"Just be careful, that's all. I... I care about you, Belle. I promised to keep you safe and I won't let you down."

The warmth and concern in his voice brought on a rush of tears. It had been so long since she'd felt like anyone gave a toss. Her family would have been behind her one hundred percent if they'd known what had been going on, but she hadn't told them about the real Nigel. At first, she'd been horribly embarrassed to admit her perfect life was a farce. Later, she couldn't get past the shame.

It was stupid, but it was the truth. The progression of abuse had been insidious. Over and over, she'd been told by Nigel it was her fault. That if she'd been a better wife, a better mother, it wouldn't happen. She had no frame of reference because she'd grown up in a lovely home and she'd been deeply ashamed to admit to anyone that she was a victim of domestic abuse.

At no point did she think it wasn't her fault. She could see now that Nigel had conditioned her that way. She believed his hurtful taunts that she was to blame for the way he acted.

If she loved him more, if she didn't give him cheek, if she had the dinner on the table on time; if the bedspread was lined up properly, if there were no bones in the salmon, if his shirts were ironed just right, he wouldn't react with anger and be forced to pull her back into line.

The last few months, she'd tried to do a little research on the Internet, but she struggled to find the right search words. Almost by accident, she'd stumbled across a site about domestic abuse and so many of the statements rang true. She'd read the statistics of how many women managed to escape and how just as many often returned...

Would she be one of those? It terrified her that she didn't know the answer.

Aware that Mason waited for her response on the other end of the phone, she replied as honestly as she could.

"Thank you, Mason. It means a lot to know you care. You're so good and kind and I don't know what I would have done without you. You gave me the courage to do what I should have done a long time ago. I'll never be able to thank you."

Mason's voice was gruff when he replied. "I don't want your thanks. And you're wrong. You're braver than you think. You're the bravest woman I know."

"How can you say that? I've lived with Nigel like this for more than nine years. Nine years! If I was truly brave, I would have stood up to him right at the outset, after the very first time he hit me."

"Don't say that, Belle. I don't pretend to know what you've been through, but I know enough about domestic abuse to know it's never as easy as that. These men are cunning, they work away at your self-respect, isolate you and make you doubt yourself, your intellect."

She heard him take a quick breath before continuing. "They manipulate you so cleverly, so insidiously you aren't even aware what they're doing. You've taken the first step to break that hold. Feel proud of what you've achieved."

Isobel swallowed the lump of emotion that threatened to choke her and swiped at a fresh burst of tears. She heard the conviction in Mason's voice and she yearned to feel as convinced about this as he was. The truth was, she was more terrified than she'd ever been in her life and couldn't help but question her decision.

When had she made good choices in the past and what was to say this was the best choice for her children?

"How are the kids?" Mason asked, his voice gentle, as if he were trying to understand her fears.

"F-fine. A little confused. Sophie wants a doll we

left behind. Ben wants his bike. And I forgot my blood pressure medication. I've already missed two doses. I...I was thinking about going back to the house to collect them."

"Belle, don't do that. Don't risk it. I can write you out another script. From the state Nigel was in when security dragged him off the ward, I'm sure that's not a good idea. He was probably ordered home for the day."

"But today he has a full theater list. They wouldn't have cancelled his surgeries."

"From the way he smelled, I'd be surprised if they let him anywhere near the operating table."

She bit her lip in indecision and considered the possibilities. The last thing she wanted to do was risk running into Nigel. Still, she could drive by their house and see. He always parked in the drive. She asked him once why he didn't park his two-hundred-thousand-dollar car in the garage, to protect it from the weather. He'd smiled at her like a simpleton and had said, "But nobody would see it in there."

It was all about appearances for Nigel: The perfect wife, two perfect kids, a house and a car that inspired envy. There'd be hell to pay if anyone had the audacity to suggest it was all an elaborate façade or, even worse, if someone destroyed his picture-perfect life by walking out the door.

"I'll drive past the house. If I see his car, I'll just keep going. He won't even know I've been by. If he's not there, all the better. I'll be quick. I'll be in and out in a matter of minutes. I'll be fine."

"Call Senior Constable Rogers first. See if he can meet you there. That way, if Nigel's home or happens to stop by, you'll be safe. You don't even know if Nigel's been served with the AVO. If he has, he'll be madder than hell. If he hasn't, he's not doing anything wrong if he approaches you. Please, Belle. Think about it. Going over there on your own is a very bad idea."

She chewed her lip and thought about what he'd said. "You're right. I'll call the police station and speak to someone. I won't go unless I can get one of them to come with me."

She heard Mason's heavy sigh of relief. "Oh, thank goodness! I mean, I'd rather you not go at all, but if you have to, having the police accompany you is the only way to go."

"I'll call you when I get there so that you know everything's all right."

"And when you leave," Mason added. "I need to know you're safe."

Once again, warmth spread through her at the tenderness and worry in his voice. It was amazing how he almost made her believe she was worthy of his concern.

"I'll call. I promise." A silence fell between them. She broke it by saying, "You'd better get back to work."

"Yes. I'll talk to you soon. Call me."

CHAPTER 13

Isobel eased her car into the street where she'd lived for the past six years, relieved to see Nigel's Porsche wasn't parked in the driveway. She looked around for any sign of a patrol car, but didn't see one.

Senior Constable Rogers had been unavailable to take her call, but she'd spoken to another officer. He'd promised to send a car over in case Nigel arrived and caused trouble while she was there, but it appeared the promised offer of protection hadn't yet materialized.

She stared at the impressive almost-new home that took pride of place on the block. They'd bought it a few months before Ben arrived. Up until then, they'd been living in a tiny apartment in Sydney's inner west. With a child on the way, having a house with a real backyard and a reasonably short commute to work had seemed like heaven. If she'd only known how Nigel would change after their son arrived and how, among other things, he'd blame her for the hefty mortgage that now hung over their heads...

"We're back home. Why did we need to pack so many bags? We only stayed away one night. Where's Dad?"

Isobel gritted her teeth and did her best to answer Ben's questions. "I think Dad's at work, honey. He usually is this time of day. We're not staying long. I'm going to run inside and collect a few things I left behind. I'll get Sophie's doll and your bike from the backyard. Then we're going back to Mason's."

"I want my bike, too," Sophie said.

"All right, honey. I'll get your bike, too."

"Why aren't we staying? I thought we were only going to your friend's house for a visit? How come we're going back? Mason isn't even home."

She wanted to squeeze her eyes tightly shut and scream, but instead, she forced a smile. "You're right, Ben. It seems a little strange, but the thing is, we're going to stay at Mason's house for a while longer. Mommy and Daddy need...a little time apart."

"Is this because Daddy yells at you?" Sophie piped up from the back seat, her expression only mildly curious.

Isobel's heart clenched. It was so wrong that her babies had witnessed her pain. If she had any hesitation about leaving, she should bury that right here and now. Her children deserved better. *She* deserved better.

"Something like that, baby." She looked around again for the patrol car, but there was no sign of it. Remembering her promise to Mason, she tugged out the cell phone he'd given her and re-dialed the number for the police station. It was answered after the third ring.

"City of Sydney Police Station, Constable Bassett speaking. How can I help you?"

"Yes, it's Isobel Donnelly. I spoke to someone there a little while ago about sending a squad car around to my house. I have an AVO out on my husband. I'm not sure it's been served yet, but I've had to return home to collect a few of my things. An officer was supposed to meet me here in case my husband arrives while I'm here. I've been waiting outside, but no one has come. Could you tell me what's going on?"

"Just a minute, Mrs Donnelly, I'll find out for you."

Hold music sounded in her ear. She closed her eyes on a heavy sigh and waited for the officer to return to the line. Mason's words of caution sounded in her head. As the seconds ticked past, her misgivings grew. She should just leave and come back when she knew the officer was here. The thought had barely formed when the officer on the other end of the phone spoke again.

"Sorry to keep you waiting, Mrs Donnelly, but it took me awhile to find the constable you spoke to earlier. The good news is, a squad car is on its way. It left here nearly half an hour ago, so it shouldn't be too far away. Are you safe there at the moment?"

Isobel cast a wary glance around her. There was no sign of Nigel. She drew in a deep breath and exhaled slowly in an effort to ease a little of her tension. "Yes, I'm fine. I guess I'll wait for the officer to arrive." After thanking the woman for her help, Isobel ended the call and tossed the phone back into her handbag.

"What are we doing, Mom? Why aren't we going inside?" Ben asked with a frown.

Isobel bit her lip, undecided about what to do. *Should she just sit tight and wait?* According to the constable, the officer wasn't far away. It would take her less than ten minutes to duck inside the house and collect the things she'd come for. She could be finished by the time the patrol car arrived. Coming to a sudden decision, she turned to face her children.

"I want you both to stay here. Don't even take off your seatbelt," she said to Ben. "I promise I won't be long."

Both of them nodded. Remembering her promise to Mason, she shot him off a brief text to say she'd arrived and then she climbed out of the car and headed toward the house.

With each step closer, the trembling in her body increased. Quickly, she unlocked the front door and stepped inside. Now that she'd decided to enter the house, a sense of urgency overtook her and she rushed down the hall to the bedrooms.

She came to the main bedroom first and pulled up with a gasp. The room had been trashed. Everywhere she looked she saw shards of broken glass. A fresh wave of fear took hold of her and she knew with a certainty that, given the chance, her husband would vent his anger like this on her. Somehow, he'd make her pay.

Turning her back on the debris, she went into the adjoining bathroom and found her bottle of blood pressure medication. With her heart thumping, she tossed back a tablet and then leaned over the sink and chased it with a mouthful of water. With the bottle clutched in her hand, she left the room. All she wanted was to collect their things and leave before it was too late.

Nigel punched the steering wheel with his fist and cursed long and loudly. He couldn't believe they'd cancelled his surgery list and had politely but firmly suggested he take the rest of the day off. He was Doctor Nigel Donnelly, Senior Registrar, directly under the Head of Surgery. How dare some fucking fat underling from HR tell him to go home?

He gunned the engine of his Porsche, impatient for the red light to change. A blond woman in the lane next to him turned her head. She looked at the car and then at him and gave him a flirtatious wink. He smiled his big, wide, charming smile at her and gunned the engine again.

For a moment, he considered following her down the road a bit and pulling over to the side. If she pulled in after him, she was as good as his. He could give her a quick fuck behind one of the abandoned buildings that littered the adjacent street and then go on about his business. That would show her. Nobody would be the wiser, least of all his wife.

His wife.

At the thought of Isobel, his anger returned full force and just as quickly, his interest in the woman in the car beside him died. Isobel was the reason why he'd been escorted from the hospital. It was her fault he'd been humiliated in front of his staff. He needed to find her and teach her a lesson. One she wouldn't forget. Nobody walked out on Nigel Donnelly and got away with it.

An image of his mother suddenly crowded his mind and an old, familiar pain surged through him and tightened his gut. The night before had been the first time in years since he'd thought of the bitch that had given him life. He hadn't seen her since junior high. For years after that, it had been just him and his dad. And that's the way he'd wanted it.

The light turned green. The car in front of him didn't move. Nigel blasted his horn and the vehicle finally shifted. Anger pounded through his veins and he realized it hadn't let up since the moment he realized his fucking bitch of a wife had left him.

How dare she leave! *Who the fuck did she think she was? Didn't she know he wouldn't rest until he found her?* He'd drag her back home by the hair if he had to and that would only be the start of it. He'd make sure she never considered leaving him again.

It wouldn't have happened if Mason Alexander hadn't come on the scene. Once Nigel realized the pair of them had to have run into each other, it hadn't taken much to work out he was involved with his wife's departure. They worked on the same ward. There was no way their paths hadn't crossed. The fact that the bitch had lied about it was all he needed to know.

Mason had always had a thing for her. Nigel had seen it from a mile away all those years ago. The way the prick would look at her when he thought no one noticed. The way he'd light up when she smiled. She smiled a lot back then. Now? Not so much.

Still, she couldn't complain. He'd provided her with the kids she wanted and a comfortable house to boot. They were the envy of many of their friends. Well, *his* friends. Isobel didn't have any. He'd made damn sure of that.

Friends took up her time, influenced her; they had a way of noticing things and putting stupid ideas in her head. Like this. It was best that she listen to no one but him. Best for everyone. His father had discovered that much too late with his mother. Nigel wouldn't make that mistake.

But for all the trouble Nigel had gone to in order to make their enviable picture-perfect family, it wasn't enough. The bitch had left without a word. He thought of all the money he'd invested in his home and family. There was no pleasing some women. She was just like his fucking mother. Except, unlike Eleanor Donnelly, Isobel hadn't left her kids behind.

Isobel glanced at her watch. It had been ten

minutes since she'd pulled into the drive. Her medication was in her handbag. The bikes were in the trunk. In her arms, she carried Sophie's doll and a handful of clothes. Quickly, she pulled the front door closed behind her, crossed the porch and headed down the steps. There was still no sign of the promised patrol car.

The familiar roar of an engine as it sped around the corner stopped her in her tracks. A few seconds later, Nigel's red Porsche pulled up at the curb. Before she could catch her breath, he flew out of the car and came striding toward her. A smile full of malice twisted his well-formed lips.

"Well, well, well. What do we have here? The fucking bitch has returned to the scene of the crime. How lucky that I just happened to stop by."

Paralyzing terror held Isobel frozen to the spot. Her mind spun so fast with frantic thoughts, she felt dizzy.

Where, oh where, was the policeman?

One thing was certain, she had to find a way to calm down her husband until the officer arrived, or she could drive away. Nigel, in a nasty mood, was a threat to everyone, especially to her and she still didn't know if he'd been served with the AVO. Trying hard to control her trembling, she forced a smile.

"Nigel, I didn't realize you'd be home. I only came by to collect a few of our things."

His gaze narrowed. "How dare you!" he snarled.

"Nigel, I'm sorry I left without speaking to you, but I was too scared to say anything. The last few years—they haven't been good—for either of us. We need some time apart. We're not good together. We... We seem to bring out the worst in each other." She glanced nervously at the kids, seated in her car watching their parents with wide eyes.

He moved up so close beside her, she could see the dark fleck in his light brown eyes. He thrust his face into hers. It was all she could do not to flinch from fear and the still-toxic smell of alcohol.

"I'll decide whether or not we're good together. You don't get to make that call. You ought to know that by now." The menace in his eyes sent a shiver of fear sliding down her spine. In panic, she tried to step out of his way. He blocked her path to the car.

"You need to put all that crap back in the house and take yourself back in there with it. Get the kids out of the damn car. Your place is here, in our home, with me."

He snatched her wrist and squeezed hard. With a cry, the doll fell from her hand. Tears burned behind her eyes. "Nigel, please! You're hurting me!"

"You haven't seen anything yet. I've barely started," he scoffed. He wrenched her arm and forced her closer until his face was mere inches from hers. She wanted desperately to look away, but was frightened of what he'd do if she dared. His eyes narrowed and his voice dropped to a threatening growl.

"I want to know Isobel, are you prepared to

even try to reconcile? Think hard before you answer because that will determine the mindset I take with you."

Terror weakened her knees. *Why, oh why, had she come alone?* Mason had cautioned her against it. She'd waved away his concerns. *Why, oh why, hadn't she listened? Or waited for the police?*

It was too late for regrets and recriminations now. From the look in Nigel's eyes, she was in for the beating of her life. His grip moved from her wrist to her hair. His fingers buried themselves in the long strands and then pulled hard. She cried out again and he laughed and yanked harder. The tears she'd tried so hard to hold at bay fell hotly down her cheeks. She heard her children crying in the car but it seemed a long way away. Too far away.

Once again, he thrust his face close to hers, his breath hot and fetid on her skin. "Listen here, Isobel Donnelly. You're *my* wife. You belong to me, in *my* house. Got it?"

In terror, she nodded frantically and winced against the pull of her hair. Nigel's grip was relentless. She bit her lip against the pain.

"Good. Now, get your skinny ass back inside and let's be finished with this leaving shit." He shoved her hard with his shoulder and at the same time released her hair. She stumbled, off balance. She took a step and tripped over. The clothes spilled out of her arms. She put her hand out to break her fall, but landed awkwardly on the paved drive.

The tears came harder. Her humiliation was complete. Blood oozed from a graze on her knee. She scrambled about on the ground, collecting Sophie's doll and the clothes. From the corner of her eye, she spied a flash of blue and white and almost collapsed with relief. The squad car had finally arrived.

A uniformed officer climbed out of the driver's seat and walked toward them.

"Excuse me, are you Isobel Donnelly?"

Standing slowly, Isobel kept her gaze trained on the policeman and nodded.

He looked from her to Nigel and back again. "Are you all right?"

Lowering her gaze to the ground, she gave another nod.

"Are you sure? Your knee's bleeding and you look a little the worse for wear."

"She's fine," Nigel snapped and then seemed to collect himself. He smiled his charming smile. "I'm a little surprised to see you here, officer. Is there something I can do for you?"

"Mrs Donnelly called the station and requested someone accompany her while she removed some personal items from the house. I'm here to see that she doesn't come to any harm."

Nigel's eyes widened, but he laughed off the constable's claims. "Harm? Why would she come to any harm? She's my wife. There must be some misunderstanding. Isobel's not here to remove anything. She lives here, with me."

"I don't think so," the officer replied. "Yesterday, the court approved an Apprehended

Violence Order in your wife's favor. I assume, from the look on your face, that you haven't yet been served with a copy. No need to worry, I have one right here."

The constable pulled a folded piece of paper out of his shirt pocket and handed it to Nigel. Her husband threw her a hard stare and then opened it. With her heart thumping, Isobel held her breath and waited for Nigel's response. She didn't have to wait long.

His face turned red with anger. "You have to be fucking kidding!" As if oblivious to the presence of the policeman, Nigel took a threatening step toward her, his hands clenched into fists.

"You fucking bitch! I don't believe it! How dare you order me to stay away from you and the kids? They're my kids as much as yours. There's no way in the world you're going to take them away from me."

"Mr Donnelly, I suggest you tone down your language and calm down a little then go and get some legal advice. Your lawyer will be able to tell you how best to proceed. In the meantime, I suggest you comply with the terms of the AVO, including staying away from your wife and children. If you breach the order, I can arrest you and have you charged. I'm sure no one wants that to happen."

Isobel snatched a breath and did her best to slow her racing heart. She could feel Nigel's anger, but she refused to look at him. Having collected the things she'd come for, she was eager to get as far away from him as she could.

The presence of the police officer was her perfect means of escape.

"Thank you for your time, officer. I've collected the things I came for and I'll continue on my way. I'd appreciate your assistance to my car, though."

The constable turned his attention to her. "Are you sure? Because I'm happy to stay as long as you need me if there are other things you require."

Isobel shuddered at the thought of going through the house and removing more things with Nigel throwing daggers at her back. No, she had what she'd come for. It was best to leave it at that.

"Thank you; that's very kind of you, but I'm done." With that, she opened the door to her car and tossed in the handful of clothes. Leaning over the seat, she gave Sophie her doll.

"Can we go now, Mom?"

She glanced at Ben where he sat in the back seat of the car, his face troubled.

"Sure, baby. We're leaving right now."

Nigel stepped forward. The officer was quick to react. With a restraining hand on Nigel's arm, he nodded to Isobel.

"You're right to go, Mrs Donnelly. Take care."

She gave him a grateful smile and tugged on her seatbelt. Wrenching his arm out of the officer's grasp, Nigel charged over to the car and banged on the window with his fist.

"Get back out here, bitch," he yelled, his fury palpable.

Unperturbed, the officer spoke to Nigel calmly and pulled him away. All the time, he shouted abuse. Isobel shook so hard, she didn't know how she managed to turn the key in the ignition, but she somehow reversed out of the drive.

She didn't look back.

CHAPTER 14

Dear Diary,

There are days when I would rather endure a thousand beatings than deal with the emotional wounds that crisscross my body and soul. Physical pain will eventually dull and fade away; my emotional pain is like a cancer; it's silent and slowly gnaws away at anything that was ever good in my life. Being with my husband has been like experiencing a living death.

How can I explain it to someone who has never been through this other than to say, it's like waking up each morning with the hope that this will be the day things will get better only to realize they won't, and with that recognition comes death all over again. Sooner or later, you start wishing for the real thing...

———————

Isobel barely made it two blocks away from her house before she broke down. Pulling over to the side of the road, she leaned her head on the steering wheel and sobbed out her relief. With shaking hands, she searched through her handbag for her phone and dialed Mason's number, all the time praying that he'd answer.

"Isobel, thank God you called. I was getting worried."

She went to speak, but all that came out was another breathless sob.

"Isobel? Where are you? What the hell's happening?"

She could hear the increasing alarm in his voice and struggled to reassure him. "I'm... I'm f-fine. N-Nigel arrived as I was leaving."

"Shit! If he—"

"It's okay. The police arrived soon after he did and I'm fine. He was served the papers right there. We're all fine."

"Thank God! Where are you?"

"A couple of blocks away from my house. I-I couldn't go any further."

"I understand. Now, Belle, I want you to listen to me. Take big breaths and calm yourself down. He's not going to hurt you again. The worst of it is over. He's seen you and realized you're never coming back. Now, hopefully he'll accept your decision and move on."

Isobel shook her head sadly, but didn't interrupt. Mason was so naïve, judging people with the same moral compass he had. He didn't know Nigel the way she did. There was no way on earth he would ever move on.

In his mind, he owned her. She was his possession. She had his kids. On top of all that, he'd be concerned she'd ruin his public image. He'd never rest until she'd paid for the damage she'd done.

"As soon as you're able, get back on the road and drive straight to my place. Don't stop anywhere along the way. I'll meet you there."

"But it's not even lunch time! You have work to do."

"Screw work. You're more important than that. You need me and I... I need to know you're okay. I'll be there as soon as I can."

Isobel nodded. "Okay." The relief she felt, knowing Mason was on his way, was overwhelming.

Thirty minutes later, she arrived at his complex and unloaded the things from the car. No doubt there was a storage area in the underground car park that she could access when Mason got home. But for now, the balcony would have to do.

With Ben's help, she stacked the bikes there. Then forcing the morning's events from her mind, she prepared a light lunch for the children, reassured them that things were fine, and put them both down for a nap.

On her way back from the bedroom, she heard the sound of a key in the lock and her heart skipped a beat. Mason closed the door behind him and she eased out her breath. He took one look at her and headed straight toward her.

"Are you hurt, Belle? Your knee! It's bleeding!"

"My knee's fine," she assured him quietly, not able to deny the hurt deep within her so easily. A grazed knee was nothing compared to that.

A moment later, his arms came around her and he held her close against his chest. She tensed and then forced herself to relax against him. Despite all she'd been through that morning, it was getting easier to lean on him and accept his comfort. Once again, tears filled her eyes and overflowed. Giving herself permission to let go, she cried like she'd never stop.

Like a broken heap of humanity, Isobel let it all out, purging her heart and body and soul of all the darkness that had taken root there. For a brief moment she felt free—free of Nigel, free of hurt and free to find the woman she'd lost so long ago. If she dared...

"I-I was on my way out," she sobbed. "I'd finished getting the things I'd come to collect. He just turned up. I didn't have any warning. If it hadn't been for the police officer, I might have done exactly what Nigel told me and marched right back inside." She hiccupped and another wave of tears poured down her cheeks.

"He-he scares me so much I can't think straight around him, but I was ready to follow his orders. Just like that, he turned me back into a snivelling, gutless wimp."

"No, Belle, no. Please don't talk about yourself like that. You're never gutless. Never weak. You're the strongest, bravest woman I know. I've told you that before and I'll keep telling you until you believe it."

She pulled back and stared at him. "How can you say that? You hardly know me. We were kids the last time we met. Clueless, carefree kids. If only I'd known the devastation ahead, I'd have wanted to stay a teenager forever."

He held her gaze. When he spoke, his words were so soft, she had to strain to hear.

"Will you tell me the rest of it? What I heard that night at the police station was bad enough, but I can't help thinking there was more and that it was even worse than the things you told them."

She looked at him, torn. She wanted to tell him, to at last get all of this off her chest. She'd told Senior Constable Rogers some of it, but no one knew the whole of it. She'd always been too ashamed and too worried that she'd be judged harshly or worse, be the one urged to leave her family—including her children.

For too many years, the thought of walking out was beyond her. Her husband appeared to the world to be such an upstanding community and family man. *Who would believe different?*

Even now, she was on edge at the thought she might be coerced to return or that he'd take her to court and get them to believe it was all her fault. And in the end, get custody of their children.

"Belle, I know how hard it must be to trust me enough to open up, but I think it might help for you to talk to someone. If not me, then a professional. A therapist. Have you ever had any counseling over the years?"

She shook her head sadly. "No, at least, not the kind you're talking about. Nigel made me go to a sex therapist for a few months. He went through a time where he... He was having difficulties getting an erection." She grimaced at the memory.

"Of course, he claimed it was all my fault. Apparently, I wasn't trying hard enough to please him. I wasn't performing as well as I should. I was too thin, too ugly; too frigid. The list went on." She drew in a ragged sigh and then quietly continued.

"It was up to me to face that humiliation and see a sex therapist alone, so that I could fix the problem. The therapist said he needed Nigel to come with me and attend the sessions too, but he never would. Instead, he just got angrier and angrier with me."

Mason remained silent, but his expression was as dark as a thundercloud. Her shoulders slumped.

"There's a lot more ugliness where that came from. Are you sure you want to hear it?"

His expression softened. With gentle fingers, he tilted her head up so that she was forced to look at him. "If you want to tell me, I want to hear it."

She stared at him and her heart filled with apprehension. At the same time, she was charged with such a strong yearning to finally share her story, she couldn't deny it a second longer. "Okay," she whispered.

He released her and she made her way over to the couch. He sat down beside her, close but not so close they were touching. She didn't feel threatened, despite his impressive size. In fact, she felt just the opposite. She felt safe having him by her side.

"When I was seventeen, I fell in love for the very

first time," she began quietly. "He was tall and broad shouldered. He was the star of the football team. I was giddy from love and had my head in the clouds. You couldn't get the smile off my face. Never once did he show any sign of the monster he was deep inside. I'm a sister, a daughter and a mother. Back then, did I think this would ever happen to me—that I deserved this? Not in my wildest dreams. And yet it did."

"How long were you married before it started?" Mason asked, his voice pitched low.

"We married a couple of weeks after our high school graduation. We were both eighteen. My parents were concerned we were rushing things and thought we were way too young, but I brushed off their concerns and Nigel charmed them with his smile. He assured my mom and dad he'd love me with everything that he had and would protect me until he died."

She sighed. "It was a fairy-tale wedding in front of our family and friends. Nigel's mother didn't attend but I wasn't surprised; he had told me she was dead. I found out later that wasn't true. Though she'd doted on him for years, when he was fourteen she just walked out on him and his dad without a word or note of explanation."

Mason nodded. "I guess that explains some things. Not that I'm defending him or making excuses. Regardless of the reasons for his warped thinking, his actions and how you've been treated are unforgivable."

"Our marriage wasn't perfect, but the first four years were pretty good. We were both busy at college, studying for our degrees. We had the occasional disagreement over things I had or hadn't done—picky little things no one else would notice—but each time, we were able to reconcile and put them behind us. At least, I thought we had. It wasn't until things started falling apart that Nigel would dredge up all the past wrongs. I was shocked that he appeared to be just as angry as he had been when each one happened."

She drew in a breath and eased it out. "But even with these minor bumps along the way, I thought we were happy. And then Ben arrived..."

"What happened? Didn't Nigel want to have kids?"

"I guess you could say he wasn't overly keen, but after many months of pleading he agreed to my request to try. I got pregnant right away. The night I brought my new baby home from the hospital was the first time he split my lip."

"Jesus!" Mason breathed and his hands clenched into fists.

She grimaced. "Yes, it was a nice welcome home, let me assure you."

Mason shook his head in bewilderment. "Why? Why would he react like that? It's not like he didn't know you were having a baby."

She shrugged sadly. "Who knows? I think in his warped mind he thought I'd transferred my love for him to the baby. That he wouldn't get his fair share. That somehow he'd miss out. He was jealous of our son!"

She shook her head slowly. "I couldn't understand it. I still can't understand it. When

Sophie came along, things got even worse. He became increasingly depressed and hostile and constantly questioned my love. He started accusing me of looking at other men and even of having an affair."

She laughed without humor. "The alleged co-conspirator was the father of a child in Ben's daycare class. It was so far from the truth, the very thought Nigel would say those things left me bewildered, hurt and confused.

"His insecurities didn't end there. I remember making a comment one night while we were watching TV about a Hollywood actor and how much I wanted to see his new movie. It was an innocent remark and nothing was made of it at the time. That night, as we were making love, he pulled away right before he climaxed. He said he'd teach me to have fantasies about other men and that he'd finish it off himself. I remember rolling over and crying myself to sleep."

Mason's frown was fierce and she could see he was trying hard to understand. "Why did you let him get away with it, even the first time?"

She shook her head sadly. "You were the one who said how these kind of men seem to know instinctively how to manipulate. It's true. They almost brainwash you, breaking you down to control your thoughts, your actions, your every waking move.

"You get to the point where you believe their comments and when they degrade you, you think you deserve it. For so long, I made excuses for his behavior: He was tired; stressed at work; dealing with a fussy baby. Or it was my fault: The dinner was later than usual; I'd forgotten to put on makeup and tidy myself up before he got home.

"There was always a reason for his mistreatment and of course, he'd be so apologetic afterwards, especially in the early days. He'd make it up to me with flowers, expensive gifts and lavish promises— whatever it took to make me believe he'd do better if I just gave him another chance and didn't try his patience.

"Of course, his remorse never lasted long and soon the pattern would repeat itself, over and over again. He'd pick fights for any and no reason. In his mind, he was always right, and until I agreed with him, he'd lecture me for hours.

"Once I left a light on in the garage. In the early hours of the morning, he woke me and made me stumble downstairs in the dark to turn it off. I wasn't allowed to switch on another light. According to Nigel, I'd already wasted enough electricity. An angry lecture followed with the question:

'Why did you leave it on? Why?'

"For two hours he grilled me and I had to work that morning. It was always like that. A careless mistake took on the quality of a major crime followed by an inquisition."

She sighed. "In recent months, I haven't even been able to figure out what might or might not trigger him. I've been walking on eggshells, bending over backwards to please him and still it hasn't been enough."

"What about the kids? How have they coped through all of this?"

She closed her eyes. It was a long moment later that she found the strength to open them.

"I used to think they were oblivious," she said quietly. "I'd tell myself they were too young to have any inkling about the kind of life we led, but I was kidding myself. Not so much with Sophie, but Ben was a lot more aware than I knew. It breaks my heart that they're growing up in such an environment. It's one of the reasons I couldn't go on. And then with the knife and the pointed threats and the sleeping tablets..."

Mason nodded, his expression solemn. "You told me."

"Yes. What I didn't tell you was when I arrived home that night before I left, the tablets were missing. He'd moved them from the bathroom cabinet. Perhaps he was worried I'd find them and draw the very conclusion I did."

"You did the right thing by leaving, Belle. There could be no good reason for Diazepam in your house when neither you nor Nigel need it."

To have her suspicions confirmed by someone else was suddenly terrifying. The knowledge that Nigel was more than likely making plans to kill her... She couldn't even finish the thought. Her body began to tremble and despite her best intentions, she couldn't help but focus on what would have happened to her children if he'd carried through with it.

As if sensing how close she was to losing control, Mason moved closer to her on the couch. His thigh brushed hers and involuntarily, she tensed. But this time, with a conscious effort, she forced herself not to shy away.

This was Mason. Wonderful, kind, thoughtful, caring Mason. He was nothing like her husband. It wasn't fair to the man beside her to react as if he were the same.

"It's all right to be frightened, Belle. You've been through more than anyone ever should. I wish I'd knocked him out when I had the chance. What he did to you, and still does to you... It makes my blood boil. Selfish, narcissistic and downright brutal, he's a bully of the highest order. I'm only grateful you got out when you did."

"It was all about the fight for him," she continued quietly, somehow seeing things more and more clearly the longer she was away from Nigel and the way they'd lived their lives.

"It's as if the fighting fueled him. The outcome didn't matter because things were never resolved. Examples of what he called my "misdeeds" kept cropping up over and over again. But first and foremost, it was about the fight. He loved the fight. I see that now."

"I've read somewhere it's always that way with abusive men," Mason added in a tone that was just as soft. "The fight's like some kind of addictive drug. It gets them high, the ultimate adrenaline rush. The more drama the better."

"That's exactly how it was," she said. "It's strange how even a few days ago, I couldn't see that."

"You've been living with it every day for a very long time. I'm sure there were a lot of days you blocked out everything other than what you needed in order to survive, to get through another day. You had two young children to see to. They became your priority. It's a natural instinct to care for your children at your own expense. You're not the first mom who's reacted that way."

Fresh tears filled her eyes and slid slowly down her cheeks. "You're right," she cried. "There were many days when I'd be feeding or bathing or changing the kids and all I could focus on was the ticking of the clock. The steady, rhythmic ticking somehow soothed me. I knew that with every tick that went by, the day was closer to its end and I'd never have to live that day again."

Her voice cracked with emotion and she was overcome with an overwhelming sense of loss. She thought of all the days and years she'd spent living in a thick fog of apathy and fear. She'd done what she had to do to make it bearable, but it should never have gone on for so long, and she would never get those moments back, to live them the way they should have been.

"I should have left him years ago," she gasped in between the tears. "I should never have let him reduce me to such a weak and spineless mess. I let him do that to me! How will my children see me? Will they ever forgive me? How will I forgive myself?"

Without conscious thought, she threw herself against the man beside her and he enfolded her in his arms. She thought she was all cried out, but there seemed no end to her tears.

She took comfort in the warmth and solid

strength of him. As her hot tears soaked his shirt all the way through, he touched her hair with gentle strokes and murmured words of reassurance.

"*Shh*, Belle; don't talk like that. It wasn't your fault. One day your kids will be old enough to understand how strong and brave you were, how you did everything you could to protect them. You've taken the hardest step of all—you've walked out on him. He'll be mad as hell that you've bested him, but you've won, Belle. You've *won*."

She lifted her head and stared at him, blinking through her tears. "I don't feel triumphant and I'm filled with so much regret. But really? You really think so?"

He leaned forward and pressed a decisive kiss against her lips. "I know so."

As if only just becoming aware of what he'd done, Mason stilled. A moment later, his eyes darkened with an emotion so raw it snatched her breath away. His gaze intensified and she found it impossible to look away. Her heart beat hard against the walls of her chest.

Slowly, cautiously, his head came down again. This time, the kiss was as light as a feather. His lips glanced off hers and left her yearning for more. Intimacy with Nigel had become a contest of wills, just another way for him to exert his dominance. The pleasure had disappeared long ago and had left behind apprehension, fear and disgust.

But with Mason, it was different. She'd never felt safer than she did in his arms. Secure, protected, cherished...*loved*. She scarcely recognized the feelings he stirred deep inside her, but there was no denying she wanted more. She *needed* more.

A rush of desire surged through her that she didn't want to ignore. She knew enough about rebound sex to know this was probably it, but she was beyond caring.

Like a match igniting a pool of gasoline, with that thought in mind, she dragged his mouth back to hers. Frantically, she kissed him. She couldn't get enough. He tasted of mint and coffee and smelled like the hospital.

All that mattered was getting closer to him, as close as she could get. To lose herself and her problems in someone who was kind and decent and good. Oh, she wanted that so badly. She broke off the kiss with a gasp and began to tear at his clothes.

"Belle, sweetheart, slow down. Take it easy."

She frowned, suddenly uncertain of his feelings. "You don't want to?"

"Oh, honey, you don't know how badly I want to, but not until I know it's what you really want and need, too. You've been through so much lately, it's natural to want to reaffirm your existence with wild, uninhibited sex, but I've waited too long for this moment to rush into it without knowing you won't regret it later on."

Her breath still came fast, despite her attempts to slow it down. Mason's words echoed through her head and when she considered what he'd said she admired his restraint. It was classic Mason—putting someone else's welfare ahead of his own—and she couldn't help but appreciate him for it.

The truth was, she wanted to forget every minute of her past by consuming and becoming consumed by Mason, even for just a little while, but wanting to be close to him wasn't just about that.

It was about Mason and his goodness and his sexy, open smile. It was funny how she'd never really noticed that about him before. Certainly not back in high school.

She reached out and traced the soft fullness of his lips and was gratified when he sucked in a breath and tensed. He stared at her, as if uncertain of her intentions.

"I want to make love with you, Mason, and I promise, I won't regret it. Not now, not ever. How could I? You're so beautiful, inside and out. You make me feel worthy and I haven't felt like that in a long, long time."

His gaze flared with emotion and desire glinted in his eyes. He took her in his arms and kissed her long and deep. She kissed him back with just as much passion. Their tongues tangled and danced in their mouths.

It was everything it should have been and it left her wanting more. As if he could read her mind, Mason bent and put one of his arms beneath her knees. With the other arm around her shoulders, he stood and made his way down the hall.

In some distant part of her mind, she remembered her children. As they passed the spare room, she turned her head and was relieved to see that both of them were still sleeping. With her hands behind Mason's neck, she pulled down his head for another soul-searing kiss and was gratified by his eager response. A moment later, he lowered her onto his bed.

After closing the door behind them, he joined her and immediately drew her back into his arms. He pressed desperate kisses against her eyes, her nose; her lips. It was as if he couldn't get enough and she felt exactly the same way.

Reaching up, she worked on his tie and when it was loose, went to work on his shirt buttons. Within moments, he'd pulled both items off and had tossed them to the floor. His hands went around the back of her short cotton sundress and sensuously and slowly, he slid the zipper down.

He pulled the dress off her shoulders and then unclipped her bra. Pulling away, she took it off and shimmied the dress down her hips. Her clothing joined his on the floor.

She came back to him and pressed up close against him, gasping at the feel of their naked skin touching.

"You're so beautiful," he whispered, his gaze full of wonder.

Isobel kissed her way across his chest, taking time to discover his nipples. A light scattering of dark hair tickled her nose. Her fingers walked down his taut belly and came to a halt at the belt in his trousers.

Undeterred, she worked on the buckle and eventually the belt came loose. The button was next, followed by his zipper. Within moments, it was down. He lifted his hips to assist her and she tugged at his trousers until they were well below his knees.

179

He kicked them off the rest of the way and then cursed softly when they got caught on his boots. Impatiently, he sat up and dealt with those too. Isobel stifled a grin. When he lay down next to her, he wore only his underwear.

"Better?" she asked and couldn't help but smile.

"Not quite."

With that, he pulled off his boxers and threw them to the floor. His hands framed her hips and slid her panties down. He stared at her while he did it and she couldn't look away. The desire in his eyes was hypnotic. She'd never experienced anything quite so erotic.

He stretched out beside her, now naked from head to toe and pulled her into his arms. Once again, she gasped from the wonder of it. His erection strained thick and hard against her belly and need stirred deep in her core. She'd been told over and over she was frigid, and it had been so long since she'd felt desire, she barely recognized it.

He lifted himself up above her, his face still and taut with need. "I want you so much, Belle, but I'm sorry, I don't have a condom. I should have thought of it sooner, but this was the furthest thing from my mind. It's been so long and I've gotten carried away in the moment and—"

She pressed a fingertip against his lips to silence him. "It doesn't matter. I'm on the pill and we're both required to take regular blood tests to ensure we're free from disease. So..." A tiny grin lifted the corner of her lips. "I'm game if you are."

He growled deep in his throat and his lips found hers in another searing kiss. Her heart thumped and her breath came fast. Heat centered between her legs. She moved restlessly against him, wanting him closer still. Not needing any further encouragement, he found her opening and eased his cock all the way in.

The feel of him stretching her wide, filling her, was like nothing she'd ever experienced. She'd been married to Nigel for nearly a decade and even in their early years of marriage, sex had never felt so beautiful and intimate.

Mason watched her as he moved slowly and she clung to him. The tension in his face and shoulders told her all she needed to know. He was holding himself back until she found her release. His thoughtfulness brought tears to her eyes.

He noticed and she could tell he was going to withdraw so she lifted her hips and surged up against him, taking him by surprise. Picking up his pace, he matched her frantic rhythm. Higher and higher they climbed until the pinnacle was just within her reach. And then, with a triumphant cry, she toppled over the edge. Moments later, Mason followed her to bliss.

She gasped and relaxed into the mattress, relishing the feel of him pulsing inside her. With a final groan, he collapsed on top of her. She held him close and was flooded with tenderness for this oh-so-special man. Tears of regret pricked her eyes, but not for what they'd just done.

If only she'd made better choices all those years ago... As if sensing her melancholy, Mason shifted his weight onto his elbows and looked down at her.

"What is it?" he asked softly.

She shook her head, not willing to explain. "Nothing. It was wonderful. *You* were wonderful. Thank you."

A shadow passed over his face, but quickly disappeared. "There's no need to thank me, Belle. I wanted this and I enjoyed it as much as you."

She nodded and closed her eyes, but not before she caught the flash of disappointment in his eyes. Her heart ached for him, but she couldn't help it. She wasn't capable of anything else. She was damaged. He knew that. He'd best get used to it and accept her response to him for what it was.

CHAPTER 15

Dear Diary,

I can sometimes hear a voice in the distance. It is sweet and gentle and beautiful. I vaguely remember hearing this voice from a long, long time ago, but I cannot place it. I used to have a voice. I used to laugh and sing and feel beautiful...but that was another lifetime ago. Now, I feel hideous.

Why would a man want to touch a woman who is nothing more than a dark and empty shell? Yes, I am expressionless and blank, no more than a husk; unworthy and most of all, unlovable.

But the voice calls to me to remember. It lures me forward with its gentleness. The closer I get, the more I start to remember that I once did live and more than anything I want to live again. If only I can figure out how...

"**M**om? Where are you? Mom?"

Mason surged upright, coming instantly awake. The afternoon sun was warm on the pillow. He glanced at his watch. It was a little after three. He must have dozed off after making love to Belle.

The memory of their magical moment of intimacy was burned forever into his brain. It had been almost all that he'd hoped for. All that had been missing was the words. Whenever he'd fantasized about them coming together, it had always resulted in both of them declaring their undying love.

But one look at the tears rolling silently down Belle's cheeks and the words he so desperately wanted to say were sealed in his mouth. To make matters worse, she'd thanked him; like she was *grateful* for his attention.

He hadn't been looking for her gratitude. People were grateful when someone held open the door for them while they were laden down with shopping. They were grateful for a nice meal someone had taken the time to prepare. They weren't grateful for someone making love to them. It just wasn't right.

"Mom! Where are you?" The child's voice had gotten more strident and it was enough to wake Isobel at his side.

"Ben? What's the matter, honey?" she said, her voice still clouded with sleep. A minute later, as if becoming aware of where she was and who she was with, she snapped to attention and came upright with a gasp. Holding the sheet up to her chest, she looked at Mason, her eyes wide.

"Oh, my goodness! Ben's right outside the door! What was I thinking? Quick! Do something! Get dressed! Get out of here."

Mason chuckled, completely unperturbed. "It's my bedroom, remember? I'm allowed to be in here."

"Yes, but not with me and not with the two of us naked." She blushed to the roots of her hair and he couldn't help but think how adorable she looked. And panicked. Taking pity on her, he climbed out of bed, collected his clothes off the floor and disappeared into the adjoining bathroom.

He heard muffled voices coming from the other side of the bathroom door and assumed Ben had found his mother. He wished he was privy to their conversation. It would have been interesting to hear what explanation she gave her young son about how she'd found herself in Mason's bed.

Pulling on the last of his clothing, Mason cracked open the door. The room had fallen silent and he was relieved to discover Ben was no longer in the room. Isobel had thrown the bedcovers aside. She'd pulled on her underwear and was hastily throwing on her dress.

"Where's Ben?" he asked as he walked back into the room.

"He's in the kitchen. He woke and couldn't find me. He got a little panicky." A guilty expression appeared on her face.

"Don't feel bad. It's not your fault, Belle. What did you say to him?"

She averted her gaze. "I told him I was tired and I'd fallen asleep in the wrong bed."

"Did he wonder why you were naked?"

A wave of crimson traveled up from her neck and spread across her cheeks. "He didn't say anything. I kept the covers pulled right up. I don't think he noticed."

Mason ignored her embarrassment. Moving closer, he pressed a soft kiss to her mouth. "I'll go and rustle up something to eat. I skipped lunch and I'm starving." He turned toward the door.

"Mason, about what happened..."

Now it was his turn to panic. *Was she about to express her gratitude again, or worse, tell him they'd made a mistake?*

"It's all right, Belle. We don't need to talk about it. I understand what you've been through. Throwing yourself into another relationship's the last thing you want to do. And it probably isn't the wisest course of action, either," he forced himself to add.

The tension in her face eased and he clenched his jaw tight against the pain. She didn't deny it. And by that she wasn't reinforcing anything he didn't already know—but dammit, why did it have to hurt so much? He'd waited for her his entire life and still the timing wasn't right. He couldn't help but wonder if it ever would.

No, he refused to go there. He wouldn't let negative thoughts intrude. He loved her with everything that he was. He had to have faith that one day she might feel the same.

"I appreciate your understanding," she said quietly. "My life feels like it's been through a tumble dryer, tossing me from side to side. I'm not yet convinced I'll survive the ordeal or that when I emerge there'll be anything left of me to give. You deserve so much better than that, Mason. You deserve so much better than *me*."

Tenderness and love flooded through him and he couldn't help but reach for her and pull her into his arms. She offered no resistance and leaned her head against his chest.

"I'm sorry, Mason," she whispered. "I'm so sorry. I'm broken beyond repair. You need to get over me and find someone else who can love you like you deserve. I'm not that woman. I have nothing to offer you. I can't imagine ever trusting a man completely again."

He heard the emotion in her voice and could tell she was close to tears. He tightened his arms around her and leaned his chin on her head. Her hair was soft and clean and smelled of some kind of berry shampoo. She fit so well against him. He refused to believe the two of them weren't meant to be together.

"Let's just take one day at a time, okay? No pressure. I'll give you all the time you need. We'll find a reputable therapist. Someone who specializes in this kind of thing. I'm sure it will help. And if and when it's time, and you want me to, I'll come along too. And I'll also ask around for a good lawyer. The sooner you talk to someone about putting things in motion with regard to the kids and your marriage, the better."

She lifted her head and looked up at him, her expression telling him she remained unconvinced it would be that simple, but to his relief, she didn't argue. Instead, she thanked him once again.

"Would you please stop thanking me?" he said, doing his best to curb his irritation. "You asked me for help. I gave it willingly, like anyone would. I'm no one special. I'm just a guy who cares for you and who wants to see you safe and happy."

She shook her head slowly back and forth. "You're wrong, Mason Alexander."

He frowned. "About what?"

"You're more than special. You're kind and generous and caring and I'm—" Her voice caught on the emotion behind her words. She cleared her throat. "And I'm proud and so very lucky to be able to call you my friend."

Friends. That's all they were? Too bad he wanted her friendship even less than he wanted her gratitude, but he did his best to accept her offer gracefully. After all, she was still in his arms, wasn't she? As long as he could keep her close, there was hope.

As if reading his thoughts, she extricated herself and moved away from him. Reaching up, she ran her fingers through her hair in an effort to restore it to some form of order. "I need to go and check on the kids."

He nodded. The moment was gone. With a quiet sigh, he opened the door and headed toward the kitchen.

Isobel plastered a smile on her face and hurried into the open-concept kitchen and living room. Since arriving at Mason's apartment the day before, she hadn't really had time to explore or to appreciate the simple beauty of his home. Classic pieces of furniture filled the small but comfortable space.

She smoothed her hand over the square dining table with four chairs that stood off to one side, opposite the breakfast bar. On the other side of the room, a modular couch the color of pale butter was positioned opposite a flat screen TV that was mounted on the wall. A coffee table squatted in the middle of a large square of white carpet with an assortment of fishing and boating magazines spread across its polished wood surface.

She crossed the living room to the double sliding doors leading to the balcony. All of a sudden, looking at her reflection in the glass, she remembered the vitriolic message from Nigel and just like that, her fear returned.

Was he still furious with her? Would he hunt her down, like he promised? Of course he was and of course he would.

The Nigel she knew didn't give up easily and was immensely possessive of his things. And that's what she was to him. A possession. Something he claimed. Something he controlled. A shiver ran down her spine and she quickly turned away to find Mason watching her from the kitchen, a frown of concern on his face.

"What is it?" he asked quietly, in deference to Sophie and Ben who sat at the table nearby.

She shook her head, as much to dislodge the disquieting thoughts as to respond to him. "It's nothing. I'm fine." Forcing a smile, she turned to her children. "So, who's ready for an afternoon treat?"

"Me! Me!" they called in unison, with identical grins. She smiled back at them and sent a silent prayer of thanks heavenward that they didn't seem affected by recent events, despite the trauma they'd both been through.

She'd taken the time to explain to them earlier when they'd arrived back at Mason's about what was happening and why their dad was so upset. She tried to keep it light and simple, but the fact was, Ben had seen Nigel hit her and both children had witnessed the awful scene outside their house. Coupled with the presence of a police officer, it was obvious, especially to Ben, things had deteriorated to a level far more frightening than he'd ever guessed.

'Why was the policeman there?' Ben had asked, his expression troubled.

'I asked him to come,' she'd explained gently. 'I've left Daddy and we're not going back. Daddy's angry about it. He wants us to come home.'

'So why don't you?' Sophie had asked.

Isobel breathed out slowly and tried to find the right words. 'I don't want to fight with your dad anymore. He gets very angry and it frightens me...and it frightens you too, doesn't it?'

Both of them had nodded, their faces solemn. It nearly broke her heart. She'd hurried to reassure them. 'I wanted to stop feeling frightened. I wanted all of us to stop feeling that way. It's not right to be scared of Daddy like that. I love you both so much. I want to look after you and shield you from the bad things and sometimes Daddy does very bad things.'

'Why?' Sophie asked.

Isobel shook her head. *Why, indeed?* She gathered both children to her and hugged them close. 'I don't know, honey. He's sick. He needs help and I can't give it to him.'

'Why doesn't he go and see a doctor at the hospital?' Ben asked then.

'He is a doctor, silly,' Sophie replied.

'Daddy needs a different kind of doctor,' Isobel explained gently. 'A doctor who can help him feel happy about things again. Until he gets better, we can't be around him.'

'How long will it take?' Sophie asked.

'I don't know, honey. It might take quite awhile.'

Ben frowned. 'Will we stay here, at Mason's all that time?'

Isobel shook her head. 'I don't know that, either, sweetheart. Mason's been kind enough to let us stay for now. We'll probably look for somewhere else to live in a little while.'

'I don't mind staying here,' Ben said, 'except there's nowhere to ride my bike. But Mason's nice. I like him.'

Isobel hugged him again and smiled. 'Yes, Mason is nice. I like him, too.'

When she'd introduced Mason to her children the night before, he'd been so natural with them. Friendly and engaging without being over the top. Ben had plied him with all sorts of questions and was curious to know how he was her friend.

'I've never met any of Mom's friends,' he'd said and she'd realized that was true. Nigel had made sure her isolation was complete.

"I think I have double choc chip ice cream in the freezer, if your mom says it's okay."

Mason's words brought a halt to her sad memories. She blinked and forced herself back to the present. She smiled softly at the man who had helped her and her babies, more than he could imagine.

"I think that's a great idea. We could sit out on the balcony and take in what's left of the beautiful day."

"Yay!" Sophie cheered. Ben just grinned and grinned. Isobel stared at him and realized it had been a long time since she'd seen her little boy with such a big smile.

"Would you like to dish it out?" Mason's question was directed to Ben. Her son's eyes went round with disbelief.

"Really?"

Mason shrugged. "Why not? Unless your mom doesn't think you're big enough?" He turned to her with a smile on his lips, his eyes sparkling with mischief.

Something tugged at her heart. Her son deserved this kind of treatment... *Where had this good man come from?*

"Please, Mom! Please!" Ben begged her, pulling on her arm.

She laughed. "Of course I think you're big enough. Look at you! You're nearly six!"

"Yeah, I'm nearly six, Mason. Did you know that?"

"Yes, your mom told me awhile ago. I can see you're the right man for the job. Here, take the ice cream scoop and these bowls and head on out to the balcony. Your mom's right; the day outside is beautiful. I'll be right behind you with the ice cream."

Ben scrambled off his seat and took the things out of Mason's hands. With Sophie right on his heels, the young boy headed toward the door.

Thank you, Isobel mouthed to the man who remained behind in the kitchen. He merely offered her a smile so sweet and tender, the warmth of it ran like melted chocolate through her veins. All of a sudden, she wanted desperately to be whole. To be normal and carefree and joyful; to take pleasure in everyday things; to forget about the ticking clock and the thoughts of what tomorrow might bring; to be free from ever-present fear and dread of what was to come; to laugh and love and sing.

She used to adore singing. Back in high school, she'd been part of the school choir. They'd performed in more than one eisteddfod and often came home with the prize. Those days seemed so long ago. She couldn't remember the last time she'd sung. And then it hit her.

It had been in the middle of winter. Nigel had

been complaining and out of sorts all evening. He'd picked a fight with her over the smallest thing and wasn't happy even when she conceded defeat early. In an effort to get her mind off the growing tension, she'd taken Ben in for a bath. She'd been six months pregnant with Sophie.

Ben had been splashing around in the water and some of it had splashed on her where she kneeled on the floor by the bath. Bubbles were everywhere. She'd laughed and dropped more bubbles on his face and he'd squealed in delight. It was then that she'd remembered a song her mother used to sing.

She didn't even hear Nigel come into the room. The first thing she knew was when he lashed out at her with his boot. He connected hard with her thigh and she'd cried out in shock and pain. An instant later, she lost her balance and toppled over onto the floor.

'Enough with that caterwauling,' he'd snarled, glaring at her where she lay on the cold tiles. 'Don't ever let me catch you singing again.' And with that, he'd left, slamming the door behind him. She could still hear the sound of it cracking against the hinges.

Of course, he'd later apologized and explained his mother had run off with a singer who performed in a local bar. It was the reason he'd reacted so badly. Isobel was quick to assure him it wouldn't happen again and that she understood his pain, but that night, like so many other nights, she'd cried herself to sleep feeling empty and alone...and joyless.

Now her chest felt tight and her heart beat fast. With an effort, once again she cleared her head of the unhappy memories. As if sensing her fragile mood, Mason encircled her shoulders with his arm and gently pulled her in close. With a sigh of relief, she leaned into him and breathed in his manly scent.

She didn't know how he knew the very moment when she needed him, but somehow he did. Now wasn't the time to question it. Now was the time to *be*. To enjoy the moment, to take the solace that was offered so freely and focus on the good things in her life.

And there were good things. The most important of them were right out on the balcony, having a bucket load of fun with an ice cream scoop and a tub of double chocolate chip.

CHAPTER 16

Mason reached for the jar of spaghetti sauce and went to undo the lid. It had been three days since Isobel and her children moved in and Christmas was inching nearer. It had always been a time of family and celebration in his house and he couldn't help but hope Belle and the kids would be with him for the holidays. He'd come home from work a little early so that he could prepare dinner for them all. It was a homey thing to do and one that he could get used to.

Careful, he warned himself. He was moving way too fast and taking some important, and undecided things, for granted. He was consumed with the thought of the four of them coming together as one happy family. He knew that despite that dream, he needed to slow things down, to give Belle time to catch up. She'd just come out of an abusive relationship. She needed time to heal.

And he was prepared to give her that time, just like he'd promised, but it was hard. All he wanted to do was love her, protect her, cherish her and keep her safe and all she seemed to want was to push him away.

He had to find the strength to accept her instinctive need to keep him at a distance and give her the time she required. He was determined to wait for as long as it took. He wasn't going anywhere. He'd decided the instant he'd offered his help that he was in it for the long haul.

"What are you doing?"

Mason turned around and spied Ben on the other side of the counter. His hair was still askew, like he'd just woken up.

"Hey, buddy, how was your nap?"

Ben shrugged. "It was okay. I keep telling Mom I'm a big boy, now. I don't need to have a nap, but she tells me to just lie down and rest; that I don't need to fall asleep."

Mason smiled. "I bet you did, though. I wish I could have an afternoon nap."

Ben laughed. "You're a grown-up. Grown-ups don't need naps."

"Some of us could use one every now and then, believe me." Mason winked and turned back toward the stove.

"What are you cooking?"

"Meatballs and spaghetti. Do you like meatballs and spaghetti?"

Ben grinned. "Yes! It's my favorite! Sophie's, too! How did you know?"

Mason winked. "A clever guess. When I was a kid, meatballs and spaghetti was my favorite meal, too."

Sophie appeared from around the corner, rubbing her eyes and yawning. "Where's Mom?"

"I think she's in the bathroom," Mason replied.

Sophie nodded and then pushed one of the dining room chairs closer to Ben. Using her chubby little arms, she pulled herself up on it and stood next to her brother. He leaned his elbows on the counter and watched while Mason worked.

"Do you know my dad?" Sophie asked.

"Yes, honey, I do. We work at the same hospital."

"Are you a doctor, too?" asked Ben.

"Yes, but I'm a different kind of doctor. Your dad takes care of people with broken bones. I look after kids, like you."

"So if I got sick and went to hospital, you could make me all better?" Sophie asked, her eyes wide.

Mason moved closer to the kitchen counter and leaned over it, bringing his face closer to the little girl's. "Yes, I guess so. Though I hope you don't get sick enough that you have to go to hospital. It's way more fun at home." He winked at her and then turned back toward the stove. Out of the corner of his eye, he caught sight of Isobel leaning against the wall, her expression full of sadness and yearning.

"Hey, there you are," he greeted her softly. "How are you doing?"

"I'm okay. Thanks for keeping the kids entertained." Sophie spotted her mom and climbed down off the chair.

"Mommy! Mommy!" The little girl ran over to

Isobel, lifting up her arms as she went. Isobel bent over and picked her up and buried her nose in her daughter's hair.

"You smell so good, Soph. Did you have a nice nap?"

"Yes, but now I'm really hungry. Mason's cooking meatballs."

"I can see that. It smells good, too."

She turned and smiled at him and his heart melted, sending his recent caution against moving too fast straight out of his head. Aware that he was staring, he turned abruptly back to the stove and got busy.

"Is there anything I can do?" she murmured.

He turned to find her way too close. His heart pounded and his mouth went dry. With an effort, he dragged his gaze away. By implicit agreement, they hadn't been intimate again and being so close to her and not being allowed to touch was an agony all in itself. It had only been a couple days since he'd made love to her, but it felt like a lifetime.

"How about you set the table?" he finally said. "We might eat inside tonight."

She nodded and moved away. Mason breathed out a surreptitious sigh of relief.

"Can I help you, Mom?" Ben asked.

"Can I?" asked Sophie.

Isobel smiled. "Of course." She bent down on one knee and gathered both of them close for a quick hug.

Mason watched them from the kitchen and was once again filled with longing. He yearned to be part of their family. That day couldn't come fast enough.

The warm summer breeze drifted across the water and lifted Isobel's unrestrained hair. She'd washed it earlier and left it loose to dry. After a relaxed evening around the table, the kids were fed, bathed and tucked into bed. Mason had entertained them with stories of his high school days and how he'd met their mom. She'd never realized the impact she'd had on him all those years ago outside his locker. She couldn't help but wonder if she'd realized it earlier, whether she'd have made better choices.

No, it wasn't likely. By the time graduation came around and Mason offered his declaration of love, she was already well and truly under the spell of the charismatic Nigel Donnelly. Mason hadn't had a chance. She was filled with sadness and regret for all that might have been. If only...

"I spoke to a lawyer today," Mason said quietly from his seat on the other deck chair. "One of the doctors at work has a buddy who specializes in family law. He gave me his number and I called him. I wanted to check him out for myself. I told him a little about your circumstances. He seemed more than up for the challenge."

Isobel listened to Mason's quiet tones and was filled with a sense of relief. She'd known she had to do something about her situation. It was important for both her and her kids that they got formal orders from the court. There was no way she was letting Nigel have custody. She wanted to get ahead of him and get a court decision in her favor before he thought to do it. She was grateful Mason had taken the first steps to that end by finding her a lawyer.

"Thank you. I really appreciate your help. With all that's gone on these past few days, finding a lawyer has been beyond me. It was hard enough to go to the police and get the AVO."

"I know, Belle, but aren't you glad you did? Imagine what might have happened if you hadn't? At least it means Nigel has to stay away from you, even while you're at work. Have you told people on your floor about it yet?"

She shook her head. "No, but I'll call in the morning. I'm rostered back on the day after tomorrow."

"Are you sure you're ready? Perhaps you need more time. If it's about the money, I—"

"It's not about the money," she interrupted. "Well, not really. Of course I need money, but it's more about my job. I love working at the hospital. It's the only place where I feel worthwhile, like I'm making a contribution. I'm not going to let Nigel steal that away from me, like he's stolen so many other things."

She drew in a breath and continued a little more calmly. "I'm going to request my shifts be changed to mornings so that I can collect the kids before closing time at their center." She grimaced. "On the evenings I worked, Nigel collected them on his way home from the hospital. Obviously that's not going to keep happening."

"I could, though. I could pick them up."

Isobel shook her head at his offer. "You've already done so much for us, Mason. I couldn't ask you to stop by a daycare center that is out of your way to collect my kids."

Mason held her gaze. "You didn't ask. I offered."

She stared back at him. His offer was tempting because it would be so much more convenient than requesting a permanent change in her shifts, but she meant it when she said he'd done enough. He was a friend, a good friend, but she needed to start standing on her own two feet. She needed to take responsibility for her new circumstances and her children and make plans for a life that didn't include their father.

"I really appreciate it, Mason, I do, but—" She held up her hand when he went to interrupt. "I need to take control of my life, starting with Sophie and Ben. It's only a small step, but it *is* a step and each and every one of them count toward helping me find my confidence." She pleaded with him silently, hoping he'd understand.

In the light that spilled out from the dining room, she noticed his frown, but eventually he nodded and then turned away to stare out across the harbor. After a while, he spoke again.

"I'm not sure what your plans are, but you're welcome to stay here for as long as you like. All of you. I... I like having you around."

She looked at him and couldn't help but wonder about his life with Sue Ann. Before she could stop herself, she opened her mouth and asked the question. "How long were you married?"

His frown deepened. He sat back in his chair, his expression wary. "Two years."

"How come you didn't have children? You work with kids every day and you're so good with them. You're good with mine, too. Didn't you want any children of your own?"

He squeezed his eyes shut as if in an effort to ward off painful memories. His shoulders slumped. "Having kids and a family of my own was one of the main reasons I got married, but as it turned out, Sue Ann was infertile. We tried for twelve months before we got tested."

He shrugged. "We were in our twenties. It didn't occur to us that one or both of us might have had problems. When we discovered Sue Ann couldn't have children, we were devastated. She wanted to try IVF. I wasn't keen. By then, our relationship had begun to deteriorate and I wasn't sure how much longer I'd be around. I look back now and can't help but think it was a blessing we didn't have kids."

He sighed and leaned over his thighs, with his elbows on his knees. His chin rested in his hands. "I'm not proud of the fact I gave up on my marriage. I could have fought harder to save it. But the truth is, I didn't want to. I married Sue Ann in the hope of forgetting a girl I'd been in love with since high school. A girl I was certain I could never have."

He lifted his head and stared at her. "It wasn't fair to Sue Ann and I lived to regret my decision to marry her, but that's how it was. How it still is."

Her heart pounded double time, but it had nothing to do with fear. The need in his eyes was obvious. She remembered the way it had felt to be in his arms, safe and secure against the warm strength of his chest. Though it still unsettled her—being held close—with Mason it almost felt right.

He pushed back his chair and came toward her and all of a sudden, panic flooded her veins. It was one thing to make love with him when she'd been overwrought with emotion and had sought oblivion in his arms. It was another to encourage him when she was calm and collected—when she had no idea if she could ever offer him a future.

Hastily, she stood and headed toward the sliding door. Mason stopped. She saw the hurt and confusion in his eyes.

"Belle..."

"I'm sorry, Mason. I think I might go inside. I... I'm tired and I need to check on the kids. Thank you for dinner. I'll...see you in the morning."

She made a hasty retreat, hating herself for her cowardice, but right there and then she was beyond giving him anything more.

———

Nigel strode out of the elevator and headed for the Human Resources Department. It had been three days since his wife had left and he'd well

205

and truly had enough. He'd taken time off from the hospital and that had been a good decision. He'd spent the first couple of days in a haze of anger fueled by alcohol. The house had taken the brunt of his rage. There wasn't a single room that hadn't sustained substantial damage. He didn't care. What was a house when he'd lost his wife, his most prized possession? Even his Porsche didn't stack up.

But slowly, he'd come to his senses and his brain had kicked back into gear, pulling him out of the haze of his anger. He'd sobered up and as the alcohol left his bloodstream, a different icy cold rage took its place. With a clearer head, his thoughts had sharpened and all of a sudden, he knew what he could do. It was so simple, he couldn't believe he hadn't thought of it sooner. He just hoped the bitch hadn't gotten there before him.

He found the door with the Human Resources nameplate on it. He knocked once and entered. A young girl of about twenty sat behind a counter. She greeted him with a friendly smile.

"Good morning, you're here bright and early. I only just sat down. What can I do for you?"

Nigel dug deep and found the charm he was renowned for. "Hello, I'm Doctor Donnelly. I was hoping you could help me."

If she recognized his name, she didn't show it. He wasn't particularly surprised. The hospital employed more than a thousand staff. She couldn't know all of them. With a bit of luck, it also meant Isobel hadn't yet contacted them.

"What is it that you need, Doctor?"

Nigel glanced at the name tag on the collar of her dress and smiled sweetly. "You see, Sally, the other day I ran into an old friend from high school. He's just started here at the hospital. I didn't have long to chat, but I promised I'd call him and get together when we both had more time. He gave me his number, but I lost it."

"Oh, that's too bad," Sally replied, looking genuinely disappointed.

"I'd really appreciate it if you could give me his address."

She frowned. "I thought you were after his phone number?"

"Yes, well, I remembered tomorrow's his birthday. I want to go by his place and surprise him." He leaned toward her and lowered his voice to a conspiratorial whisper. "You see, he lost both of his parents to cancer when he was only a small child. He didn't have any birthday celebrations after that. I think he was eight when it happened. Very sad."

"Oh, no! How awful! That poor boy!"

"Yes, now you can see why it's so important to me. I've even ordered a cake." He smiled again and gave her a wink.

She bit her lip. "I'm not supposed to give out private information, even to other staff."

"But he and I are old friends. Besides, who's going to know? I'm not going to tell anyone. Are you?"

She still looked unconvinced. "Maybe I could just give you his cell number. After all, he's already given you that." Her expression turned hopeful.

He forced back his impatience and threw her another smile. "That would be great, Sally and I'd really appreciate it, but see, apart from the cake, I've also bought him a birthday gift. It's a top of the range mountain bike. We used to love riding together when we were boys. I want to leave it in his driveway. Can you imagine his surprise when he comes out in the morning and finds it?"

Sally's eyes went wide with astonishment and a wide grin creased her lips. "Wow, I wish someone would buy me a cool gift like that! You must be really good friends."

Nigel smiled and nodded, knowing the information he sought was now as good as his. "Oh, but we are. The best."

Chapter 17

Dear Diary,

People say you remember your first kiss, your first crush, the first time you make love. While I have had all those firsts, I add another to that list of memories. I can also remember the first time he hit me and that experience will be forever imprinted in my mind.

It doesn't matter that more beatings came afterwards, it's the first one that leaves the lasting impression because with that single act of violence the seeds of fear are sown and with each hit afterwards, that fear grows until it spreads and spreads and spreads...

The fear took hold of me, choking the very life out of me, squeezing me like a vice until I uttered that final gasp of breath...

I still have nightmares about that night. I re-live his fury in microscopic detail each and every time. And those nightmares remind me that I have walked through the valley of the shadow of death... And yet, I still live.

I pray to God that he will restore my soul and some day bring me to greener pastures because, despite everything, I have to believe that You are watching and somehow protecting me...

Isobel listened to the sounds of her children playing in the other room and smiled. She loved how comfortable they were in Mason's home. She'd been worried that they'd miss their large backyard and their regular visits to the park, but so far the confines of Mason's apartment hadn't concerned them.

Picking up her phone, she made the second call of the morning to the director of Benn and Sophie's daycare center. Ten minutes later, she ended the call and let out a sigh of relief. The woman had been more than understanding when Isobel explained the change in their circumstances and as difficult as it had been to speak about, it had lifted a weight off Isobel's mind.

It was unfortunate she couldn't remove the children altogether and place them somewhere else, somewhere Nigel didn't know about, but openings in daycare centers in and around the city were hard to come by. Besides, her children were comfortable there.

It was a familiar environment where both of them had plenty of friends. So much of their world had been turned upside down. For their sakes, it was important that she retain a little stability. She'd make sure the center had a copy of the AVO so that if Nigel happened by, they'd know what to do. She hoped it wouldn't come to that, but it was best to be prepared. The only other call she had to make was to HR.

Earlier, she'd spoken to her boss. Georgie had urged her to notify Human Resources of the AVO. Isobel had been relieved Georgie had been sympathetic to her situation and was willing to switch her two evenings and one night shift over to mornings. From now on, she'd only be rostered on the day shifts, a time when Mason would often be in the hospital, too. The thought brought her comfort.

Doing morning shifts meant that she'd have to drop Ben and Sophie off at the center before seven, which wasn't ideal, but for the moment, it was all she could manage. She certainly didn't expect Mason to care for them before he left for work. Besides, there would occasionally be times when he was on night shift and he wouldn't arrive home before it was time for her to leave—and of course, staying with him was only short term.

Despite his generous offer to stay as long as they liked, his apartment was set up as a plush bachelor pad, filled with expensive furniture and carpet as white as fresh laid snow. She shuddered. White carpet! She only hoped the kids didn't spill anything on it. She was pretty sure Mason wouldn't mind. So far, he seemed casual and laid-back in the extreme. But, even so...

She couldn't help but think of Nigel and how he'd react to stains on the carpet or dirt on the floor. Once, he'd forced her to mop the same strip of linoleum until her fingers were chafed and raw. It was never good enough, never clean enough and he insisted she had to do it better. That went on for hours.

At the thought of her husband, she was once again flooded with fear. He'd been livid outside their house. *If not for the police officer...*

Despite the AVO restricting Nigel's access to her and their kids, she still didn't believe he'd get over her departure and simply move on. It wasn't in his makeup. She needed to be on her guard for when he tried a second time to convince her she'd made a mistake. And she had no doubt there would be a second time.

She wandered out onto the balcony, hoping the beautiful summer morning unfolding outside her window would lift her spirits. Warm sunlight danced on the water below, turning the harbor into a sparkly wet playground. Soon it would be Christmas. For the first time in years, she looked forward to it.

Her spirits rose at the thought that she wouldn't be spending another holiday with her husband. For years, Christmas with Nigel had been anything but joyous. The criticism, ridicule and constant demands that she do better seemed to increase exponentially as the holiday season approached. The kids were showered with presents from him, but there was never anything under the tree for her.

Not that the holiday was all about gifts, but the fact he didn't believe she was worth celebrating or spending money on hurt. When she'd gotten the courage to approach him about it one year, he'd confessed, after a particularly vicious fight, that his mother had left on Christmas Eve, as if that explained everything. It didn't.

Her gaze drifted to her left to where the street came to an end at the pier. The sound of the water lapping the shoreline far below was soothing. She turned to take a seat in the deck chair and a flash of red caught her eye. A shiny red car was parked on the opposite side of the road, directly across from Mason's balcony.

She froze. It was Nigel. Even six floors up, she recognized him. He sat in his distinctive cherry-red Porsche Boxster Cabriolet. He had the hood down and she could see the top of his head. As if sensing her scrutiny, he looked up and his gaze locked on hers, pinning her to the spot. With her heart in her throat, she ducked back inside, but not before she'd caught a glimpse of his mocking smile.

He'd found her. Oh, God, he'd found her. The words kept echoing in her head. In panic, she rushed around the apartment and locked all the windows and doors, including the door that led onto the balcony. The apartment might have a security system and be six floors up, but she wasn't taking any chances.

She ran down the hallway, her breath coming fast. The kids were playing quietly in their room. They stared at her curiously and she forced a smile and pretended that everything was okay. It was incredibly hard to do.

"What's the matter, Mom? You look kind of funny."

"N-nothing, Ben. I'm... I'm fine. I just wanted to check that you were okay. Is everything all right? Would you like something to eat?"

"No, we're okay. Soph and I are doing a puzzle."

"All right, kids. Well, you have fun." She turned and walked back down the hallway toward the kitchen and immediately picked up her cell phone. She dialed Mason's number and prayed silently that he'd pick up.

"Belle, how nice to hear from you."

She could hear the smile in his voice. Any other time, it would have made her smile in response, but she was too frightened to do anything other than blurt out the reason for her call. "Nigel's parked outside your building."

"Are you sure it's him?"

"Yes, I'm sure. He looked up, right at me. I was out on the balcony."

"I'll come home. I can be there in an hour. In the meantime, call the police. He's not supposed come within fifty feet of you."

"Technically, he hasn't done anything wrong. He was at least that far away. And I'm probably overreacting. Just because he saw me on the balcony doesn't mean he knows what apartment I'm in." She drew in a deep breath and puffed it out, trying hard to stem her panic. "Stay at work. You're busy. I'll be fine."

"You saw him outside my building, Belle. I don't care if he's within his rights, I'm going to make sure he's moved on. I'll see you soon."

"O-okay," she whispered, secretly relieved. The thought of Nigel waiting for her downstairs—

"Is he still there?"

She forced herself closer to the balcony door and found the courage to release the lock. She stepped out only as far as she needed to in order to get a view of the street below. It was clear. She blew out a sigh of relief. "No, he's gone."

"Good, but I'm still coming home. I need to make sure for myself. Where are the kids?"

She heard the concern in his voice and it warmed her through. "They're playing in their bedroom. They don't know Nigel was outside. I didn't see any point in telling them."

"You did the right thing. He shouldn't be there, anyway. He knows the terms of the AVO. He's thumbing his nose at us."

"He's not going to give up easily, Mason. It's just not in his nature to concede defeat."

"Yeah, well, we'll see about how tough he is when we report him to the police. I don't care that technically he hasn't done anything wrong. He's also not supposed to intimidate you and he's sure as hell managed to do that. I wish I could get five minutes alone with him and teach him to pick on someone his own size. I bet he wouldn't be so brave, then."

Isobel listened to Mason's words in quiet awe. She couldn't remember anyone ever supporting her like that. Even when she was a child, she'd never had a person champion her cause. She was older than her sister by five years and it had always been Kat who needed protecting. As the older sister, Isobel had only been too willing to take on that responsibility.

She'd assumed when she'd married Nigel that she'd be able to turn to him for protection if and when she needed it. She never imagined it would be him she needed to be protected from.

"Thank you for understanding, Mason, and for all your support. It means the world to me."

There was silence on the other end of the phone. A moment later, his voice thick with emotion, he said, "I'm glad to hear it." He cleared his throat and then added, "Keep the doors locked. I'll see you soon."

She shuddered. "Don't worry, I'm not going anywhere."

"Turn the TV on. Find a movie. It will take your mind off things. I'll get there as quickly as I can."

Isobel ended the call with a small sigh and then forced herself out of her funk. Mason was right. A good movie was just what she needed to distract her and make her forget her fear. The doors were locked, the windows were shut. Like she'd told Mason, she was fine. She was safe. Everything was going to be okay.

She was halfway across the living room, intent on switching on the TV, when the doorbell rang. Her nerves immediately flew into overdrive. She dashed back for her phone and had already started to dial Mason's number when she came to her senses and put it away.

It was just a knock on the door, for Pete's sake. Something as commonplace as blowing her nose. If she hadn't spied Nigel outside the building ten minutes earlier, she'd have thought nothing of it. Did she really want to let him turn her into a blithering mess of fear and indecision? *Hadn't she lived enough years like that?*

The knock came again, more impatient this time and she suddenly made up her mind. She walked over to the door and looked through the security hole. All she could see was the back of a man's head. It was covered in a faded blue ball cap.

"Who is it?" she called in a voice that was still a little shaky.

"Mail courier. I have a delivery for Doctor Mason Alexander. Is he home?"

The man's voice was a little muffled. Probably because of the thickness of the door. She decided to play it safe. "No, I'm sorry, you'll have to come back later."

"The parcel's been sent as high priority. Are you sure you can't just sign for it? It won't take long."

Undecided on the best course of action, she bit her lip. She pulled out her phone and tried Mason again, intending to ask him if he was expecting a parcel. The phone rang out and eventually went to voicemail. She ended the call without leaving a message.

"Hurry up, lady. I don't have all day!"

She peeked through the security hole again and saw no more of the man than before. It was time she stopped jumping at every shadow, thinking Nigel was behind every door. His car was gone. He'd done what he'd come for—to frighten her out of her wits and to remind her he could find her no matter how far she ran. With a bit of luck, he was already miles away.

"Are you gonna open the door, lady? I've got a lot more deliveries to make."

The man's whine propelled her into action and all at once she made up her mind. Reaching up, she undid the locks and unclasped the security chain. She started to open the door.

Nigel burst in, knocking her out of the way. She screamed and spun on her heel, intent on getting away. She took a step, and a second before he grabbed her hair and dragged her back again.

"You stupid bitch! Who the fuck do you think you are? You should know better than to try and run. No one runs from Nigel Donnelly."

With terror flooding her veins, she tried to find the breath to respond. "Get out of here, Nigel, before I scream the roof down. This is an apartment building. The walls are thin. Someone will hear and come running."

He spun her around to face him and he stared at her with eyes filled with hate. She shuddered and went icy cold. Everything inside her froze.

"This is all your fault, Isobel. You've fucking driven me to this. You've got no one to blame but yourself." He sucked in a harsh breath and appeared to make an effort to get himself back under control.

"You need to come home, Isobel. You're my wife. I want you to come home. Now, go and get the kids and your things and let's go."

Isobel heard his words and felt their impact all the way to her bones. Yet again, he was ordering her about, telling her what he wanted, telling her what to do. She'd put up with it for nine long years. The time she'd spent with Mason had shown her how much easier it was meant to be.

Mason. Where was he?

The thought of his constant reassurances, his caring and concern gave her a strength she never realized she possessed until that moment. Knowing he was right now on his way over to protect her and keep her safe filled her with courage. With a narrowed gaze, she took a step backward and stared Nigel straight in the eye.

"Go to hell."

Nigel's bellow of rage echoed all the way through the apartment. He raised his fist and brought it crashing down. With a scream, she ducked out of the way and managed to avoid it. He came at her and she screamed again, unmindful of her children, knowing that having someone nearby to hear her could be a matter of life and death. Hers.

"Help! Please! Somebody help me!"

She could hear her kids screaming. A moment later, they ran toward her from the direction of the bedrooms and she nearly keeled over at the shock and terror on their faces.

"Mommy! Mommy! Mommy!"

With no other choice, she turned her back on them and ran toward the open front door and continued to scream at the top of her lungs again. "Help! Somebody help me!"

A door across the hall opened and then another a few doors down. Two male neighbors appeared, looking concerned.

"What's going on?" one of them said.

"Are you all right? Do you want me to call the police?" asked the other.

Nigel was right behind her, but as the neighbors appeared, he came to a sudden halt. He lowered his fists, but his hands remained clenched. His breath came harsh and fast.

"Are you all right, lady?" the man who lived opposite Mason asked.

"Please, just keep him away from me. Please," she begged and indicated Nigel. The stranger stood taller and shouldered his way in between them. She almost collapsed when she realized she was finally safe.

"What's going on?" the other neighbor asked, again to no one in particular.

"Mind your own business," Nigel growled. "This has nothing to do with you. She's my wife. We're having a little argument. It's nothing to worry about."

The man who'd placed himself between her and Nigel frowned down at her. "Is that right? Are you two married?"

Isobel nodded, still trembling with shock. "Yes, he's my husband, but four days ago I left with my children and took out an AVO. He-he hasn't taken it well and now he knows where we're living..."

The man grimaced. "What are the terms of the AVO? I assume he's meant to stay well away from you."

She nodded. "Yes."

"I'll call the police," the other neighbor said, tugging out his cell phone.

"There's no need to call the police," Nigel said

abruptly. "I'm leaving." He pushed his way past her rescuer and eyeballed her before he stepped onto the open elevator. "This isn't over, Isobel. Not by a long shot."

The malice in his eyes sent a shiver down her spine. Her limbs suddenly refused to hold her upright. She gasped and stumbled and fell against the kindly neighbor.

"Lady, are you sure you're okay? Perhaps I should call an ambulance?"

Isobel heard him as if from far away, but managed to shake her head. "No, please. I'll be fine. I don't need an ambulance. Can you... Can you just stay with us for a while and if I need a witness to what happened today, will you help me?"

"Of course," the man responded and helped her back inside. The other neighbor nodded as well and followed, still looking unconvinced that she was fine.

"I think we should call the police. You need to report that guy. He's crazy."

Isobel managed a nod. "You're right, he is. And I'll definitely report this to the police. I spoke to an officer earlier in the week, when I approached them about getting the AVO. He knows all about my husband and I'll make sure he knows about this. My friend can take me there later."

The neighbor who'd helped her inside nodded in agreement. "I think that's a very wise idea. The man's unhinged. There's no telling what he might do now that he knows where you are."

Ben and Sophie ran toward her and threw

themselves in her arms. "Mommy, Mommy! Are you all right? Why was Daddy here?" Sophie asked.

"Did he hurt you again?" asked Ben, his face pale, his eyes still wide with fear.

The two men made eye contact, squared their shoulders and once again looked ready to protect Isobel and her children from any threat.

Even so, Isobel's heart broke in two. It was happening all over again. How many times would she allow her husband to put their children through so much trauma? She steeled her spine and determined there and then that it would never happen again.

Bending down, she put her arms around her babies and hugged them close. "I'm fine, darlings. I'm fine. Daddy's gone. He's not going to hurt anyone again. We're going to be all right, I promise you."

She refused to believe otherwise.

CHAPTER 18

Dear Diary,

I once heard a work colleague say the most dangerous time for an abused woman is when they find the courage to leave. It is then that they are at their most vulnerable. It didn't mean anything to me at the time. I was living a hellish existence, but my sense of self was so depleted, I didn't recognize myself as being that kind of woman. Besides, back then, I couldn't imagine ever being free.

But now I am—I'm free. I wish I could tell you I feel better, lighter, freer, but he'll never let me go. I know this with as much certainty as I know the color of my hair.

It's bright red, by the way. Hot and fiery and passionate. A woman who could never be subdued. That's what people think. If only they knew...

I'm none of these things. I'm a woman who isn't strong and assertive. I measure my worth through sheer hard work and the results of my labors. When those are flawed, then I am, too.

My husband knows this about me, knows my weakness and he does all he can to exploit it. The beds are never made well enough, the dinner is too cold; the dishes aren't clean enough, the children are out of control...

There's always something to criticize and it has eroded my confidence and any feelings I once had of self-worth. And now I am free... It's funny, I don't feel free. I feel like a woman who's running for her life with no clear destination in mind. Any moment, he'll catch up to me and I'll be back where I started.

Once again, I'll be consumed by the darkness and this time, I won't be strong enough to resist. I'll let it swallow me whole...

"How could you have answered the door? You let him in! He could have killed all of you!" shouted Mason, his temper getting the better of him.

"Please don't yell at me."

Isobel's quiet request and the sight of her frightened face penetrated the anger, frustration and helplessness that had assaulted him the moment he'd arrived home and learned about Nigel's attack. He sucked a deep breath into his lungs and willed himself to calm down. Yelling at the victim wasn't fair and doing it to someone who'd gone through as much trauma as she had... *What the hell was he thinking?*

"I'm sorry, Belle. I didn't mean to yell." He closed the distance between them and pulled her into his arms. She tensed and resisted his attempts to offer comfort and he immediately released her.

She looked at him, her eyes shadowed with hurt. "I told you. I'm fine. Two of your neighbors very kindly helped me out. They made him leave." She shuddered.

"Did anyone call the police?"

"No, I told them not to. He was gone by then and...I wanted to wait for you to get home so we could go to the police station together."

He gritted his teeth in frustration and tried hard to hold on to his patience. "Belle, if the police had been called right away, they might have even found him in the vicinity. They could have arrested him on the spot for breaching the AVO." He pulled his phone out of his pocket and started dialing.

She crossed her arms defensively over her chest and a mutinous expression filled her eyes. "You can't keep saving me, Mason. I need to stand up and fight this battle on my own. I appreciate everything you've done for me and my children, but I have to prove to myself that I can do this."

Mason clenched his jaw so tightly he was sure the bones would break. She just didn't get it. He ended the call and blew out his breath on a heavy sigh. "Belle, you don't have to prove anything and you sure as hell don't need to do this on your own. Nobody deals with the kind of crap you've been through on their own. And why would you want to? It doesn't have to be so difficult! I want to help you! I want to be there for you! I... I *love* you!"

He threw his arms out wide as he said it and all the exasperation and pent-up anger and fear over what had happened to her boiled over into those words. He stared at her, his chest heaving.

Isobel looked stricken. She buried her face in her hands and her shoulders shook with the force of her sobs. Overwhelming hurt and disappointment held him frozen to the spot. He'd just declared his love for her—a second time—and she was sobbing like he'd broken her heart.

She lifted her head and already her eyes were red and swollen with tears. The sight tore at his gut. He wanted to go to her and reassure her, promise her everything would be all right, but he couldn't move.

"I-I don't deserve your love, Mason," she hiccupped through her sobs. "You're wasting it on me. I'm unworthy, broken beyond repair. Can't you see?"

He shook his head slowly. "No, Belle, I can't. What I see is a beautiful, courageous woman who's been brave enough to leave a violent and hellish life—for herself and for her children. Somewhere deep inside you, you know you deserve better and you know your kids do, too."

He drew closer as he spoke to her, hoping against hope to convince her. "Nobody can imagine how hard it must have been for you to take that step, but guess what? You *did* it! You found the courage, determination, sheer *guts* to pack up and walk out on a man who made you fear for your life—who *still* makes you fear for your life. And you're right to feel that way. He's utterly and totally insane."

He reached out and tenderly cupped her cheek. She stared at him, her eyes wide, but this time she didn't move away. "It's not your fault he's the way he is. It's never been your fault. Stop beating yourself up about it. If you let him destroy you like this, he'll have won! Don't give him that power," he implored her, desperate to get through to her. "Seek out the woman you were not so long ago and embrace her, give her permission to breathe again, to laugh and sing and dance in the rain. To *live*."

The air between them was charged. His face was inches from hers. Her breath came in short, sharp pants, but her gaze remained locked on his. He lowered his gaze and stared at her mouth, her lips slightly parted. Need to claim her surged through him, hot and hard and fast and left him breathless.

Slowly, he inched toward her until his lips grazed hers. It was only the slightest of touches, but it was electrifying. His hands came around to frame her face and all of a sudden, he couldn't get close enough. It seemed like she felt the same way.

They came together in fierce desperation, their kiss went on forever, explosive in its passion. He didn't want it to end. Her arms came around his neck. She clung to him and pressed her sweet curves against him. He crushed her against his body and kissed her over and over again.

"The children...?" he muttered, fast getting to the point where he couldn't stop.

She pulled away, panting. "They're at my sister's. I called her straight afterwards and asked her if they could stay with her for the night. I needed to get them away from here, from everything. I told Kat about Nigel, about the way things have been for the past five years.

"She was shocked that she hadn't seen it and hurt that I hadn't confided. She doesn't understand I didn't tell anyone—how even now, I can barely bring myself to speak about it." Her voice cracked with emotion and tears glistened in her eyes. Mason sighed again and dragged her back into his arms.

He'd call the police and report Nigel's breach, but not right now. Nigel was probably long gone. Besides, they had the testimony of the two witnesses as well as Belle to support what had happened. There were also security cameras at the entrance to the building. It would show Nigel coming in and going out. He hoped, together, the statements and evidence would be enough to have the prick brought in.

Belle pressed herself against him and threaded her arms around his neck. Knowing they had the night alone was almost more than he could bear. His lips found hers once again and this time, some of the urgency eased. Now that he knew they had all the time in the world, he intended to savor every moment.

His lips trailed over her cheeks and nuzzled her ears. His tongue swept over the whorls. He caught her sharp intake of breath.

"Do you like that?" he murmured.

He felt her nod and smiled. He wanted so much to please her. Moving lower, he kissed his way down her neck, pushing her soft cotton T-shirt out of the way. His hands reached up to cup her breasts and his thumbs stroked lazily over her nipples. They hardened under his touch.

Dragging his head back to hers, she subjected him to another mind-blowing kiss. He pressed himself against her, needing so much to be close. He tugged at the bottom of her T-shirt and sighed when it came loose from her shorts. The feel of her silky, warm skin beneath his fingers was heaven. She arched into him and he slid his hand up higher, caressing her. Suddenly, he needed to feel her naked against him, pressed together from head to toe.

He swept her up in his arms. She let out a little gasp. He caught it in his mouth. With purposeful strides he walked down the hallway. Lowering her gently to his king-sized bed, he quickly followed her down. Impatient, he pulled her T-shirt over her head.

He made short work of her bra and then started on her shorts. She lifted her hips and he shimmied them down her hips. Naked but for a scrap of white lace that only just covered her womanhood, he pushed back on his haunches and took a few moments to simply take in the beauty and perfection that was Isobel West.

"You're so beautiful," he breathed, feeling in awe of the woman spread before him. When he thought of all that she'd been through, he was blown away by her fortitude. The fact that she'd managed to escape that horror was a testament to her resilience and inner strength. All he had to do was make her believe it.

Tugging at his tie, he pulled it loose and threw it

on the floor. For a moment, the buttons on his shirt stalled him, but soon it, too, joined the growing pile of discarded clothes. Belle reached up and splayed her hands over the taut muscles of his chest and he gasped.

Heat ignited across his skin, wherever her fingers touched. His heart beat double time. Slowly, she moved her hand over his chest. Exploring, curious, her fingernails grazed his nipples. He did his best to stay still until she'd had her fill, but it was a torturous effort. All he wanted was to hold her and kiss her and love her for the rest of his life.

"I love the way you feel," she whispered.

His gaze locked on hers. All the love and desire he'd held inside him came rushing to the fore. He tore off his trousers and underwear and slid her thong down her legs. A moment later, they were skin to skin as he lay there, fully on top of her. He sighed in relief.

Drawing in a lungful of air, he breathed in her unique scent. The smell of her hair, her skin, her *essence*. It was like no other and he loved it. He loved every part of her. He could barely remember a time when he hadn't.

Slowly, he moved his head and kissed her, softly, tenderly, teasing her with his tongue. His cock lay thick and hard between them, throbbing with desire. But he was determined to take this slowly, one kiss, one touch at a time. He wanted to drive her so wild with need that she'd forget everything but him.

He kissed her eyes, her mouth, her nose and then once again found the sensitive spot near her ears. She groaned and moved restlessly beneath him, but he refused to be hurried.

"Relax. Enjoy. Tonight is all about you. I want you to know how special you are, how beautiful, how brave, how unique. Let me love you the way I want to, Belle. Let me give this gift to you."

She stared at him, her eyes wide with hope, yet he saw a shadow of uncertainty. He could tell she didn't know whether to go with it or not, whether she could trust him not to let her fall. A fresh wave of determination surged through him and he vowed silently to do whatever it took. One way or the other, and over as much time as was needed, he'd convince her his love was real and nothing was ever going to change it.

He shifted his weight until most of it was on his knees and then leaned over to suckle one nipple. The hard nub was pink and sweet and tasted like heaven. He turned his attention to her other breast and gave it the same kind of attention.

His hand kneaded the soft skin of her thigh while his mouth continued its exquisite torture. Small sounds of pleasure escaped from her throat and once again, she stirred beneath him.

"Please, Mason," she gasped.

"Not yet," he murmured and moved his lips lower across her belly. He kissed the taut planes of her stomach and dipped his tongue into the indentation made by her belly button. Easing himself further away, he nuzzled his way lower. Burying his face in the warmth between her legs, he lapped at her sweet, soft lips.

She gave a half-hearted protest, but he paid it

no heed. With his lips and his tongue, he stroked her until she was a whimpering ball of need. With his fingers, he parted her soft folds and she surged upwards against his hand. Slowly, he eased two fingers inside her and moved them in and out.

Once again, her hips came off the bed and her hand came down to cover his. Pressing herself against him, she tried to increase the rhythm and pressure.

"Take it easy, honey. We have all night. There's no need to rush."

"But I want you, Mason. I need you. It's been so long since I felt anything. I need to have you deep inside me, now."

His cock swelled with her words and the throbbing grew almost painful. He levered himself up until he was poised above her and began to inch his way into her warmth.

"Faster, Mason, faster. I want you to love me now. Please," she whispered.

The desperation in her voice and the wildness in her eyes pushed him over the edge. With a guttural sound way back in his throat, he plunged all the way inside her. He groaned his relief aloud.

"Oh, sweet Jesus, you feel so good," he gasped. "So hot and wet and willing. You don't know what you do to me, Belle. I could love you like this forever."

A tiny smile of satisfaction turned up the corners of her lips. She gazed at him with eyes full of wonder. He moved against her and it was like nothing he'd ever experienced. Even their first time couldn't compare to this.

The first time, she'd been so distraught and broken and vulnerable, it had been all about offering her his comfort and reassurance and love. Now, it felt like she really saw him, Mason, the man who would give her the moon. He marveled at how good it could be when he was making love to the woman who'd stolen his heart, his soul, his everything. Nothing else could ever come close.

Isobel clung to Mason's broad shoulders and rode the waves of pleasure until she thought she'd die. Until Mason, her husband had been her one and only lover and sex with Nigel had been nothing like this, even in the beginning. She'd always been too focused on pleasing him and seeing to his needs. Later, it seemed like from start to finish, she'd done nothing but brace herself for his inevitable climax then criticism.

But with Mason, it was nothing like that. He was a gentle and considerate lover, putting her needs way above his own. It had been that way the first time they were together, but she hadn't been in the right state of mind to appreciate it. Now, feeling stronger and more in control of the nightmare that had been her life, she was able to see and feel how special and truly wonderful he was.

Standing up to Nigel earlier in the day had felt amazing. Okay, she'd taken the brave step of walking out of his life, but she'd spent every moment since then looking over her shoulder, terrified that he'd reappear and force her to come back home.

When she told him to go to hell in front of Mason's neighbors, she could barely describe the feeling of power that had surged inside her. She'd still been scared out of her wits, but somehow knowing she had Mason's support and encouragement behind her and the protection of his neighbors, she'd found the courage and determination to do it. She'd stood up to her husband and had come away the winner. It was an incredible moment. And she had Mason to thank for it.

Not that it was gratitude pulsing inside her right at that moment. The white-hot desire pouring through her veins and setting her nerve endings on fire couldn't be described in any way, shape or form like that. This was want and need and sizzling attraction all rolled up into one and she couldn't get enough. She wanted to remember every moment of this magical experience...

She caressed the well-defined muscles of his chest and luxuriated in the light smattering of hair. It was silky and dark, just like the hair on his head. Her hands moved lower and skimmed over his taut belly, loving the way muscles clenched and tightened beneath her fingers. That she had that effect on him was mind blowing.

With Nigel, it had been all about him. Never once had he complimented her or told her how much she turned him on. It was all about him and his gratification and then her humiliation became his favorite way to play.

She couldn't bear to think of all the things he'd done to her just because he knew she didn't want him to. It had become a twisted game to him. A game played by a selfish, manipulative, controlling man who got a kick out of seeing her distress and her humiliation.

With an effort, she forced the dark memories aside and concentrated on the man she held in her arms. He was good and kind and gentle and giving. He was everything her husband was not.

Mason continued to thrust into her and she clung to him like she might cling to a kayak being tossed over the rapids. He was her lifeboat, her rescuer, her hero and somewhere from way down deep inside her, she thought maybe, just maybe, he could lead her back toward love.

CHAPTER 19

Dear Diary,

I am so confused. My world has been turned upside down. I want to trust in another man's love, but I'm terrified to be wrong again. I thought my husband was the love of my life and he turned out to be my worst nightmare. I look back and don't understand how I didn't see the ugliness that lay in his heart; the anger and control and selfishness that dominated our relationship almost from the start.

I don't know whether to feel pity or sorrow or anger toward him. Maybe I feel all three, irrevocably entwined together, never to be separated. One thing I do know is that I will never let him close enough to hurt me or my children again.

Maybe this is my fault because all I saw was who he wanted me to see. The perfect man, the perfect husband... I know now that he was no such thing. Our love was never meant to be; an illusion from the very beginning.

Every day I am away from him, a little more light penetrates the darkness. I am beginning to see clearer all

the things I couldn't and perhaps wouldn't see before... I
dream that someday I'll see a rainbow...and when I do, I'll
know I have returned to the land of the living.

I sobel turned to look over her shoulder as she backed out of the car space reserved for Mason in the underground garage of his apartment complex. It had been nearly a fortnight since she'd left Nigel and Christmas was less than a week away. Staying at Mason's apartment had been exactly what she'd needed to nurture and heal her broken spirit, but she couldn't hide out there forever. It was time for her to take control of her life and the first thing on her list was to return to work again.

After the attack in Mason's home, she'd telephoned Georgie and had been given another week off. The time had served her well. She felt stronger every day. Knowing that Nigel had been arrested and charged with breach of the AVO also helped her feel that finally, God was on her side. The fact that her husband had been released on bail was something that played in the back of her mind, but she tried not to let it affect her decisions and the way she lived.

She'd even managed to take the kids to the park just down the street. They'd played on the swings and had enjoyed the sun. It had only been for ten minutes, but it was something. She'd also gone to the nearest bank and had opened up an account in her own name. Returning to work was another milestone she had to achieve.

She'd always loved her job as a nurse and working on the children's ward was even closer to her heart. She loved children and had wanted a whole bunch of them. Nigel had put an end to that dream. She'd had to beg and plead and promise him the world for him to agree to try for Ben. According to Nigel, Sophie had been a mistake.

At the time, Isobel had been taking antibiotics for a chest infection and they'd interfered with the effectiveness of her contraceptive pills. Nigel had been livid. He'd demanded she have an abortion, but she'd adamantly refused. Her defiance had cost her a black eye and a couple of loose teeth, but as far as she was concerned, the dental work was well worth it.

When Sophie was born, she was overjoyed and instantly fell in love. To Nigel's credit, he grudgingly came around. Isobel was cynical enough to guess that unlike Ben, it had something to do with the fact Sophie looked just like her father.

Now, she made the turn that would take her to Ben and Sophie's daycare center and continued driving up the street. She glanced in the rear view mirror. "We're almost there, guys. Are you ready to go back?"

"I am!" Ben announced from the back seat. "As cool as Mason's place is, there's nowhere to ride my bike. We didn't even take it to the park! At least I get to ride bikes at daycare."

Isobel sent up a silent prayer that her son had

recovered from the trauma of witnessing the latest fight between her and Nigel. She'd made sure she spoke to both of her children and explained what had happened as best she could. They both understood their daddy was unwell and needed time to become less angry. She'd told them they wouldn't be seeing him until he'd learned how to be around them without yelling or hurting anyone.

'I don't like it when Daddy yells,' Sophie had said, her big eyes dark and solemn. Isobel had hugged her close and had whispered against her hair, 'I don't like it either, baby.'

She settled them into their daycare rooms and was relieved when Sophie gave her a bright smile and a wave good-bye. It would do them good to have a little normalcy back in their lives. Their teachers and daycare center friends were like a second family.

Closing the door to Sophie's room behind her, Isobel walked up to the administration desk. From her handbag, she pulled out a copy of the AVO. The girl behind the counter greeted her with a smile.

"Hi, Isobel. I haven't seen you for a while. Have you been away on a holiday?"

Out of habit, Isobel ducked her head in embarrassment. A second later, she realized the enormity of her accomplishment by getting to this point, and raised her chin again. Obviously this person hadn't been informed. Better to be embarrassed than dead. She had to remember that.

"No, I... I've had some trouble at home. I spoke

to the director a little over a week ago. Nigel and I have...separated. The police are involved. I have an AVO against him." She shoved the papers over the counter. "I'd appreciate it if you make sure the rest of the staff are aware. Nigel's been ordered to stay away from me and the children. Under no circumstances is he allowed to collect them."

The girl's eyes went wide with shock, but to her credit she remained professional. "Of course, Isobel. If there's anything I or any of the other staff can do—?"

"I appreciate your offer, but I think we're all okay. Just keep an eye on my babies. They might seem a little upset. They've been through a lot lately and while they seem all right at times, the stress of this situation sometimes manifests in unusual or unexpected ways."

"Yes, of course I'll make sure all of the other staff are made aware, too."

"Oh, and my contact details have changed," Isobel said at the last minute. Handing over Mason's address and her new phone number, she thanked the girl, said good-bye and left.

Hurrying now, she headed toward her car and prayed she wouldn't be caught up in morning traffic. It was her first shift back and she didn't want to be late and she still had to give a copy of the AVO to someone in HR before she went on the floor. Mason was almost certain HR was where Nigel had obtained the address to Mason's apartment. There simply wasn't anyone else in Sydney who knew where he lived. Isobel couldn't help but feel guilty that she hadn't phoned them at the start.

The police had urged her to tell everyone who needed to know, despite any embarrassment it might cause. It was better to have people looking out for her and to react with offers of assistance if Nigel happened to approach. Especially given that they worked in the same hospital. It would be impossible to get an order restraining him from attending his workplace. All they could hope was that he'd abide by its terms and stay away from her.

She sent a silent prayer heavenward that he'd see sense and keep out of her way, but she was terrified that he wouldn't. Still, she had to keep on living. *What choice did she have?* She had children, a job; responsibilities. She couldn't expect Mason to support them. Besides, she refused to let Nigel dictate the way she lived her life. She was done with that, and with him, forever.

She pulled into the staff parking lot and breathed a sigh of relief. She'd made it with a few minutes to spare. Long enough to attend upon the HR staff. Climbing out of her old Toyota Magna, she locked it and hurried across the asphalt.

"Isobel."

She spun her around, her heart leaping into her throat. Nigel stood not ten yards away. Despite her brave assurances only moments earlier, her legs went to water.

"Stay away from me, Nigel! I swear, I'll call the police." Her voice was shaky with fear, but she meant every word she said. She opened her handbag and scrambled through the contents, looking for her phone. The sound of Nigel's menacing laughter chilled her to the bone.

"Go ahead. You think a piece of fucking paper's going to stop me?"

He took a step toward her and Isobel let out a shriek. "Stop right there! Don't come any closer. I mean it, Nigel. Don't dare move another step."

He held up his hands in surrender. "Okay, okay, take it easy." He shook his head slowly back and forth and gradually appeared to calm down.

"Why are we fighting like this, Isobel? I don't understand. I love you and you love me. Come home. I promise I'll try harder. No more shouting, no more violence. I promise not to hit you again. I don't want to hurt you, Isobel. Please believe me. I love you. I want you and the kids to come home."

This time when she looked at him she was filled with pity. "I'm sorry, Nigel. It's over. I might have loved and respected you once, but not anymore. I'm not coming back, now or ever."

His face became more frantic. "I'll kill myself! I swear I'll do it! I'll take pills! You know I'll do it!"

She shook her head sadly, but didn't reply.

"It's Mason, isn't it? You're fucking him! I can see it in your eyes."

"Please don't blame Mason for this. It has nothing to do with him. This is about you and me and always has been. I haven't loved you for a long, long time and if you're honest, you'll admit you don't love me, despite your claims. You want to own me, control me—like a possession, but you don't love me. People don't hurt those they love the way you've hurt me."

"It's the way my father taught me to love! My mother worked hard to please him every second of the day!"

"Yes," she agreed softly, "and look how that worked out."

Nigel's expression turned desperate. He came toward her again, his eyes pleading. "Don't do this to our family, Isobel! I beg of you! I swear, I've changed! Please, please come home."

She stared at him a moment longer and once again was filled with pity. He no longer had the power to hurt her and with that realization, the terror with which she'd regarded him for so many years eased.

"Good-bye, Nigel. Take care." She turned back toward the hospital and walked away. She didn't look back.

———————

Mason headed straight for the children's ward the moment he entered the hospital. Isobel had left for work before him. He'd offered to take the kids and drop them off at their center before work, but she'd turned him down.

He understood her need to retain some independence and to explain things about the AVO personally to the daycare staff, but it was ridiculous having to leave for work half an hour earlier than normal just so she could do that drop-off. He certainly intended to revisit the arrangement and could only hope the next time they discussed it, she'd be more willing to accept his offer.

He caught sight of Georgie Whitely behind the high counter that bordered the nurses' station and greeted her with a friendly smile. Though he'd been at the Sydney Harbour Hospital for less than a month, the staff had made him feel welcome, and a necessary and trusted part of their team. The Nursing Unit Manger returned his greeting with a short wave.

"Hi, Mason. You're bright and early. We've just finished the handover with the nurses. Your patients have had an uneventful night. I'd like you to take a look at Jody Collins in bed six. She came in late last night with a nasty chest and throat infection. She's responding well to the antibiotics that were prescribed for her last evening, but if you could pop in and see her, that would be great."

"Sure, no problem. I'll be there in a minute. I don't suppose you know where Isobel is?" He did his best to keep his tone casual. Isobel had insisted they keep the fact that she was staying with him a secret. It was bad enough that half of her colleagues had been on the floor and witnessed Nigel's angry accusations a fortnight earlier, but until it was confirmed by her or Mason, no one would know the truth for sure.

Of course, he'd wanted to argue with her. As far as he was concerned, he was with the woman he loved and would love forever. He wanted to shout it from the rooftops. But for Belle, their relationship was new and uncertain and she still hadn't made any kind of commitment. As much as he didn't like it, he understood her reluctance to go public and for now, acceded to her wishes.

Georgie didn't even raise an eyebrow. Either she was an excellent actress or she really didn't have a clue he and Isobel had a thing. Or perhaps she was the ultimate professional and didn't think it was any of her business. Whatever the reason, Mason was relieved when she merely said, "I think she's in the treatment room preparing to change a patient's dressing."

He gave the nurse a quick smile. "Thanks, Georgie. I'll check in on the child in bed six in a moment."

"No hurry, Mason. Let me know when you're ready."

He nodded and strode off in the direction of the treatment room. He opened the door and came to a stop. Isobel was bent over a stainless steel trolley, checking its contents. Mason's heart melted at the sight of her. Although it had only been a couple of hours since he'd seen her, he'd missed her.

Leaving her and the children at home in his apartment each day had been difficult, especially after knowing Nigel knew where they were. Mason was beyond grateful they hadn't heard from the prick since the police had arrested him, despite the fact he'd been set loose. Mason could only hope the stint in the lock-up, before the bastard made bail, had been enough to bring the prick to his senses. Mason didn't know what he'd do if the asshole showed up again.

Isobel looked up from what she was doing and smiled at him. His stomach somersaulted with sudden nerves. It was just like in high school. The moment she appeared in the corridors or the bleachers, he'd be tongue tied and stumbling over his words. It had happened every single time. No wonder she'd never noticed him. Now, he did his best to hide his nervousness with a grin.

"Hi," he said.

"Hi."

"How are you?"

"I'm good," she said with quiet reassurance.

"Good."

"I ran into Nigel in the car park."

"*What*?" He blinked in disbelief at her calm statement. "You saw Nigel this morning?

"Yes. He approached me in the car park as I was heading inside to work."

Mason stared at her, his heart pounding. She was taking this latest Nigel meeting way too calmly. He drew in a breath and tried to match her composure.

"What did he say?"

She glanced up at him and then returned to filling the trolley. "He begged me to come home; told me he still loved me and tried to convince me he'd changed."

Mason blew out his breath. "Wow. How did he seem? Was he angry?"

"He was at first, but after awhile, he kind of got

a grip on himself. In the end, he was just sad and desperate. All I felt was pity."

"He didn't try to hurt you or threaten you in any way?"

"No, the only threat he made was to himself."

"You mean he threatened to harm himself?"

"Suicide, to be precise. He told me he'd take pills. Don't worry, it isn't the first time he's made that kind of threat. It used to tear me up inside and I'd be riddled with guilt. Now I can see it was just another way he exerted his power and control over me."

Mason shook his head, unable to believe she was taking it so calmly. She'd had a run-in with her crazy, violent husband. A man who'd recently attacked her and had served up years of abuse. It didn't make sense that she wasn't fearful or at least showing signs of apprehension.

"What did you say?" he asked, trying to make sense of it.

"I reminded him of the AVO, and told him I didn't love him, that I hadn't loved him for a long time. I told him it was over. What I didn't tell him was that I felt sorry for him." She sighed quietly and then continued.

"For so long, I lived in a vacuum where all I wanted was for each day to end. Yet I was afraid of the nights I had to spend in his bed and what he'd force me to do. I lived in a constant state of fear and tension and it eroded everything else away. Thanks to you, I've now had the chance to spend time away from that, away from *him*, and I can see things much more clearly. I can see him for who he is. A sad, desperate, sick man who needs serious professional help."

"You're no longer afraid of him?"

"I think I'll always be a little afraid of him. I lived so long in fear. It will take a long time to unlearn and forget. Maybe I never will. But I'm hopeful his hold on me will lessen over the months and years and that one day I'll look back and shudder, not with terror but with regret that I let him steal joy from me for so many years."

"You're not old," he whispered, drawing closer. "Not by a long shot."

She smiled and rested her hand casually on his chest. Even through his white lab coat, he swore he could feel her heat.

"And you are a beautiful liar."

"Hey!" he protested. "You and I are both the same age and I know darn well I'm only now coming into my peak!"

She laughed and the sound of it filled him with joy. Her laughs had been few and far between and he cherished every one of them. She reached up and pressed a playful kiss on his cheek. It started out as a casual caress, but the feel of her lips on his skin sent a surge of electricity dancing along his spine. They hadn't made love since the night her husband had broken in, and he was as taut as a piano string.

Until now, she hadn't made any move toward him and he'd respected her need to take things slow. He was waiting for her to give him a sign that she was once again ready to proceed. It was slowly killing him...

He grabbed her hand and pressed it against his heart. "Belle..."

"*Shh*, Mason. Not here. Let's wait until we're home."

Home. He was thrilled that she'd referred to his apartment that way. It filled him with warmth and hope. He took a step back and cleared his throat.

"How did Nigel take the fact you told him it was over between the two of you?" he asked in an effort to distract himself and the erection he was trying to ignore.

She shrugged sadly. "It's hard to tell. I want to believe he'll see sense and let me walk away, but I'm not sure he'll give us up so easily. To him, we're possessions—ones *he* chooses when to give away. It's not supposed to happen the other way round."

"Maybe when word spreads that you're separated, he'll be forced to accept it and move on?"

She shrugged again. "Maybe. I guess all we can do is live with that hope. In the meantime, I intend to do all that I can to learn from this, and forget about it and him. It's time I put my energies into building the kind of life I've always wanted for me and my children."

He stared at her, but couldn't bring himself to ask if that life included him. It was too soon to be putting her under so much pressure. Instead, he said, "I've spoken to some colleagues. They've recommended a couple of therapists who specialize in domestic abuse. I have the contact details if you want them."

"Thanks; I do."

He handed her a piece of paper and she tucked it into the pocket of her uniform. When she looked up at him her eyes were full of gratitude.

"Thanks again, Mason. Thanks for everything. I don't know what I would have done without your help. You're the reason I found the courage today to stand tall and tell Nigel it was over. You gave me that, Mason, and I'll never forget it."

"No, Belle, you're wrong. You did that all on your own. All I did was give you support and encouragement and share my belief that you could do it. I'm so proud of you." His voice turned husky with emotion and once again, he cleared his throat.

She moved closer. So close that if he moved slightly, he'd brush her with his coat. She reached up and brought her hand behind his head and slowly exerted pressure until his lips were inches from hers.

"Kiss me, Mason," she whispered and he did.

Long moments later, he pulled away. His chest heaved with the effort it cost to curb his passion. They were in the treatment room, after all. Anyone could walk in at any moment. It was funny how Isobel didn't seem to care. Throwing caution to the wind, he spoke from the heart.

"You know how I feel about you, Belle. I don't care how long it takes. I'll wait for you forever."

Emotion shadowed her beautiful green eyes. A moment later, they sparkled with tears. A tiny smile trembled at the corners of her lips.

"What did I do to deserve you, Mason Alexander?"

Chapter 20

Nigel flicked through shot after shot of the photos he'd taken of his wife and her new man and his anger burned hotter with every frame. They'd been taken from a distance, on the other side of the staff car park, but with the expensive lens Nigel had attached to his phone he was able to zoom in until their images were crystal clear.

He stared at the smile on Isobel's face and the proprietary way Mason had thrown his arm around her shoulders. He'd pulled her in close to his side, as if he didn't care if their secret got out; as if he didn't care he was fucking another man's wife.

A fresh wave of fury burned through Nigel's gut. His eyes narrowed and his lips curled up in a snarl. Reaching for the decanter of scotch that stood on the low table near his elbow, he refilled his glass and then swallowed a healthy mouthful. It had been a month since the bitch walked out. Christmas had come and gone and yet he was still forced to endure the sideways glances of his colleagues and the sniggers from other staff. He was the source of whispers, innuendo and downright lies and there was nothing he could do.

Well, he'd had enough of doing nothing. It was time he wrested back control. The bitch would pay for what she'd done to him. Of that, he was certain. All he had to do was to come up with a plan; a plan so fantastic, so amazing, it would blow his mind and more importantly, would finish off Isobel Donnelly.

He took another two mouthfuls of scotch and then set the empty glass aside. The alcohol burned its way down his throat and he welcomed the heated feel of it. He stared at the fireplace set into the wall on the other side of the den. It was cold and dark and lifeless, like the rest of the house. It didn't matter that it was the middle of summer and that a fire wasn't needed. Some would also argue he didn't need a wife and family.

And they'd be right—the wife, at least...

And then it came to him. The plan he'd hungered for. The plan he couldn't wait to set in motion. The plan that would mean the end, once and for all, of Isobel-fucking-West and open the door for another, more deserving Mrs Donnelly, a woman who would appreciate all he had to offer.

———

"Watch out, Mason! I'm coming through!" Ben

shouted, giggling and ringing the bell attached to the handlebars of his new bike.

Isobel stood beside the swings, idly pushing Sophie back and forth. She laughed at her son's antics and shook her head, her heart filling with gratitude and love. She couldn't remember the last time she'd seen such uninhibited joy on Ben's face. The fear that had been a constant shadow in his beautiful green eyes for so many months had disappeared. He looked like an older version of the little boy she remembered.

Mason neatly sidestepped out of the way and Ben shot past him, his legs peddling with furious concentration. Mason's laughter reached her from where she stood with Sophie at the swings, across the other side of the small park. She couldn't help but smile.

"That's it, buddy! Go your hardest!" Mason called out to him. Ben turned and threw him a cheery wave and then continued biking around the path.

They'd spent Christmas together in Mason's home. It had been the best Christmas she could remember and she was sure the kids felt the same. Their shouts of laughter had filled every room and there had been a joy in the air that had never been there before and it was all thanks to the man who even now stayed close to her son, watching him with a protective eye.

As far as she knew, Nigel still worked at the hospital, but she hadn't seen him since the day he'd confronted her in the car park. She could only hope something of what she'd said to him had finally gotten through and he'd decided to let them go.

She and Mason had settled into a comfortable routine of work and children and down time. It was all so normal and nice. No. Nice was the wrong word. There was nothing *nice* about Mason. He far exceeded nice.

Nice didn't come close to describing the caring, considerate, supportive friend and lover he'd become. The way he treated her and her children with kindness and respect. He sought out her opinions on every little thing and genuinely appeared interested in her response. She'd never experienced that kind of easy, respectful camaraderie with her husband and now she couldn't imagine being with a man who treated her with anything less.

And then there was the way Mason looked, wet and tousled from a shower, with just a towel draped loosely around his hips. She'd have had to be dead not to notice his appeal. His chest was broad with well-defined muscles. She remembered how it felt against her breasts.

The memory made her blush, but warmth tingled low in her core. She moved a little restlessly and wished they were home. Home. With her family.

Her family. Is that what they'd become? Is that what she wanted them to become? Her therapist had urged her to embrace life again. He'd even suggested she start to date, and be open to a new relationship; one that was safe and normal and made her feel good. She hadn't been able to bring herself to tell him she had already done that.

Mason was all of those things and though the thought of completely trusting a man again terrified her, she wanted desperately to find the courage to try.

'If you don't open your heart again, then your victimization will be complete.' The words of her therapist echoed in her head and all of a sudden, she didn't want to remain a victim. A surge of determination flooded through her. Dammit, she deserved a happy life, to be loved and cherished for who she was, imperfections and all.

"Push me, Mommy! Push me!"

Sophie's high-pitched squeal penetrated her heavy thoughts and she blinked and focused on the face of her beautiful daughter.

"Okay, honey! Hold on tight!" She stepped forward and pushed Sophie until she once again swung high. Her little girl screamed with laughter and Isobel laughed. Out of the corner of her eye, she spied a flash of red. The meaning of it hit her brain and quickly activated her heart. She gasped and her pulse took off at a gallop.

A red car. Nigel. Oh, God. He was here at the park. Mason. Ben. Where were Mason and Ben?

With her thoughts surging in a frenzy of fear, she looked around in a panic. The red car eased its way along the street that bordered the park. Isobel stared at it. A moment later, she breathed a sigh of relief. It was a red car, but not a convertible. It wasn't even a Porsche. Just an ordinary sedan with an elderly couple in the front.

She sucked in a deep breath of air and eased it out between tight lips. It wasn't Nigel. It was just a red car. It was all right. They were all right. *It wasn't Nigel...*

Mason jogged up beside her, Ben not far behind, on his bike. She saw the frown on Mason's face and the concern that clouded his dark eyes.

"Are you okay?" he asked. "You look like you just saw a ghost."

She drew in another breath and offered him a shaky smile. "I'm fine. I-I thought I saw Nigel, but it was someone else driving a red car. I'll be okay. It just...shook me up."

Mason nodded, his expression filled with understanding. "It's normal to react like that, Belle. It'll take time to heal, to trust yourself enough that you can ignore the triggers, to forget the fear and pain and feel safe again."

She nodded and was grateful when he closed the distance between them and drew her in close for a hug. She leaned against him and breathed in deeply of his unique scent. With a soft sigh, she looked up at him.

"Thank you. For everything. For believing in me, for giving me strength, for caring."

His eyes darkened with emotion. "I love you, Belle."

She held his gaze. Her heart pounded. The air around them grew charged. "I... I love you, too."

His eyes widened in amazement. A moment later, a grin split his face in two. "Do you mean it? You love me? You really *love* me?"

She smiled and nodded and laughed and

cried. Until that moment, she hadn't realized it was true. Somehow, somewhere along the way, she'd fallen in love with this beautiful, gentle man and she couldn't believe how right it felt.

She stood on her tiptoes and kissed him, long and lovingly on his lips. His arms tightened around her and he matched her kiss for kiss. Their tongues entwined, their passion grew until both of them came up gasping for air.

"Mommy and Mason are kissing," Sophie sang from her position on the swing.

"Do it again!" Ben cheered, smiling hard.

Isobel laughed along with Mason and it felt more than good. She wanted to cherish the feeling and hold it close to savor over and over again. And then she remembered she didn't have to. This was the start of her new life, a life where love and laughter flowed freely. A life where she felt safe and protected and cherished, along with her children.

She turned back to Mason and kissed him softly on the mouth. "Let's go back home."

His eyes lit up with happiness and he smiled his beautiful smile. Bowing low, he swept off his ball cap and waved it with a flourish.

"Your wish is my command."

———————

A few days later, Isobel turned up the car radio and sang along with the up-tempo song playing through the speakers. She moved her head to the beat and even tapped the steering wheel. The kids giggled and chattered cheerfully from the back seat. It was early, but the sun was already shining brightly and the day promised to be a good one.

Since declaring her love for Mason she'd never felt happier. Right now, she felt as free as a bird. She almost believed she could soar up into the clouds and drift aimlessly across the perfect, clear sky, counting each and every one of her blessings. Her therapist was right. Embracing life and love and all they had to offer was the best thing she'd ever done.

If there was an occasional dark moment when she'd remember the way it had been with Nigel, she'd quickly and deliberately force it aside. She refused to let her past destroy her or intrude in any way on the peace and tranquillity of her existence and the joy she'd found with Mason.

Mason. Just the thought of him set her heart racing and she'd only just left his side. He'd been rinsing dishes as she'd kissed him good-bye and hurried the kids to the car. The fact that she'd see him at the hospital in an hour or so made her feel all warm and gooey inside. While they hadn't gone out of their way to announce their relationship to their colleagues, neither had they kept it a secret. She no longer saw a need to.

Okay, she was still legally married to Nigel and he continued to work at the hospital, but she wasn't prepared to let either of those things stand in the way of her happiness. She'd contacted the lawyer and set the divorce proceedings in motion and though she'd never wanted to break up her marriage and her family, her situation left her with no other choice.

It was like her therapist clarified: It wasn't Isobel who'd made their lives so unbearable that she had to walk out the door. She'd left in response to Nigel's actions and in the end, it had been a matter of life and death. She truly believed if she'd stayed, he'd have killed her. And as much as she'd never wanted her children to come from a broken home, the thought of leaving them motherless was even worse. The thought he might not have stopped with her was too unbearable to contemplate.

In the end, there had been no other decision to make and she was grateful for the therapy and for Mason for helping her to see it the way it was. It would take a long time before she stopped looking over her shoulder... Who knew? Maybe that instinctive reaction never went away? But she was determined to get a hold on it and not let the fear get in her way.

Now she wove through traffic on the way to the daycare center to drop off Ben and Sophie. The two chatted in the back seat as she approached a set of traffic lights. They switched from orange to red ahead of her and she eased her foot off the accelerator. Slowing down, she glanced in her rear view mirror and her heart leaped into her throat. A red car pulled in behind her.

She drew in a deep breath and did her best to slow her pulse. Despite all the pep talking, she was still as skittish as ever. It was just a red car. There were thousands of them in the city. She needed to stop being so jumpy every time she spotted one.

Still, she flicked on her indicator and eased into another lane. She couldn't help the need to put a little distance between them. It was silly, but the urge was too strong to ignore. She'd discuss it with her therapist at her next appointment and ask for some strategies to deal with it. For now, she'd give in to the need to move as far away from the vehicle as the traffic would allow.

The lights turned green and Isobel pressed down steadily on the accelerator. She'd always been a careful driver and she refused to become the cause an accident just because she'd been spooked by a red car. She drew in another breath and forced it through her dry lips, telling herself to relax. The sound of a throbbing engine beside her caused her to glance across.

Nigel sat behind the wheel of his cherry-red Porsche, sneering at her. Isobel's stomach dropped to the floor. Almost instantaneously, fear, thick and visceral clawed at her belly and throat. She snatched desperate breaths and tried hard to focus on the road. A moment later, he disappeared from sight and she wondered frantically where he'd gone. She glanced again in the rear view mirror and found him.

He sat so close behind her, if she braked, he'd run into her tail lights. She tried to keep her pace steady while she worked out what she could do. Nigel would guess where she was going this time of the morning and would know the children were also in the car.

What would she do if he followed her to the daycare center and confronted her as she got out of the car? It was normally a busy time, with lots of parents coming and going. She didn't think she was under any physical threat, but she could do without a nasty argument, especially in front of their kids.

Perhaps he wouldn't follow her... Perhaps he just wanted to give her a fright—because he could. It was so typical of Nigel, she could believe that was his intent. She prayed she was right and that sooner or later, he'd tire of the game and go his own way. He was dressed in his usual suit and tie. She assumed he was also heading into work.

That thought didn't rest easily with her, either, but it had been weeks since she'd seen him. She could only hope he wouldn't confront her in the hospital car park again. Her gaze strayed to her handbag where it lay on the front passenger seat. She wanted to call Mason, but she didn't dare take her concentration off the road. She wished for a moment that her old Magna had Bluetooth, but there was no point wishing that way now.

The traffic had thinned as she wound her way through the suburban streets, but with Nigel still close behind her, she was forced to stay focused. He gunned his engine behind her again and this time, he was close enough that she could see the expression on his face. His eyes were wild and unfocused and he appeared to be laughing at her. He caught her eye in the mirror and slowly ran his index finger from one ear to the other in a slicing motion across his throat.

Her blood ran cold at the implicit threat and she jammed her foot down on the accelerator. The car leaped forward, hurtling down the road. Her breath came faster and faster. As if sensing the tension in the car, Ben and Sophie fell silent. Nigel matched her pace, just inches from the back of her car. She pressed the accelerator down further and gripped the steering wheel.

A set of traffic lights loomed up ahead, still showing green. A second later, they switched to orange. With her heart in her throat, she floored the pedal and prayed she'd make it in time. She heard the sound of Nigel's engine and knew he was still very close behind.

The light turned red and she squeezed her eyes shut with her foot still pressed to the floor. She caught a glimpse of a truck and the horrified look on the face of the driver and then it was all too late. A sickening, squealing grind of metal on metal reverberated through the car. She screamed through lungs that were short on air and pain raced through her chest. The car went spinning round and round and she thought it would never stop.

After what seemed like an eternity, the spinning motion ended and she breathed a sigh of relief. The car was still on its wheels. They'd been hit, but they were okay. She struggled to get herself free of the seatbelt that was cutting into her chest. At last, it snapped open and she turned to reassure her children.

One look was all it took. She screamed and screamed and screamed...

CHAPTER 21

The blue and red of the emergency strobe lights surrounded her. Everywhere she looked, there were police cars, fire trucks, ambulances. Dazed and confused and more terrified than she'd ever been in her life, Isobel pushed her fist against her mouth and tried to retain a sliver of self-control. Blood poured from a gash on her forehead and tears streamed down her cheeks, but she paid no attention to either of them as she searched frantically for her kids.

She grabbed hold of the shirt front of the nearest paramedic and begged him. "Please, my children, where are they? I need to see them! I need to know they're okay!"

"I'm sorry, lady. You'll have to step away. They're being treated at the scene. We have to get them stabilized before we can take them to the hospital. Please, you need to stay out of the way."

His tone was gentle, but firm and he tried to steer her away from the scene. She shook off his hands in increasing panic.

CHRIS TAYLOR

"No! Don't touch me and don't tell me to move away! They're my children! I need to see them! Ben? Sophie? It's Mommy. Please tell me you're okay!"

Her desperate plea remained unanswered and fresh fear settled heavily in her heart. *Oh, God, what if they didn't make it?* When she turned around in her seat and saw them... There was so much blood. She'd seen enough trauma victims to know that amount of blood meant things were far from good.

"Are you the driver of the Toyota Magna?"

She spun around and then gasped as pain tore through her chest. It must have been caused by the seatbelt pulling tight upon impact. A uniformed police officer regarded her solemnly, a notebook and pen in his hand.

"Y-yes," she stammered. She reached out and clutched his sleeve. "Please, officer, my children. How are they? I need to see them."

The police officer's expression remained solemn, but compassion filled his eyes. "I'm sorry, it isn't good. The paramedics are working on them now."

Her legs nearly collapsed out from underneath her. She grabbed his arm and held on to him, trying to stay upright. "Are they still alive? Please, tell me they're still alive." A harsh sob caught in the back of her throat and hysteria gripped her chest. She breathed so fast she was dizzy, but the panic wouldn't subside.

"I need you to answer some questions. We'll start with your full name and address."

The officer's gentle but insistent manner gradually broke through her fog of panic and fear. She gave him the information he requested. When he asked her to tell him what had happened, fury struck her full force.

"My husband...Nigel Donnelly... He was chasing me. He'd been tailgating me for miles. It started along Parramatta Road. I-I accelerated to get away from him. I... I just wanted to get away." She looked around at the crowd of people, trying to find him. "Where is he? Nigel, where is he? You need to speak to him. He'll tell you what happened."

"We have. He said he was traveling behind you when you suddenly sped away. You went through a red light. There was a truck coming the other way. You were lucky the driver was still gaining speed. If he'd been traveling faster, you all could have been killed."

Isobel shook her head back and forth at the enormity of what had happened. "Oh, my God! Oh, my God! Please, tell me my children are all right?"

The officer looked at her sympathetically. "You're bleeding, Mrs Donnelly. You need to be seen by a paramedic. I wish I had better news. All I know for sure is that when they were pulled out of the car, they were breathing."

For the second time, her legs went weak and she used the officer's arm once again for support. He waited for her to become steady before gently disengaging himself and stepping away. A moment later, the doors to one of the ambulance vehicles snapped shut and sped away, its lights and siren blazing. It was quickly followed by a second.

"My babies..." Isobel gasped, following the progress of the emergency vehicles with her desolate gaze. "Where are they taking them?"

"I overheard one of the paramedics say they were being taken to the Sydney Harbour Hospital. I need you to answer a few more questions and then you'll be free to go, for now."

She frowned in confusion. "For now? What do you mean, 'for now'?"

"We're not entirely sure yet what happened. The truck driver said you came through a red light. Your husband confirms it. Depending upon the reason for your negligence, charges might be laid."

"Charges? Against *me*? You have to be kidding! It wasn't my fault! I was trying to get away! I have an AVO against Nigel. Call Senior Constable Rogers at the Sydney City Police Station. He knows all about it. Nigel kept coming closer and closer, forcing me to do what I could to get away. If I'd slowed, he'd have crashed right into me, that's how close he was." Her voice cracked and fresh tears ran down her cheeks. "I had no choice! You have to believe me! I had no choice..."

"We're talking to a few other witnesses. We'll see what they have to say." He looked at her, his expression now curious. "Why was your husband chasing you?"

Isobel drew in a deep breath and let it out on a

shudder. "We have a violent history. For years, I've been a victim of domestic abuse. About a month ago, I left him and took our children. He... He didn't take it well."

"Was he aware of the AVO?"

"Yes, of course he was. Speak to Senior Constable Rogers. He'll tell you everything you need to know. There was another incident before Christmas. It was also reported to the police."

"Were any charges laid?"

"Yes. My husband was charged with assault and breaching the AVO. He's currently out on bail."

The officer wrote in his notebook and then looked back at her. "I'll look into it. If what you say is true, it might be enough to relieve you of any responsibility, regardless of running the red light. The courts take domestic violence cases very seriously. In the meantime, let's hope your children survive."

He turned away and his solemn words echoed around and around inside her head. The blood from the gash on her forehead had slowed and the bruising on her chest from the seatbelt was nothing compared to the pain in her heart. She looked around, searching for some way to get to the hospital.

An unfamiliar woman broke away from the crowd and came toward her. "Would you like a ride to the hospital?" the woman asked quietly, with kindness in her eyes.

Isobel stared at her and then nodded quickly. "Yes, thank you. I would. I need to see my children. I need to make sure they're all right."

"I'm parked over this way," the woman replied, indicating with her hand.

Isobel looked past her and spied the wreckage of the Toyota Magna. The door behind the driver's side was unrecognizable. It had been pushed into the body of the car so far, she couldn't imagine how anyone sitting next to it could have survived. *Ben.* Ben had been sitting behind her. Oh, God, no... She couldn't complete the thought.

A whimper of pain escaped through the fist she held to her mouth. She heard herself crying as if from afar. She felt the stranger's arm go around her shoulders to steady her. As if in a dream, they walked past the mangled wreckage and toward the woman's car. Stumbling more than walking, Isobel didn't know how they made it, but a few minutes later, the kindly stranger helped her into the front seat, watched her belt herself in and then took her place behind the wheel.

"I'm going to take it slowly so you don't panic on me, but rest assured, I'll get you there as quickly as I can. Your children will be okay, I'm sure of it."

Isobel wanted so much to believe the woman's words, but she knew as well as anyone that what the lady said, meant nothing. The police officer wasn't even sure of the status of her children. There was no way a bystander would know. Still, the woman was showing extraordinary kindness and Isobel kept her desolate thoughts to herself.

"What happened?" the woman asked as she pulled out onto the street.

Not sure if she could even bring herself to think

about it, Isobel surprised herself by blurting out the awful course of events that had led up to the tragic accident. When she finished, the woman simply nodded.

"I can see it in your eyes that you're telling the truth. I've been there, too."

Isobel gaped, shocked to her senses as she realized the woman wasn't talking about the accident.

"I've also escaped a violent marriage, although it was many years ago now. He was a lawyer and well thought of in the community. I was his picture-perfect bride. We were the perfect couple, or so everyone believed. Little did my friends and family know I lived in fear and isolation for nearly twenty years before I finally found the courage to leave." Her voice softened.

"Your eyes are such a beautiful green, but I recognize the hurt and the horror. It's there every time you mention your husband. You don't have to try and deny it. Over the years, I've come to realize my experience has given me a sixth sense about these things."

Isobel stared at the stranger and slowly shook her head. "*Twenty* years? You poor, poor woman."

"Don't feel sorry for me, honey. Yes, it was a long time and yes, it was as horrible as you can imagine, but I'm free now and I've found the love of my life. My children are grown and most of the time they're happy. My second husband is the gentlest, kindest soul on the earth and I thank God every day that I found him. I'm blessed and these days, I feel like I'm the luckiest woman in the world."

She turned to Isobel and gently touched her hand. "I just want you to know you've taken the first step toward a better life. Whatever happens, you'll never be trapped like that again, with fear and depression your constant companions, always by your side. Be proud of yourself for finding the courage and for doing it so early into your marriage. I'm sure it feels like you've been living like this forever, but believe me, you'll look back and realize it wasn't."

Returning her attention to the road, the woman continued to drive them to the hospital. Isobel tried to come to terms with what the stranger had said. How could she have known just by looking at her that she'd suffered those years of horror? Was it that plain to see? As if she could read her mind, the woman spoke again.

"Don't upset yourself, honey, over what people see. I see it because I've lived through it. I know exactly how it feels. I know how it overwhelms you until you feel like you're drowning, like there's never enough air. You're gasping for breath and nobody knows. Nobody sees a thing. People see what they want to see. It's just the way it is." The woman drew in a deep breath before continuing.

"You need to try harder to make the police see. They need to know what you've been through. They need to understand the sheer terror you felt when your husband drove up behind you today. They need to know you had no choice; that you had to get away. You have to make them see,

Isobel, for all of us. And there are a lot of us, the victims of our silent pain.

"Out of shame, we hide it from our friends and neighbors, but we're not the ones who should feel ashamed. Our only mistake was marrying a man who was unwell. And it is a sickness. Their need to control and hurt and humiliate isn't normal. It's a disease, just like any other. It's a pity most of society doesn't see it that way. People like you and I can make a difference, if we're brave enough."

She reached into her handbag that sat between them and handed Isobel a business card. *'Women Without Weapons'* was printed on one side with a phone number.

"We think we're helpless, but we're not. As individuals, maybe, but as a united voice, we can make a difference and it doesn't take a caustic tongue or a pair of wayward fists. We're a peaceful organization and more and more people are paying attention. For too long, domestic violence has remained hidden behind closed doors and that's exactly how the perpetrators like it. It's time we turned the spotlight on it and exposed it and all its ugly truths. It's the only way we can change things for the better."

Isobel took the proffered card, her thoughts in a whirlwind of disbelief, confusion and panic. *How had this woman picked her out of the crowd and known exactly what she'd been through?* She didn't know how and right now, she didn't have the time or energy to think about it.

The car pulled up outside the Emergency

Department of the Sydney Harbour Hospital. Isobel shoved open the door and scrambled out. She turned to the woman who'd helped her and held the card up to her lips. She mouthed a silent thank you and then slowly turned away. A moment later, she stepped into the ED. Her fear and panic returned full force as she headed straight for the counter.

"My name's Isobel Donnelly. My children and I were in a car accident. They were brought here by ambulance. Please, can you take me to them? I really need to see them."

The nurse looked up at her and noticed Isobel's uniform. She frowned. "You work here?"

"Yes, on the children's ward."

"Have you been seen by anyone? It looks like that cut on your forehead might need some stitches."

"No, I'm fine, please, I need to see my children."

With a shake of her head, the nurse turned her attention to the computer screen. "What are their names?" she asked.

Isobel gave the woman the information and waited on tenterhooks for her reply.

"They've both been taken to surgery. You'll—"

"Please, which theater? I know my way around. If you can tell me where they're being operated on, I can wait in the visitors' lounge."

The nurse looked a little doubtful. Eventually, she nodded. "I guess that's okay. They've been taken to James Russell Theaters in D Block."

Isobel didn't wait another second. Pressing the

button for the exit, she ran down the corridor toward the bank of elevators, her chest heaving. She pulled out her phone while she waited and called Mason. It seemed like an agony of time had passed before he answered.

At the sound of his voice, she broke down. Gasping and sobbing, she could barely get the words out.

"Stay right there. I'll be with you in a minute."

His steady reassurance calmed her and she managed to get a grip on her breathing, but when he arrived in front of her moments later, she collapsed against him and started crying again.

"Mason! Oh, Mason! I ran a red light! They're hurt! My babies are hurt and it's all my fault."

Moving her away from the people who were gathered around, waiting for the elevator, he shielded her with his body and asked her to tell him what happened.

With gasps and sobs, she managed to fill him in. When she finished, his face was pale, but his eyes were hard. He stared at her, his gaze intense.

"This isn't your fault, Belle; don't ever think that way again. If that bastard Donnelly hadn't been chasing you, this never would have happened. He's the one who must take the blame, fairly and squarely."

"But—"

"Don't do this to yourself, Belle, I mean it." His face was sterner than she'd ever seen it.

"Right now, we have to concentrate on the children. I'd heard there'd been an accident and two children were being brought in, but I've been flat out all morning. I haven't yet been to the ward. I didn't know you hadn't arrived."

She nodded, trying hard to take in what he said, but all she could think of was her babies. "I need to see them, Mason. I need to know they're okay."

"They're likely still in surgery. We'll have—"

"Please," she said more urgently, "please take me to them."

Taking her hand, Mason led her to the fire stairs. "It'll be quicker this way."

She followed after him, keeping up with his pace despite her shorter stride. Urging him silently onward, she ran down the three flights of steps that would bring them out on the level where the James Russell Theaters were housed. It was cooler down there and was kept that way on purpose. She shivered, but she couldn't say if it was from the sudden cold or because any moment, she'd find out the fate of her children.

They walked into the outer room where the nurse who checked-in the incoming patients worked. A woman dressed in scrubs looked up as they approached her.

"Hi, can I help you?" she asked with a smile, her gaze on Mason.

"Yes, we're enquiring about Ben and Sophie Donnelly. This is their mother, Isobel."

The nurse's gaze sharpened. She looked at Isobel and took in her uniform. "You work in the hospital?"

"Yes," Isobel managed. "Please, tell me, are they all right?"

The nurse drew in a deep breath and eased it out. "They're both still in surgery. Your son was more badly injured than your little girl as he was sitting on the side of the vehicle that received most of the impact."

Isobel bit her lip and nodded. "Yes, yes, he was." Her voice cracked and hot tears sprang to her eyes. *If he didn't pull through...* Her breath caught on another sob.

"Who are the surgeons?" Mason asked quietly.

"Doctor Stephens is in Theater Three with Sophie. Doctor Barrington and Doctor Rogers are in Theater Two with Ben."

Isobel's heart plummeted. Doctor Barrington was a neurosurgeon. She didn't need to be told what that meant. With a howl of pain and disbelief, she collapsed against Mason. His arm came around her and pulled her in close.

"You can wait in the visitors' lounge. I'll come and get you as soon as I know—"

"Where are they? Let go of me! Where the fuck are my kids?"

CHAPTER 22

Mason heard the familiar, loud and angry voice and tensed. Isobel's face lost all color. A moment later, Nigel appeared in the doorway. Almost instantly, he spied them near the nurse's desk and pulled away from two colleagues who were doing their best to restrain him. He stormed toward his wife.

"You bitch! You fucking slut! This is all your fault!" His face was suffused with an angry red flush, his fury was palpable.

Instinctively, Mason pushed her behind him, determined to protect her. His gaze narrowed on Nigel.

"Back off, Donnelly. I understand you're upset, but you're not going to speak to Isobel like that. Now, step away and calm down. Throwing accusations around like that isn't going to help anyone."

If anything, his calm and measured words had the opposite effect. Nigel's face turned purple with rage. Out of the corner of his eye, Mason saw the nurse reach for her phone.

"Don't you dare tell me to fucking calm down, Alexander," Nigel spat, his eyes filled with venom. "They're not your kids lying on a stretcher, fighting for their lives."

A shaft of pain went through Mason. He knew better than anyone that Ben and Sophie weren't his. That didn't mean he couldn't love them like they were, but it sure as hell wasn't something Nigel was ready to hear. He drew in a deep breath and did his best to remain calm.

"I understand that, Donnelly. It doesn't mean I don't care. I care for both of them, just like I care for their mother."

Nigel let out a bellow of rage and charged at him. With his hand in a fist, Nigel threw a punch in the direction of Mason's head. Isobel screamed and Mason felt her duck. His anger simmered just below the surface, but he tried hard to keep it in check. Assaulting another doctor could mean the end of his career, no matter the provocation.

Staring at Nigel, Mason held his ground. When the man swung a second time, he caught his wrist and effectively stopped the blow. The action infuriated Nigel and all of a sudden, his anger knew no bounds.

"You fucking bastard! You prick! You couldn't wait to get into her pants. Even when we were in high school, you wanted to fuck her. Don't bother denying it. Everyone could see. The only one who couldn't was Isobel. She was too fucking dumb to notice. And of course, I kept her busy sucking my cock. She didn't have time to look at you."

Mason tensed again. Despite his best efforts, his

anger boiled over. His hands clenched into fists. "You filthy scum. You're not fit to wipe her feet. You're nothing. You hear me? *Nothing!*"

Nigel let out another roar and swung his fist again. This time, it glanced off Mason's cheek. Isobel screamed again. No longer able to restrain himself, Mason drew back his arm and let Nigel have the full force of his fist. As it connected with the man's nose, he heard a satisfying crunch. Blood spurted out from everywhere. Nigel stumbled backward and fell to the ground, holding his injured nose.

"You fucking asshole! You broke my nose! You fucking bastard!"

Two security guards rushed into the area and came to a sudden halt. They looked from Nigel to Mason and back to Nigel again, as if unsure who they needed to assist.

"Get this asshole out of here," Mason growled.

"Doctor Donnelly needs to be escorted off the premises," the nurse added in support of Mason and appearing more than a little upset herself.

The security guards hauled Nigel to his feet, ignoring the torrent of abuse that spewed from his mouth. He struggled with them momentarily until one of them, a hulk of a man, pulled Nigel's arms back hard behind his back.

"Fuck off! Let go of me!" Nigel yelled. "You'll break my arms in a minute. I'm a surgeon. If you so much as lay a bruise on me I'll sue your ass off." Unperturbed, the guard turned and marched Nigel out of the room.

Mason turned to Isobel and she collapsed against him. He put his arms around her and held her close. She buried her head against his chest and breathed a sigh of relief. A moment later, she looked up and touched the tender spot on his cheek.

"He hit you! Are you all right?"

"I'm fine."

She felt around with her fingers, her touch soft and cool against his heated flesh. "I don't think anything's broken. You were lucky."

He pressed a quick kiss on her mouth. "I'm sorry you had to witness that."

She shuddered, but her expression remained resolute. "I've seen and heard a lot worse over the years."

Mason grimaced and tightened his hold. He couldn't even begin to imagine what she'd been through. He'd only had a glimpse of Nigel's temper and the madness that lay behind it. "I'm still sorry," he whispered. "Nobody should have to put up with that."

"Mrs Donnelly?"

Isobel twisted out of his arms and turned to face the nurse. "Yes?"

"I've just had a call from recovery. Your daughter's in there now. She's groggy but awake and asking for you."

Isobel cried out in relief and unmindful of her injuries, threw herself back in Mason's arms. His heart warmed with love that she'd turned to him in her hour of need: for help, for reassurance, for comfort. He didn't care what or when. The fact that she needed him and wanted him close when it came to times of trouble was enough.

"Can I go in and see her?" she asked.

"Yes, I'll show you the way."

Isobel looked back at Mason. "Is it all right if Doctor Alexander comes with me? We're... We're together."

The nurse smiled softly and nodded. "Of course. Follow me."

Mason's heart filled with love. He reached for Isobel's hand and squeezed it. She looked up at him with tenderness and love and returned the pressure. It was more than enough.

Isobel caught sight of her baby girl lying so still and pale against the crisp white hospital sheets and cried out loud. All of her years of nursing training went out the window. Nothing could prepare her for the sight of her three-year-old with a drip in her arm, her leg in plaster from ankle to thigh and an oxygen mask over her face. Isobel rushed over and restrained herself from dragging the little girl into her arms. Instead, settled for a gentle kiss on her baby's cheek.

"How did the surgery go?" Mason asked the nurse who hovered nearby.

"Fine. Doctor Stephens is pleased with how it all went."

Isobel focused in on the conversation. "What... What kind of injuries did she sustain?"

"She's a very lucky girl, from what I understand," the nurse replied. "A broken femur but it was a fairly straightforward break. No need for pins or plates. Doctor Stephens reset it under general anaesthetic. Far less trauma that way."

"Of course," Isobel agreed. "Did she have any internal injuries?"

"Not as far as anybody can tell at this point. She was unconscious when she was brought in, but by the time she'd been prepped for theater, she was alert and aware of what was happening. They did a CT scan on her brain to be certain, but everything looked fine."

Relief surged through Isobel and she leaned against Mason for support. Once again, his strong and reassuring presence was there for her. He put his arm around her and drew her in close to his side.

Her thoughts turned to Ben and she couldn't help trembling at the thought of what injuries he might have sustained. She forced herself to ask the question.

"Do you know how much longer they might be with my son?"

The nurse shook her head. "He was injured pretty badly. Quite a few broken bones, but it was the head injury they were most concerned about. They called in Doctor Barrington."

A fresh wave of dread settled heavily in Isobel's stomach and sent a swirl of nausea up her esophagus. She swallowed hard in an effort to keep it at bay. Ben had a serious head injury and it was all her fault.

"It's not your fault, Belle," Mason told her quietly, his voice firm.

She shook her head. In less serious circumstances, she would have been amused. "How do you do that?"

"Do what?"

"Mind read."

"Is that what I was doing?"

"Yes, and it isn't the first time," she gently accused, letting him know she wasn't upset by his uncanny knack.

Mason shrugged. "I'm not sure. I don't do it consciously. I guess I just sometimes know how you're going to react. You're good and kind and generous and you love your kids more than your life. Despite Nigel's part in the accident, it's easy to guess you're not done blaming yourself. I'd be the same," he added and squeezed her arm.

It was more than an hour later when the door that connected the recovery room and the operating theaters swung open and two staff members in green scrubs appeared. Between them, they pushed a gurney. Ben lay small and still among the sheets, swathed in bandages from head to toe. She barely recognized him.

His eyes were nearly swollen shut and the parts of his body that weren't swaddled in bandages were covered in dark bruises. Tears sprang to her eyes and she held her hand up to her mouth in an effort to hold back a sob.

"Oh, Ben! My baby! My poor little baby boy!"

"He looks a little worse for wear, but I can assure you, we're all happy with how the surgery went."

Isobel turned and stared at the doctor who'd followed Ben into the room. Belatedly, she held out her hand. "I'm Isobel Donnelly, Ben's mom."

"And I'm Beau Barrington," the surgeon replied.

"The best neurosurgeon around," Mason added. "We're so lucky he was on call."

Doctor Barrington held out his hand to Mason and shook it. "Mason Alexander, it's been awhile. It's good to see you again."

Mason nodded and turned to Isobel. "Beau and I went to med school together. He and I and one of my cousins made a good team."

Beau chuckled. "Oh, those were the good old days. If only we'd known how tough it was going to be when we graduated college and set foot in a real hospital."

"You've done very well for yourself, Beau," Mason replied. "You have a formidable reputation. We're so grateful you were available to operate on Ben."

Beau acknowledged Mason's praise with a modest shrug. "I did what any one of us would have done."

"You saved his life," Isobel said, her voice trembling. Beau tilted his head and nodded slightly in agreement.

"It was a little tricky there for a while. He'd suffered a subarachnoid bleed. We managed to find the source of the bleeding and got the flow to stop. He'll spend a day or two in the intensive care unit where we can keep a close eye on him. He still has a little swelling on the brain."

Isobel gasped and her heart beat faster. Her

little boy wasn't out of the woods yet. Beau saw her distress and hurried to reassure her.

"I can tell you're imagining the worst and it was pretty bad when we first examined him, but we're confident we stemmed the bleeding. The damage to the brain itself was minimal. Once the swelling goes down, we anticipate he'll make a full recovery."

"How long will he remain unconscious?" Mason asked quietly, coming to stand close to Isobel's side.

"It's hard to tell," Beau replied. "Hopefully once the swelling subsides, he'll wake up and be almost as good as new. He'll be sore for a while and the two broken legs will slow him down, but all that's temporary, we hope."

Isobel tried to take comfort from his optimism, but the truth was, her little boy was still very sick. She wanted to curl up in a corner and cry her heart out and wallow in her guilt. Once again, Mason showed his support by thanking the doctor and then steering her away, in the direction Ben had been taken.

"Come and say hello to your son," Mason said. "It will comfort him to hear your voice. Talk to him and tell him how cool it's going to be watching him get around in a wheelchair. With Sophie on a pair of crutches, we're going to have some fun for a while. It's lucky there's an elevator in my building."

Isobel focused on Mason's chatter and was grateful for it. She knew he was doing his best to take her mind off the trauma of the past few hours and help her concentrate on the positive. Besides, what he said was true. There were plenty of studies that showed coma patients responded to external stimuli and many had later reported hearing the conversations of their loved ones during the time they lay unconscious.

"Yes, of course. I-I can't wait to give him a kiss and say hello."

Mason stared down at her and all of a sudden, dragged her in close. He squeezed her so tightly it almost hurt. She clung to him, drawing strength from his solid presence. She lifted her head and he met her lips with a soft and tender kiss.

"I love you, Isobel West. Don't forget it."

"I love you, too, Mason. And thank you. For everything."

"For better or worse," he murmured. "Like I said, I'm here for the long haul."

EPILOGUE

Twelve months later

Dear Diary,

With the passage of time comes healing and with healing comes the hope that some day things will be normal and happy again. You have given me that gift of hope, dear Mason and I'll love you for it forever.

For so many years, there was nothing but darkness and needles of icy cold rain. My tears would flow in time with the water that fell from the sky, scorching me with their pain.

But now when it rains, I see the beauty of a rainstorm and my tears are nowhere to be found. The air is cleansed, along with my soul and when the storm is done, I see the sunshine. Beyond it, I look for that rainbow and for the first time in a long time, I can see it.

Within the arches of bright color, I see life, I see love; I see hope. I see my smiling reflection and the happy faces of my children and I am reminded that I have finally returned to the place where I belong. With you by my side, I have returned to the land of the living.

———————

Isobel didn't think there was anything she loved better than the sound of her children squealing with laughter. The fact that Mason was the cause of their frivolity made it all the more special. She pulled her light jacket closer around her to ward off the chill that drifted off the ice rink, all the way over to where she sat in the stands.

"Come on, Mommy! Come and join us!" Sophie squealed as Mason twirled her around the ice, taking care to hold her tight.

Isobel smiled and shook her head, content to watch from the sidelines. "You guys go ahead. You look like you're having a lot of fun. I'm happy to sit here and take photos." She raised the camera she held in her lap and snapped off a few more shots. Ben skated close and threw a pose. Isobel couldn't help but laugh.

He'd recovered well from his injuries and she thanked God every day for bringing her little boy through. As far as anyone could tell, there were no lasting effects, at least not physical ones. Both children were still seeing a therapist regularly to ensure their mental status achieved the same level of health as their bodies, and the regular updates Isobel received from their doctor were positive.

Mason skated over with Sophie in his arms and climbed off the icy surface of the rink. Sitting down beside Isobel, he attended to the little girl's skates. A moment later, they clattered to the floor and he smiled at her.

"You did great out there, Soph. We'll make a skater out of you yet!"

She giggled back at him. "It's easy to skate when I'm up on your shoulders. It feels like I'm flying way up in the sky."

Mason pulled her in against his side and kissed the top of her head. Isobel's heart melted at the demonstration of love he gave so freely to her children. The kids weren't the only recipients of his love. As if reading her thoughts, he looked over Sophie's head and his gaze tangled with hers. Her pulse jumped, like it always did when he was near.

"Thank you," she said softly, her eyes filling up.

"For what?"

"For everything; for being you."

"Why the tears?" he asked, reaching over to gently wipe the moisture from her cheeks.

"They're happy tears. My emotions are all over the place at the moment."

"Any reason in particular?"

She blushed and ducked her head. She reached for her handbag on the seat beside her and pulled an envelope out of it. In silence, she handed it to him.

He took the envelope without hesitation and opened it. Tugging out the single sheet of paper, he scanned its contents. Eventually, he looked up at her, his eyes full of understanding.

"Your divorce papers came through."

"Yes."

"It's a big moment. I remember when mine arrived."

"I can't believe it's been more than twelve months since I walked out on Nigel. It's incredible how quickly time passes when you're happy."

"And in love," Mason added, giving her a wink. He smiled his beautiful smile and she went warm and gooey all over. Even after a year, she still reacted to him that way. She didn't ever want to stop feeling like she did right there and then.

She thought of Nigel and felt sad. He was serving six years for dangerous acts causing grievous bodily harm, stalking and a string of other offenses. She believed justice had been served, but she still couldn't help feeling sad about the way his life had turned out. She only hoped that he'd learned his lesson and that when he was eventually released, he'd accept she'd moved on and he'd go forward without her in his life.

She was also relieved the circumstances of the accident and their history of domestic violence had been considered and she hadn't been charged for her part in the accident. After everything they'd been through, it would have been awful to have to front up to a court of law and answer for her actions.

Thankfully, the police had investigated her story and several witnesses had come forward, including the kindly stranger who'd given her a ride to the hospital. Isobel hadn't forgotten what the woman had said and she still had the woman's business card tucked into the side pocket of her purse.

When the time was ready, she'd join the crusade to bring an end to domestic violence. Too many women left it too late and were murdered or permanently maimed. She couldn't help but feel relieved and immensely grateful she hadn't been one of those.

"Now you're a single woman again, I guess we ought to celebrate."

Mason's statement brought her out of her sad musings and she managed a smile. "We should. What did you have in mind?"

"Ice cream!" Ben shouted, making his way over to where they sat.

"Yay! Ice cream!" Sophie echoed with a grin.

Mason nodded. "Ice cream sounds good and we'll definitely get to it later. Right now, I have something else in mind." He turned back to Isobel, his expression suddenly serious.

A wave of nerves tightened her stomach. She looked at him with curiosity, wondering what had caused his change of mood. As if sensing her confusion, he reached over and took her hand.

"I love you so much, Isobel West and I love your children, too. You can't know how happy you make me feel."

"You make me happy, too, Mason. Happier than I ever dreamed," she said softly, meaning every word of it.

He squeezed her hand. "There's only one thing that would make me happier."

Surprise shot through her and she shook her head with a laugh. "How did you know? I should have guessed with you being a doctor, you'd take notice of these things."

Mason frowned. "What things? What are you talking about?"

"The baby, of course!"

"The baby?"

"Yes! I'm pregnant!"

Shock flooded his features and all of a sudden, Isobel realized the tiny new life growing inside her was the last thing he'd been thinking about. The shock on his face was replaced with disbelief and he shook his head back and forth.

"You're pregnant? I don't believe it! How?"

Her smile faded and she couldn't help but wonder if he was pleased. He loved Ben and Sophie like his own, but they'd never discussed having their own children. She shrugged.

"I'm not sure. I was still on the pill when I found out. I guess your swimmers were more determined than either of us. Sometimes it can happen."

Mason's smile grew wider. "Absolutely! I need to thank those little swimmers of mine."

"So, you're happy about it?"

He drew her in close beside him and pressed a warm kiss upon her lips. "*Happy?* Happy doesn't even come close, but I'd be happier still if you'd agree to be my wife."

This time, it was her turn to be shocked. "Are you...proposing to me?"

"Yes, it's what I was about to do before you interrupted and dropped your big news. I even asked Ben and Sophie a few weeks ago what they thought of the idea."

Isobel turned to her children, fresh tears threatening. "Is it true? Did Mason ask you what you thought about the two of us getting married?"

"Yes!" they shouted in chorus, their smiles wide and bright.

"And what did you say?" Mason asked.

"We said yes!" Ben announced, still grinning madly.

Isobel turned back to Mason, who had gotten down on one knee. In his hand, he held a beautiful emerald ring. It was surrounded by diamonds. She gasped in surprise.

"You already have the ring?"

He grinned, unabashed. "I've been carrying it around for weeks. I knew your divorce would become final any day and I wanted to be prepared. As soon as you became available, I wanted to claim you for my own. So, what do you say? Isobel West, will you marry me?"

All the love and joy she felt for him welled up inside her. This time, she couldn't hold her tears back. "Yes!" she gasped. "Yes! Yes! Yes!" She held his head between her hands and pressed kisses all over his face. She'd never felt more loved.

How had she gotten so lucky? From the darkest depths of despair and pain, like a phoenix, she'd risen from the ashes. She'd claimed back her life and protected her children and she'd done it all with the love and support of the man sat by her side.

"I love you, Mason Alexander. I'll love you until the day I die."

He kissed her softly, tenderly, and she felt the love he had for her in his heart all the way down to her soul.

"You're my life, my everything, Belle. I love you with all that I am and all that I have and I will until the end of time."

NOTE TO READERS

I do hope you have enjoyed reading Isobel and Mason's story. If you've enjoyed this story, please feel free to leave a review for The Perfect Husband. Every review is very much appreciated.

If you would like to receive news on upcoming stories, release dates, book launches and other snippets, please feel free to sign up for my newsletter. You can do this by visiting my website at www.christaylorauthor.com.au and clicking on the "Subscribe to my Newsletter" link on the right.

The Body Thief is the next book in the Sydney Harbour Hospital Series.

Here's a sneak peek:

A race against time...

Samantha Wolfe is no stranger to death. As a senior forensic pathologist at the Department of Forensic Medicine in Sydney, she's lost count of the number of post mortems she's performed in the quest to find answers. But something strange is happening in the Glebe morgue. The number of bodies coming through with donated organs has surged upwards and there doesn't appear to be any valid reason for it.

Has the government's initiatives to increase the number of organ donors finally paid off, or is something far more sinister at play? The more Sam delves into the mystery, the more she's certain evil lurks nearby.

Detective Sergeant Rohan Coleridge is put in charge of the investigation and he's not exactly happy about it. The last time he spoke to Samantha Wolfe, they were both in college and she accused him of walking out on his responsibilities. Taking on the investigation means significant hours spent up close and personal with her and he's not sure if either of them will walk away unscathed.

But the more Rohan investigates, the more he's convinced something is definitely amiss, but is the perpetrator one of the doctors of the prestigious Sydney Harbour Hospital, or is it someone far closer to home....?

The Body Thief will be released on 27 December, 2015 and is available for pre-order from your favorite digital retailer.

About The Author

Chris Taylor grew up on a farm in north-west New South Wales, Australia. She always had a thirst for stories and recalls writing her first book at the ripe old age of eight. Always a lover of romance and happily-ever-afters, a career in criminal law sparked her interest in intrigue and suspense. For Chris to be able to combine romance with suspense in her books is a dream come true.

Chris is married to Linden and is the mother of five children. If not behind her computer, you can find her doing the school run, taxiing children to swimming lessons, football, ballet and cricket. In her spare time, Chris loves to read her favorite authors who include Richard North Patterson, Sandra Brown, Kathleen E Woodiwiss and Jude Devereaux.

You can find out more about Chris and sign up for her newsletter at her website:

http://www.christaylorauthor.com.au

68333392R00184